Rodric watched as Eva
river. A wicked and powerfu
Below, she was caught in the
vortex.

A deep rumble moved through the air. Laughter,
Rodric realized. The demon was laughing.

"Damn you!" Rodric yelled. "You're a coward
controlled by your mistress."

As thunder boomed, the water shot up and Eva
Grace was level with Rodric. Treasures the faeries had
given her gleamed at her throat, and the demon made the
earth shake.

"Give those to me," the creature roared.

The demon couldn't just take them, she'd have to
give them to him. Which meant Rodric could save her.
But how?

"Help me," he called to his ancestors. "Help us!"

A thick rope appeared in his hands. He made a loop
and threw it with all his strength toward her. She fought
to get the loop over her head, but the effort cost her.

The demon roared at Rodric. "Tell her to save
herself. Give me what I need."

"She's not giving you anything," Rodric shouted.

"Maybe to save you." A lightning bolt struck just
feet from Rodric.

Summoning all the magic in his blood, Rodric
slowly began to pull Eva Grace up from the river.

Healing Magic

by

Neely Powell

The Witches of New Mourne

Healing Magic

Cover Art by *Debbie Taylor*

The Wild Rose Press, Inc.
PO Box 708
Adams Basin, NY 14410-0708
Visit us at www.thewildrosepress.com

Publishing History
First Edition, 2021
Trade Paperback ISBN 978-1-5092-3960-3
Digital ISBN 978-1-5092-3961-0

The Witches of New Mourne
Published in the United States of America

Dedication

For Bill Crowell with love.
Jan Hamilton Powell

In loving memory of Richard, my true inspiration.
Leigh Neely

Chapter 1

Eva Grace Connelly stepped outside her kitchen and smiled. Fall was her favorite time of year, and the backyard of the stone house she'd recently purchased brought her joy. Tonight, she'd light a fire for the first time, and she was looking forward to a quiet evening.

Deep in the woods a dog barked, and the sound reverberated through Eva Grace's chest.

The wind changed.

The chill of October gave way to a wintry blast. Frozen air punched her from behind and threw her into her woodpile. Logs tumbled, and the wind held her down.

She gathered her magic, arming herself against the descending evil as she climbed to her feet. Her mind opened, and her family, the Connelly coven, responded. She felt the alarm of cousins Brenna and Fiona, the startled fear of her grandmother, Sarah. However, their strength flooded her and allowed her to step directly into the wind.

"So, you're back," she shouted into the storm. "I've been waiting."

Against the night sky, an ice funnel formed. Though the wind continued its fury, the tornado moved with deliberation down the side of the ridge behind the house. Trees snapped, and the earth gleamed white and frozen in the path of the approaching monster.

A face appeared in the spinning cloud, and Eva Grace recognized the demon—her coven's enemy and this small, north Georgia town's worst nightmare. She knew this demon well. It had killed the man she loved. It would kill again.

The demon's sharp teeth dripped crimson ice. Laughter joined the roar of the storm.

Eva Grace lifted her arms and stared into its face. "Bring it on, you bastard, bring it on."

"Noooooooo!" The scream of her sister witches rang in her head and was echoed by a masculine voice to her right.

Dr. Rodric McGuire fought his way toward her. How was he moving through this wind? Only magic kept her from falling. What propelled him?

"Don't challenge it," Rodric yelled.

Stubbornly, she faced the demon again. Her coven's magic surged through her. The funnel stopped. The demon's roar turned into a shriek of despair. Rodric reached her side as the funnel exploded.

Ice shards flew like spears. Rodric shielded her against the stone wall of the big house. Only the sudden drop of the wind saved them. The ice fell harmlessly to the ground just inches away.

Heat radiated from Rodric's body as his arms curved around Eva Grace. "By the Goddess, I thought it was coming for you. I thought …" The emotion in his voice deepened his Scottish accent.

Eva Grace clung to him in relief. She wanted to fight the demon, but this attack was unexpected. Rodric's ragged, deep breaths were the only sounds in a night that was abruptly cold and still.

"I told you it would be back," she whispered. "When

it's around, so is the Woman in White. She's coming for me this time."

"But she can't have you." Rodric's arms tightened around her. "Let's go inside."

****

In the living room, Eva Grace flicked her wrist to spark a flame in the fireplace. The blaze took quick hold of the dry kindling, and Rodric added a couple of small logs. They stood in silence a moment, warming their hands. The nightmare outside seemed a distant memory.

"We need some tea." Eva Grace headed for the kitchen. "The others will be here soon."

The front door flew open, and Sarah Connelly rushed inside. The coven leader's eyes were bright in her pale face as she crossed the room and took Eva Grace's hands. "Are you okay? Were you hurt?"

"You know I'm all right," Eva Grace said as her grandmother hugged her. "You made sure I was."

Eva Grace welcomed the embrace of this tall, powerful witch in a denim jacket, T-shirt and faded jeans. No doubt Sarah had flown here, crossing the miles from the family home to reach Eva Grace as soon as possible.

Sarah had raised Eva Grace and her cousins, Brenna and Fiona. With Sarah, they always felt safe. But could she protect against the demon and the other, vengeful spirit who was coming? They all knew the Woman in White always got her tribute—from every generation of Connelly witches.

In moments the living room and porch were filled with witches. Sarah's sisters—the elder aunts, Doris and Frances, with their gray hair and still vibrant green eyes. Fiona and Brenna and the other aunts and cousins who made up the coven. All of them were emerald-eyed and with hair from various shades of auburn to red. Eva Grace could see herself in all of them.

She remained quiet as they all talked about how the wards around her house held and how their combined power blocked the demon. At times like this, she felt they could survive anything, but then she recalled the funnel of ice ripping through the woods and knew the power they faced was more than equal to theirs.

But tonight, Brenna was exhilarated. "The demon made a direct attack this time, and we stopped him. Maybe that's a sign."

Eva Grace's gaze met Rodric's and she saw her own doubt mirrored there.

He went into the kitchen, leaving the women to their chatter about the demon and the curse that hung over their family.

The Woman in White already haunted this land that the Connelly witches settled in the 1700s. The coven and their families had fled a Second Ice Age in Ireland, but the cold followed them. Snow came before Samhain. They were days away from starvation when their coven leader bargained with the Woman. And so began their terrible sacrifice.

The coven had pieced together a history—the Woman's real name was Catriona MacCuindliss. Her father was possessed by a demon, and he killed her Cherokee husband and their son. The coven believed the Woman had killed her father and perhaps herself. That murderous rage had turned her into a powerful, malevolent spirit. The demon craved the Woman's strength and sought to steal the magic of the Connelly coven in its quest. The Woman took great pleasure in allowing the demon to pursue the young witches.

In the end, she always claimed a Connelly and sent the demon away. She had taken Eva Grace's mother nearly 30 years ago.

Twice the demon had visited this summer and left death in its wake. The Woman came, too, but did not take a Connelly witch's life. Eva Grace knew tonight had been the opening shot of the next round with their foes. But the rest of the coven did not share her view.

Rodric appeared at her side with a tea cup. His smile reached his warm, brown eyes. "Sugar and lemon."

"Thank you." The rusty-haired Scot knew exactly how she liked her tea. During the past months of chaos, she had come to trust the paranormal expert's support and understanding. Lately, she'd begun to feel more than gratitude.

But Rodric could never be more than a friend.

She turned to her family. "Who wants something hot?"

Tea was poured and cookies shared. No Connelly gathering was complete without food. Eva Grace was surprised they didn't whip up a cake or two.

As the last witch swept out the door, she dropped onto the sofa. "I'm not sure what's been more exhausting tonight. The demon or my family."

Rodric smiled and sat beside her, stretching out his long legs. "They are a lively group."

Eva Grace frowned. "And they're wrong."

"I agree," Rodric said. "Why didn't you argue with them tonight?"

"They were all feeling so pleased with themselves."

"I wonder how Brenna can be so sure the demon can be held, or the Woman is not coming back," he said as he stroked his close-cropped beard.

"She fought the demon and won. So did Fiona. Along the way we learned a lot about the Woman and why she made the bargain with our family. After the last battle, the Woman wept. They all felt those were tears of remorse."

"No one can be sure of that."

"I may not be a medium like Fiona or have the ability to command the elements like Brenna, but I can feel what's coming."

"Many beautiful women are not so perceptive." Rodric's smile was unexpectedly rakish.

"I'm a witch, not just a woman."

"Indeed." An emotion she couldn't name flashed in his gaze.

Eva Grace turned away. Her fiancé Garth was murdered by the demon in June. She had spent most of her life planning to marry him, and attraction to another man didn't seem right.

She changed the subject. "How did you happen to be here tonight, anyway? I wasn't expecting you until tomorrow."

"I caught an earlier flight from London."

He had been in Europe for two weeks, investigating claims of a haunting at an inn in the South of France. Internationally known and respected, Rodric was in New Mourne because of his friendship with the county sheriff, Jake Tyler.

Jake and Garth were shapeshifters who once served together in an elite, multi-national military team of supernaturals. Rodric was an expert consultant to the team, and the three men became close. Eva Grace hated that it wasn't until Garth died that Rodric came to New

Mourne.

But he was now a soldier in their fight against the evil spirit. He was researching the Woman in White's family, searching for clues about her and the demon who had once been her father.

Rodric said, "When I was getting close to New Mourne this evening, I got a weather alert. I checked the radar, and it looked like a weird bit of energy was headed south, out of the mountains in North Carolina."

"Storms don't move south here."

"That's why I broke every speed limit to get here. We all know the effect of paranormal activity on weather. When the demon descended on us at the Summer Solstice, the heat was unbearable."

"And the storms were fierce," Eva Grace said.

"When we talked the other day, you said it has been colder than normal for October. That's not a good sign."

A puff of smoke billowed from the fireplace at Rodric's quiet words. Both of them stood, on guard.

When nothing more happened, Eva Grace gave a shaky laugh. "It would be just like the Woman or the demon to slide down the chimney like some perverted version of Santa Claus."

"Don't mock them," Rodric warned. "It's the same time of year the Woman first cursed your family."

"That's one of the reasons I know she's coming." As if in response, the wind moaned outside.

"We can't give in to the Woman." Rodric's hand on hers was warm and reassuring. "Do you feel like this house is too big for you? Do you feel safe out here?"

"I do. There's so much love in this house. Cousin Inez raised her family here. This is where she wrote all the journals that have helped us trace the family history.

I feel at home here."

Rodric squeezed her hand again. As a healer, Eva Grace always divined knowledge from touch. His quiet confidence flowed through her. And there was more, a hint of otherness.

Rodric never presented himself as anything but human. But sometimes, just beneath his calm surface, she sensed wildness. How had he fought through the wind tonight? Or known instinctively she needed help?

Maybe it was that hint of something more that drew her in now, made her lean toward him.

He touched her face. Anticipation built between them.

A hard knock on the front door startled them both.

Rodric glanced at his watch. "It's nearly ten."

"No one in the coven would knock." She stepped forward.

Rodric stopped her. "Let's be careful."

"There are wards in place," Eva Grace said. "They stopped the demon tonight."

"With help from your sister witches. Black magic is full of trickery."

The loud knock sounded again. "I'm looking for Eva Grace Connelly," a masculine voice said from the other side.

"Who are you?"

"A traveler in need."

Eva Grace heard that entreaty often. No one but family, friends, and those truly in need could penetrate her protective wards.

Rodric shook his head, but Eva Grace opened the door. A blast of cold air swept in. A man stood in the glow of the porch light. His black leather jacket was open to reveal an Angel Witch T-shirt. Eva Grace recognized the heavy metal group's name from her grandmother's eclectic music collection. The man's jeans were worn, and his motorcycle boots were scuffed and dusty. Silver laced the dark hair pulled back in a ponytail.

"Are you Miss Connelly, the healer?"

"Who are you?" Rodric's voice was sharp.

The man retreated half a step, hands up. "I'm not looking for trouble." His quick grin was disarming.

Recognition stirred in Eva Grace. How did she know him? "Is there something you need, Mr.—"

"Mick Phillips," he said and relaxed his stance. "I'm sorry to interrupt, but my granddaughter is ill. She needs help."

Eva Grace sensed he was struggling, trying to control emotion.

"Why not go to a doctor?" Rodric studied Mick with unease.

"I fear the cause of my granddaughter's fever can't be treated at a hospital. I've heard you can help with such things."

Eva Grace opened the door of the closet nearby, grabbed a coat, and slipped it on before retrieving a small, leather bag, purse and keys. "Where do you live?"

"We're at Callie's RV Park. My crew is doing some work here before winter sets in."

Rodric's disapproval was clear.

"I can't pay you, but I'll be happy to take on some projects around the house."

"I'm sure we can work something out." Eva Grace understood Rodric's caution, but she felt safe. "Let's go."

"I'll go on." Mick ambled toward the truck he had

parked behind Eva Grace's BMW convertible.

Eva Graced locked the door and turned to Rodric. "You don't have to— "

"You're insane if you think I'm not going with you."

"People I don't know come to me for help all the time."

"In the guise of a handsome man, the demon knocked on your cousin's door this past summer and tricked her into betraying the coven. After what happened tonight, how can you go with him?"

"My magic is more powerful than my cousin's," Eva Grace said calmly. "There's true need in this man's voice."

"And these are dangerous days."

As they hurried to her car, the wind gusted. Leaves from the old oak in the front yard fell in a dry shower.

"I promise you this will be okay," Eva Grace reassured him.

"I hope so. You mean so..." Rodric stopped and cleared his throat. "You mean so much to your family. You can't be careless."

The powerful engine of the man's truck roared to life.

"I don't trust him," Rodric said.

In answer, Eva Grace got in the car. Still grumbling, Rodric settled into the passenger seat.

She smiled. "Fasten your seat belt. This could be a bumpy ride."

Chapter 2

The night closed around them as they followed the old truck down one dark, winding road after another.

Rodric wished he'd insisted on driving. "I don't believe I've been this far west of town before."

"I know every road in Mourne County. Don't worry."

Rodric had every confidence in her ability to take care of herself, and he was not without weapons of his own. But after the demon's attempt to get to her earlier, his senses were on alert.

The wind gusted hard. Eva Grace's grip tightened on the steering wheel. Rodric knew better than to comment. This beautiful, red-haired witch had a stubborn streak.

"We're going to a campground run by a family of shifters," she said.

"I guess they attract an interesting clientele."

"Callie runs the business. Her family's been in New Mourne for a long time."

"As long as the Connellys?"

"Almost. They were good friends with Garth. That's why I'm not worried tonight. Callie and her family wouldn't allow anyone dangerous in their park."

Rodric refrained from comment. Eva Grace was extremely smart, but when someone came to her for help, she was likely to take chances.

"The park probably won't be full since it's so cold," she continued. "Normally the fall colors mean the town is full of visitors, but the leaves peaked early this year. We haven't been busy at all at the shop."

Eva Grace owned Siren's Call, a shop specializing in crystals, herbs, local arts, and metaphysical aids.

"With less people to be concerned with, perhaps your family's magic will be even more powerful."

"I never thought of it that way. Even before I fully understood the curse, I knew that we were born to protect others—human and supernatural."

Rodric thought of how she challenged the demon. She was a protector, a warrior witch with a healing touch.

And he was in love with her.

This was an impossible situation. She was still grieving Garth and preparing to be the Woman's next tribute. Even if she survived the curse, she might never be able to love anyone else.

His chest tightened. He'd been with beautiful, intelligent women many times, but none had ever opened his heart like Eva Grace.

Tonight, when she faced that icy storm of evil, his every instinct had been to protect her. He came close to losing control of his true self. And if he revealed his own alter ego, he wasn't sure how she or anyone else would react.

Steady, he told himself. *Keep it steady.*

Eva Grace slammed on the brakes.

"What the hell?" Rodric peered ahead. Eyes glowed in the headlights.

"It's a dog," Eva Grace said with a shaky laugh. "Just a dog." She was more on edge than she pretended.

"Just a dog," he agreed. However, the canine didn't run away. What was this? The night was full of magic and made him even more apprehensive about this trip.

In the nearly-empty RV park, people sat around a campfire next to the largest trailer. A few of them stood as the vehicles approached. Beyond them was a smaller travel trailer.

Eva Grace pulled her car to a stop behind Mick's truck. "It's like a gypsy wagon."

Rodric had seen others like it in the hills of Wales and England. The trailer had rough-hewn wooden walls and what appeared to be a thatched roof. Light glowed through curtains at the windows.

Mick got out of his truck and waited for them. Rodric placed a protective hand at Eva Grace's elbow as they walked forward.

Mick nodded toward the tiny home. "Randi has been sick since yesterday. Fever, weakness, out of her head."

"Could it just be the flu?" Rodric asked.

"It came on suddenly. One of our women said she just fell to the ground."

"One of *your* women?" The possessive tone irked Rodric.

The man's dark gaze met his. "We're family here."

"Let me check on your granddaughter." Eva Grace went past the men and up the steps.

Rodric followed close on her heels. He wanted to stay between her and this arrogant stranger. His hand kept going to his waist for a weapon that would appear if needed.

The trailer was dimly lit but clean. A young woman lay on a long bench, huddled under blankets. Perspiration gleamed on her ashen face. An older woman sat nearby, hands clasped to her chest as she chanted. Mick spoke to her sharply, and she hurried out.

Rodric was fluent in ten languages, but he didn't recognize this one.

Eva Grace leaned close. "Black magic. Can you smell it?"

A rank odor scented the air, but he couldn't pinpoint the source. He looked at Mick, but the man's attention was focused on his granddaughter, his expression inscrutable.

Eva Grace took off her coat and pushed up the sleeves of her soft cream sweater.

Mick knelt in front of his granddaughter, put his hand on her arm and squeezed. "Randi? Miranda? Can you wake up for me?"

She mumbled as her eyes fluttered open. Mick crooned to her in that same unfamiliar language.

"Her body is fighting," Eva Grace said. "An infection and maybe something magical."

"Should you talk to some of the others? Sarah or Brenna?" Rodric asked.

Eva Grace's face set with determination. "I think I can handle this."

"Just don't take any unnecessary chances."

Eva Grace put her bag on the kitchen counter and washed her hands in the stainless-steel sink.

"Let me check her," she told Mick and he moved away. "Do you two want to go outside? She may be more comfortable with me if we're not disturbed."

"I'm not leaving," Mick said.

Rodric wasn't going anywhere.

She sighed and turned back to Randi. "Has she been chilling?"

"Some," Mick explained. "My aunt thought we needed to sweat the infection or the spell out of her."

"Not a bad idea, but I think we need to cool her down." Eva Grace pulled the heavy blankets back. In a long, pink nightshirt, Randi looked fragile and very sick.

She placed a hand on Miranda's forehead. She asked Mick to fill and plug in the electric teapot as she got teas from her bag. She placed citrine crystals at Randi's head and feet.

"They'll help her body heal," she explained.

When the water boiled, Eva Grace poured it over a tea ball in a cup. The sharp, clean scent of peppermint wafted through the room. "This will lower the fever and flush toxins out of her system."

Mick sat on the bed and lifted his granddaughter to a sitting position while Eva Grace coaxed her to drink the tea. Faint color stained Randi's skin, and she began to whimper, her limbs stirring restlessly.

"No," she croaked. "No, no…" She began to jerk and twitch, caught in a seizure.

Eva Grace drew back, alarmed.

"Randi," Mick pleaded. "Randi, please wake up."

Rodric stepped forward. "What's wrong?"

Eva Grace glared at Mick. "What have you done?"

Momentary fear crossed the man's features. "I would not harm her. Whatever harmed her is not from me and mine. I tell you it's not."

"Please leave," Eva Grace told him. "Leave me with her."

Rodric took hold of Mick's arm. "You need to go."

Mick jerked away. "You'll not order me out of my home."

"Then I can't help her," Eva Grace said. "Do you

want her to get better?"

Mick's internal struggle was clear. Finally, without another word, he stormed out of the trailer.

"This isn't safe," Rodric said.

"Get a blue candle from my bag." Gaze fixed on Randi, Eva Grace raised her arms and began to chant.

Rodric put the candle on the table. Flame flickered to life. He was fascinated by the power emanating from the witch who owned his heart.

Her strong, confident voice filled the room. "Black as night and full of spite. Evil comes and uses her. Tell us now, tell us how. Where you go, what you show—"

Randi sat up and looked at Eva Grace, her eyes black and fever-bright.

Rodric stepped forward, ready to drag Eva Grace outside. Randi's rough, guttural voice stopped him.

"Evil is coming, and its hunger is deep. This town will suffer, death will spread. You witches can't fight this time. You can't win. You won't see Samhain. Not this time. You bitches will lose. All will be lost..."

Randi's body bowed backward and lifted off the bench. Then she dropped, limp and still.

Rodric pulled Eva Grace back against him. She was trembling. This witch who lived calmly with the constant threat of death was afraid. He couldn't bear it. "Let's get out of here."

"There's no danger. At least not right now." Eva Grace straightened her shoulders and took a deep breath. "Look at the candle."

Rodric saw the flame was burning bright and high.

"I called for a prophecy, and I got it." She laid a hand against Randi's forehead. "Her fever has broken." She smoothed Randi's damp hair away from her face and drew a blanket over her legs.

"I don't understand," Rodric said.

"This confirms what we were talking about earlier. We were led here tonight to get confirmation that the Woman isn't finished."

"But why here? Why these people? You've never met them before, have you?"

Eva Grace regarded their surroundings with a frown. "There's something familiar here. Does she remind you of someone?" She looked down at Randi who now appeared to be comfortable and sleeping.

To Rodric she seemed like an ordinary dark-haired young woman. "I don't see it."

"Something tells me we will."

"Let's get out of here."

"Just let me make sure she's okay." Eva Grace extinguished the candle and said a quick, calming spell.

Randi woke with a start and looked at Eva Grace with fear.

"Your grandfather called me to help," Eva Grace soothed. She introduced herself and Rodric. "I think you're going to be all right now."

Eva Grace had Randi drink more peppermint tea and took her temperature again.

"Where can I get you a dry gown?" Eva Grace asked.

Randi pointed to the little room at the end of the trailer. "Grandfather sleeps out here. I sleep there."

Rodric went and found another nightgown in a chest. When he came back Eva Grace was wiping the girl's face with a cloth. He turned while she dressed Randi. Only then did she go to the door and invite Mick back in.

"I doubt her fever will come back," Eva Grace told him as she packed her bag. "Just give her the teas I left and broth. Be sure she gets plenty of other liquids."

"I can't thank you enough. I'll be happy to work off this debt," he said. "Is there anything you need done around your home?"

"No," Rodric said fiercely.

Evan Grace glared at him. "I'm sure we'll talk again," she told Mick.

Mick followed them out of the trailer.

The temperature had dropped several degrees. Eva Grace shivered. "It feels like it could snow."

"I think it will," Mick said, studying the looming clouds. "I don't think it's just weather, though."

He smiled. "Sorry, I tend to get dramatic. Some people think it's my Slavic heritage. Thank you again."

Rodric insisted on driving, and Eva Grace didn't protest. He was anxious to get away from this place and the man who was still watching them.

Once out of the campground, Rodric said, "You know what they are."

"They travel around and do home improvements and the like."

"They're scam artists, con men who take money from honest people, and either do shoddy work or don't even do the work at all."

"People used to call them gypsies. They're called Travelers now," she said.

"We have real problems with them all over the UK. You need to stay away," Rodric said more forcefully than he intended.

She didn't reply.

As always, his brogue came out when he was angry

or anxious. "You canna believe anything Mick Phillips says. Just be aware of who—and what—he is. And if you were led here tonight, why?"

She was silent, and Rodric knew her well enough to understand he couldn't argue this point any further.

At her house, she said, "Would you like to come in for a nightcap or a cup of tea?"

"It's late. You should go to bed." He shut off the car and started to get out.

Eva Grace leaned forward, her mouth opened in shock.

"What's wrong?" Rodric said.

She pointed beyond him. "Look at that. The flowers are covered with frost. They were smiling at the sun today and now they're dead."

The autumn blooms were all coated with heavy frost and leaning under the strain.

Frost continued to settle like ice, and Eva Grace said, "This is a very bad sign."

He couldn't disagree.

"Randi said there would be suffering and death before Samhain. She said it was coming and it had a deep hunger."

He couldn't resist putting his arms around her, and she didn't move away. He turned his face to her hair to inhale her sweet scent. He should feel guilty, but all he could think of was kissing her. Imagining her mouth under his, he allowed his control to slip, and he pulled her closer.

"She's coming for me, isn't she?" Eva Grace murmured. "That's why I was called out tonight. So the Woman in White can begin the torture."

"Nothing about this curse is predictable. Remember

all we've learned about her. She suffered before she died. There's still a chance she could be merciful."

Eva Grace pulled away, and they stood in the cold, their silence awkward.

"I have to tell the coven what happened tonight," she said finally. "Will you come with me to Sarah's in the morning?"

"Of course."

She nodded and went in without looking back.

Shivering, not dressed for the sudden cold, he drove to the inn. In his lonely bed, he dreamed of Eva Grace.

He awoke bathed in sweat, wanting her so badly he gave himself the only release he could. She called to the blood of his ancestors, to the self he hid from human view. He loved her, a beautiful witch who might be doomed.

What in hell was he going to do?

Chapter 3

Eva Grace hoped Rodric wasn't aware of how much she appreciated the way he looked in his jeans and leather jacket this morning. There was something unexpected about him, no matter what he wore. She wondered again about the otherness she'd felt from him last night.

Angry voices spilled into the entry as she led him into her grandmother's home. A pungent, herbal aroma permeated the air.

"Oh, sweet goddess," she murmured. "The elder aunts are making a potion."

Rodric smiled and shut the front door on the morning's bitter wind. "Sounds more like a brawl."

"Because that's how their magic works best." At his puzzled look, she laughed. "Every year the coven makes a potion for good fortune to sell at the Samhain Festival in town. Aunt Doris and Aunt Frances insist on making it, and they always get into an argument about it. Brenna and I think that's how they make the spell work—because the two of them brewing or cooking anything together requires lots of luck."

They hung their coats on a hall tree and entered the large dining room where her family gathered for the coven meetings. Eva Grace loved the rubbed pine table that seated eighteen. The log-paneled walls were original to the first cabin built by the coven long ago. A fire crackled in the old stone fireplace, which was made with rocks from a nearby creek.

Eva Grace and Rodric headed for the welcome warmth as various members of the coven called out greetings.

She wondered if the Connellys who built this house were as lively and quarrelsome as those who occupied it today. Through an open door to the kitchen, she could see the two elder aunts, her grandmother's twin sisters, Frances and Doris. They were bickering over a large pot on the stove.

Their daughters, Estelle and Diane, carried in platters of bacon, eggs and fruit, and they bemoaned the fact that no one had thought to bring a coffee cake or apple fritters, and they would have to make do with pumpkin muffins. Cousins Maggie and Lauren were complaining about carbs even as they helped themselves to the muffins.

Delia, Brenna and Fiona's mother, was seated at the table, flipping through *The Connelly Book of Magic* and mumbling to herself.

Fiona laughed as she filled a cup of coffee from an urn on the sideboard. "Welcome to our jungle, Rodric. Can I get you some tea?"

"I'll take your devil's brew," Rodric replied.

"You're becoming addicted to all things American." Eva Grace poured hot water from an electric pot and selected Earl Grey. She needed a pick-me-up this morning.

"Fast food burgers are my favorite." Rodric sighed as he took a steaming mug from Fiona. "I fear for my cholesterol levels."

Fiona tucked a strand of dark auburn hair behind her

ear. "Eva Grace can brew a remedy for you. It's convenient to have a healer in the family."

"Even my magic doesn't easily unclog arteries." Eva Grace eyed the butter Lauren slathered onto a biscuit.

"What?" Lauren demanded. "Are you saying I'm clogging my arteries?"

Maggie, who had been filling a plate with eggs and bacon, frowned. "So, you're saying we shouldn't eat?"

Diane and Estelle immediately fussed about the food they'd prepared getting cold. Eva Grace sipped her tea, knowing she couldn't say anything right when the coven was in this mood.

Rodric flashed a charming smile, brown eyes twinkling behind his glasses. "Ladies, this all looks amazing. I'm ready to eat."

The Connelly witches did love feeding their men and hurried to fill a plate for him.

Eva Grace looked around for Brenna. Their special magic began when they were born at exactly the same moment on a raw February evening, the festival of St. Brighid. Unfortunately, Eva Grace's mother, Celia, had died when the babies were only weeks old—the tribute for the Woman in White for her generation.

Brenna, Eva Grace, Fiona, Lauren and Maggie were the current potential victims of the Woman in White. Brenna was the most powerful witch of their generation; the elements fed her magic. She was fierce in her determination to thwart the Woman's curse. Eva Grace was eager to hear Brenna thoughts about last night's encounter with the demon and what happened later at the RV park.

There was someone else missing, she realized.

"Where's Sarah?"

"She isn't feeling well this morning." Fiona cast a worried glance toward the hallway.

Raised voices from the kitchen distracted them.

"That crazy old bat is being ridiculous," fumed Aunt Frances as she led the way into the dining room. "The potion just needs to simmer."

She threw up her hands and told the assembled group. "Doris will mess up the potion just like she did the potatoes at the family reunion. She always thinks she can make the recipe better."

Delia shoved the book of spells and potions away. "The recipe isn't even in the book. I don't know how this thing stays in such a mess. I've straightened it out over and over again."

Aunt Doris appeared in the doorway. "We don't need the recipe." She tapped her temple. "I have it all up here."

"Then why did you put in so much rosemary?" Frances demanded.

"There was a time when the book would have spoken the recipe for us," Estelle said. "But it has been silent for years."

The room virtually exploded with opinions. Holding a full plate of bacon, eggs and biscuits, Rodric edged close to Eva Grace again. "They really are fierce."

"You should see them when they're baking. The flour actually flies."

"Enough." The command preceded Sarah and her husband, Marcus, into the room. Her green eyes chilly, she flicked one hand toward the Book of Magic. Pages ruffled back and forth before settling.

"There it is," Delia declared. "The recipe called for

three palms full of rosemary."

"I told you!" Doris said in triumph.

A warning look from Sarah hushed the squabbling twins. Though eleven years younger than her sisters, she was the coven leader by the gift of her immense magic.

She asked Eva Grace, "Do you have the crystals for the spell?"

Eva Grace took a small packet out of the pocket of her gray pants. "Right here."

"Frances, you take those, and after the potion has simmered on low for two hours, you'll cast the spell together. Diane, Estelle and Delia, you need to participate. Your generation has to take over some of these tasks."

Noting Sarah looked drawn and tired this morning. Eva Grace went to her grandmother and laid a hand on her arm. "You're not well."

Marcus answered for her. "No, she's not. What little she slept last night, she was tossing and turning."

"Some unsettled dreams," Sarah said. "It's nothing." Her gaze sharpened on Eva Grace. "You don't look rested yourself. I hope there was no further disturbance from the demon."

"I had a late call last night and maybe I missed more of my beauty sleep than I should have," Eva Grace said.

"Who was sick?"

"A young woman at Callie's RV Park," Eva Grace said. "Her grandfather came by the house to get me."

"You have no business going out alone like that at night, especially after the demon appeared to you," Aunt Frances said, her lips a grim line.

"I went with her," Rodric said. "And I was glad I did. I'm concerned about the group of Travelers we met."

A look passed from Frances to Sarah, puzzling Eva Grace. Before she could ask more, however, Sarah sat down and the din of noise rose again.

Marcus excused himself as soon as he finished eating. He was a master furniture craftsman, and Sarah was a renowned artist who used the region's natural gemstones in jewelry and decorative items. During the onslaught this summer, the demon burned the workshop to the ground. The structure was rebuilt, but men were coming to help Marcus install new wood-working equipment this morning.

Dishes were soon cleared, and the coven began their meeting.

"I assume there's a reason you're here," Sarah said to Rodric. With her long, white braid and dressed in jeans and peasant top, she shouldn't have been regal, but Eva Grace thought Sarah comported herself like a queen.

Rodric responded in kind. "I hope you will permit me to stay. There are some weather anomalies occurring that concern me."

"We all realize that this cold is unusual," Sarah agreed. "I'd like to discuss a few other matters and give Brenna a chance to arrive before you start."

Eva Grace grew impatient as they talked through plans for Samhain. Her family seemed more focused on celebrating than ending the curse. Samhain signaled the "light into darkness" phase of the year, when summer ends and winter begins. The old Celtic beliefs had slowly diluted into the traditional Halloween rituals, but not in New Mourne. The coven would decorate a special altar in the heart of their magic, a clearing in the forest behind this home place. Together they would honor and celebrate their ancestors.

"I think we should take advantage of the most important evening of the year to cast a spell to banish the Woman and the demon forever," Delia said.

"That's part of what I want to talk about," Eva Grace said. "At the RV park last night, I sensed black magic. Shouldn't we be worried about what might happen before Samhain?" She looked to Sarah.

Sarah nodded. "It appears Brenna is running late. Let's start with what Rodric has found, and then talk about what happened at the RV park."

Rodric retrieved a leather satchel from a nearby chair.

Delia said, "Aiden told me you were studying some of the outside influences surrounding visits from the Woman in White in the past."

Dr. Aiden Burns was her husband and the father of Brenna and Fiona. The couple had traveled the globe studying and teaching about legends, folklore and magic. While they roamed, they left their daughters with Sarah, a choice that was still a sore spot in their family.

Last summer, Aiden and Delia returned to New Mourne so the coven was united in the fight against the Woman and demon.

Rodric pulled papers out of his satchel. "I've made some studies about weather patterns that coincide with appearances of the Woman in White."

He passed stapled packets around the table. "If you'll open this to page six, you'll see the weather we're having doesn't show up on any other weather maps. While your weather is always cooler here in the mountains, outside of here they're having a normal autumn."

"Even Highlands, North Carolina, is warmer than we are," Fiona murmured, looking concerned.

Rodric continued, "These maps come from the National Weather Service, the Weather Channel, and—"

"You know, my coleus was dead this morning," Doris cut in. "They'd been sticking around despite the cold, but today, they were black and shriveled."

"My backyard looked like a war zone," Frances said sadly. "Some of the hardier plants survived but the ones I planted for fall blooming are all gone."

"That's what Rodric wants to talk with us about. Let's let him continue," Eva Grace said with impatience.

She stopped as the front door slammed. Brenna ran into the dining room. Her eyes sparkled with happiness. Her fiancé, Sheriff Jake Tyler, followed, grinning widely.

In their smiles Eva Grace saw something she had overlooked until now. She was usually more in tune with Brenna, but preoccupation with the Woman had dulled her perception. With effort, Eva Grace swallowed the anger and sadness that rippled through her body and made her grip the table's edge until her knuckles were white.

She looked away from the glowing couple and found Rodric watching her. She knew he saw beneath the smile she struggled to maintain. He most likely felt her jealousy. How could he know that? How could any human have that kind of precognition?

"I'm pregnant!" Brenna said. Jake wrapped her in his arms.

The group at the table rose as one to surround them. Eva Grace lagged behind as grief overwhelmed her. But when Brenna turned to her, she was able to hug her cousin with genuine and heartfelt gladness. This was her sister in all the ways that counted. She couldn't be anything but happy for Brenna and Jake.

"Blessed be," Eva Grace said. "You're going to be a wonderful mother."

Now Brenna looked hesitant and sad. "It should have been you first," she murmured as she hugged Eva Grace closer.

The enthusiasm of the group swept them apart.

Eva Grace could see this wasn't the time to discuss black magic or defeating the family curse.

Despite the early hour, the aunts broke out sparkling wine. Expectant grandmother Delia led the toast. "Brenna, I know I have not been the greatest example, but I believe you will be an amazing mother, just as you are an amazing woman." She hugged Brenna and turned to Jake. "And you've got a wonderful man to help you."

Rodric smiled as an excited Fiona pulled them into a group hug. "I'm going to be an aunt! I can't wait to tell Bailey." Fiona and the savvy television producer were engaged to be married and planning a wedding next spring.

Delia pulled out her cell phone. "Let's call your father."

Feeling her control beginning to waver, Eva Grace said, "I'd love to stay and continue the celebration, but I need to get Siren's Call opened." She kissed Brenna's cheek. "Come over tonight so I can check you out." She was a licensed midwife and had delivered the Connelly babies of the younger generation.

She spared a thought for Rodric, who had driven from town with her, but Eva Grace could not look at him.

She desperately wanted out of this house and away from the happiness that was no longer hers. The others were too overcome with the good news to notice how she was struggling, but Rodric did. She couldn't stand that, couldn't face him. She hurried into the hall, grabbed her coat and ran outside.

She was almost at her car when Rodric caught up to her. "Please wait. Are you okay?"

Eva Grace opened the door and flung her bag and purse into the backseat. "Oh, I'm just fine. My cousin is living out my dream in every way, and I have to pretend I'm happy about it while my heart feels like a fist was slammed into it."

He slid an arm around her shoulders. "I know how long you and Garth were planning to marry and have a family."

Eva Grace put her face in her hands. "I thought it would be me. Garth and I wanted kids quickly because of his service in the military. We waited so long. Too long." She pounded her fist against the side of the driver's door. "It should have been me."

Rodric pulled her against him. She buried her face in his shoulder. The tears she had held back so long could no longer be controlled. He stroked her back as the laughter and chatter inside the house drifted out to them.

"I've never been a jealous person," she whispered. "I'm so ashamed."

"Don't. You should feel exactly what you feel. You don't have to pretend with me."

"Yes, thank the goddess for you." The truth of those words startled her. She started to pull away.

Rodric cupped her cheek with his broad but gentle hand. She looked up at him through wet lashes.

Then his lips were on hers.

For a moment, Eva Grave gave in to the comfort of this intimate contact. But her relaxation quickly turned to something deeper. All semblance of restraint disappeared. With a groan, Rodric urged her against the side of her car. Their bodies pressed together, and she could feel how he hardened. She liked that. She was losing herself, giving in to feelings she had been fighting.

It took all her willpower to pull away. "Stop, Rodric. Please..."

He released her, and she turned.

"Eva Grace—"

"What am I doing? Garth has only been dead a few months and I'm making out with another man." She gave Rodric a pleading look. "Please forgive me. I'm so sorry."

He fell back a step, looking so hurt that she wanted to cry again. How in the world had she allowed this to happen?

"I have to go. This can't happen again."

She opened the car door and got in, not looking at him as she started the engine and drove away.

Chapter 4

Freezing air stung Rodric's face as he stalked through the woods outside the town. Dead, brown leaves swirled to the ground. Gray clouds hovered over the mountains, and fog danced among the trees. The landscape suited his mood—dark and angry.

After Eva Grace left him at Sarah's, he hitched a ride with Jake to the inn. His friend was filled with excitement over his impending fatherhood and didn't notice Rodric said very little. Eva Grace's immediate and hungry response had destroyed all his guards. He was afraid he might give his feelings away to Jake.

What could he say? That his tenuous hold on his attraction to Eva Grace had finally broken? That he had screwed up in every way imaginable?

Rodric couldn't stay in town when he felt this way. He couldn't hide who he was while this upset and sexually aroused.

He didn't know how it happened. He never allowed himself to care as he did for Eva Grace or to respond to a woman so roughly.

Raised by a devoted and largely female house staff, he learned early to listen and appreciate the intricacies of the female mind. He chose to cloak himself as a bearded and somewhat ordinary professor committed to the study of the paranormal. But women were always drawn to him, and he enjoyed the benefits. He thought most of the women enjoyed their time with him, too. He generally moved on before there was a hint of anything serious.

So how in the world had he allowed himself to fall in love with Eva Grace Connelly, the woman who still loved his close friend?

He didn't delude himself that today's kiss was anything other than her simple need for comfort. Instead of drawing her closer, he should have stepped away, protected her dignity and squashed his desire.

"You want her."

The voice came from all directions. Rodric spun around, his keen senses springing to life. "Who's there?"

Laughter spilled from the trees. The fog circled, and a putrid smell permeated the air. He recalled the sulfuric odor from the demon's attack on Siren's Call earlier this year. Now the damned monster was here.

Rodric cursed. He had wandered beyond the most protected boundaries of the town, and once again ignored his guards. He lived in a careful way, but his distraction with Eva Grace allowed evil to creep up on him.

"You should take her." The voice came from behind the fog screen. "The little witch is very skilled. I watched sweet Eva Grace with her man the night before I killed him."

Fury shattered Rodric's human form. Leather and hammered steel replaced his wool coat and professor garb. A spear appeared in his hand as he leapt into the air. "You filthy scum. Don't say her name."

A gasp rewarded Rodric's transformation. So the demon was unaware of who or what he was. That proved how weak the Woman kept her slave.

A tree to Rodric's left burst into flame. He spun and heaved a spear that split the flames in half. In the blur of heat, he saw the black, oozing creature that slunk in the shadows of the trees.

"You weak, miserable shite. Come out and fight."

Fire consumed another tree. Rodric flung another spear.

The demon dared to laugh, and Rodric plunged forward, an axe coming out of his hand. His family coat of arms gleamed on the cold iron blade. He wished for the ultimate weapon, the one his uncle had lost, but the tools he could still call from his ancestors would have to do. It was time to kill this demon and stop the torture of this town and the Connelly coven.

"Ferguson." The demon's hiss brought Rodric up short. "Spawn of Aife."

"Yes, I'm of her," Rodric shouted. "And I will kill you." A battle cry rumbled from the depths of Rodric's soul as he rushed forward.

The demon ran, trailing sparks. Trees turned to torches as Rodric raced in pursuit. The creature's knowledge of the landscape was an advantage. Rodric closed in, but the demon plunged under a rock. A long, snake-like tail disappeared just as Rodric swung his axe.

The blade split the stone, but the hole beneath sealed into the frozen earth.

Rodric roared in frustration. Trees and underbrush whooshed into flame, and he looked around in alarm. The last thing New Mourne needed was a wildfire. The axe disappeared, and Rodric raised his face to the leaden sky beseeching his ancestors again.

Rain fell, extinguishing the fire. The moisture turned to ice in an instant. The cold sealed around him, and Rodric drew upon his human form. He was once again Dr. Rodric McGuire, son of the late Rhona and Finn

McGuire, nephew of his despised Uncle Boyd Ferguson, laird of his family's lands and keeper of their gifts and burdens.

The demon was the Woman in White's father who came to the New World in the guise of a missionary and remained because she enslaved him. How did the demon know of his mother's family? Why had the creature challenged Rodric and used such vulgarity about Rodric's feelings for Eva Grace?

Turning back toward town, Rodric tried to reason through it. The demon had confronted them twice in twenty-four hours. The Woman was preparing to strike. He picked up his pace. The vengeful spirit would have to go through him to get to Eva Grace.

****

By the time he reached town, Rodric had control of himself. It was important he be calm and show his strength and confidence. No doubt the demon was watching from somewhere beyond the wards around New Mourne. He could not reveal his panic to the creature.

His focus was protecting Eva Grace and ending the curse. That began with setting things right between the two of them.

On Main Street he spoke with Gladys, the sheriff's department dispatcher. He chatted briefly with Fred Williams, the local pastor who was head of the Board of Commissioners and a secret friend of the Connellys. He stopped by the bakery, and the pretty kitchen witch packed up two chocolate cupcakes that smelled of sugar and magic.

He strolled up the sidewalk to the small, pre-Civil War house where Eva Grace had opened Siren's Call.

The parking lot to the right was almost empty. The unseasonable cold had definitely chased away tourists.

Inside, Rodric forced himself not to rush to Eva Grace. She was at the cash register, chatting with the shop's lone customer. Her smile faltered as she saw him, but she completed the transaction and sent the woman on her way with a cheerful blessing.

Rodric set the small, blue bakery box down. "I bring you apologies in the form of cake." He forced a lightness into his voice that he didn't feel.

Her green eyes were shadowed with unhappiness. "I'm the one who should apologize."

"Nonsense."

"But I shouldn't have been so emotional. You aren't responsible for my feelings or—"

"I am responsible for being your friend," he interrupted. "I'm responsible for momentarily losing my head when I found a beautiful woman in my arms."

Color stained her cheeks. "Please don't try to make it your fault."

"But it's not yours, either." He put out his hand, and she took it with obvious reluctance. He drew her around the counter. "We had a moment, Eva Grace. It doesn't mean we can't still be friends."

"I'm so embarrassed."

"Don't be, please." He squeezed her hand and looked directly into her beautiful green eyes. "I know how much you loved Garth, how much you'll always love him."

"Of course I will," she said quickly.

"And he was my friend. The reason I came here to help was for him, because he and Jake were my closest mates. I've stayed because of you."

Her gaze sharpened in alarm.

He forced himself to laugh. "I want to do everything I can to end this curse and protect the woman my friend loved."

He thought—or hoped—he saw disappointment in her eyes, but he couldn't be sure.

She took her hand from his. "Thank you for being so kind."

"So, we're good?" He picked up the bakery box. "Can we share some cake and tea? I have something else to tell you. It's about my meeting with the demon this morning."

"What?" Her alarm was clear.

"Let's have the cake, and I'll tell you."

And he did, leaving out the parts about his heritage as the son of a goddess and fighting the demon with supernatural force. It was sufficient to tell her he got away.

Some secrets couldn't be shared with a friend, or even the woman he had so foolishly and hopelessly allowed to claim his heart.

Chapter 5

Eva Grace was relieved Rodric agreed with her—
they must convince the coven that the Woman was still
a threat. The demon was back again and stronger it
seemed. Soon it would begin playing havoc in the town.
With the veil between worlds thinned by the approach of
Samhain, New Mourne was especially vulnerable.

Convinced knowledge would give them more
power, Rodric had headed back to the inn to continue his
research. He told her he was sure ending the curse could
be done if they gathered more information about the
Woman. She was convinced, however, that they needed
to connect with the woman on an emotional level.

It was good to be on steady footing with him again.
Eva Grace wasn't ready to examine all of her responses
to kissing him, but more than anything, she needed him
as an ally.

How could she get everyone to see danger from the
Woman was imminent? Eva Grace planned to tell them
about Rodric's experience in the woods, but she feared
that once again they would only see that the demon
backed down.

There were too many distractions—the coming
festival, the excitement of Fiona's engagement to Bailey
and now the news of Brenna's pregnancy.

An ache started in Eva Grace again. If Garth hadn't
died...

Determined not to give in to self-pity, she went to the shop's small kitchen to wash the teacups. Her cousin Lauren called out a greeting from the back door.

Eva Grace gave herself a quick beauty push to hide any evidence of anxiety. She was worried her cousins had noticed her jealousy and anger this morning. It wasn't in her to hurt Brenna, and right now, the coven needed to be united.

"No customers?" Lauren asked with a grimace.

"Just one this morning. I saw from the receipts that yesterday was no different."

"We had such a good September, but we may need to let our extra help go," Lauren said as she took off her coat and scarf.

"I hate to do that."

"Your heart is almost too tender for business."

"That's why I have you," Eva Grace retorted.

Lauren did the books and managed marketing and staff.

Tall and curvaceous with luxuriant, long auburn hair, Lauren was easily the family beauty. Males had been chasing her since puberty, and she had a reputation for taking her pleasure and leaving broken hearts behind. People often underestimated her intelligence—she was smart and savvy.

Sales had increased on the web significantly when Lauren took over the website and social media, which brought more foot traffic into the store.

While Lauren stowed her things in the office, she called out, "Whose dog is in the parking lot?"

"What dog?"

"A big black Labrador mix was just standing out near the street. He looked friendly, but I didn't mess with him. He seemed kind of lost."

Eva Grace went to the window. "I don't see him now." She thought of the dog she'd almost hit last night and was suddenly uneasy.

"He probably just got out of his yard." Lauren turned toward the storeroom, all business again. "Our online sales are good this month. Since we're so slow, we can concentrate on getting some shipments out. Most of these are rush orders for Samhain."

Eva Grace pushed aside unnecessary anxiety about a dog and followed Lauren. They were interrupted by a knock on the back door and found their cousin Maggie juggling boxes.

Maggie was married and the mother of four-year-old Rose. Physically, she was a less voluptuous version of Lauren, her auburn hair a shade deeper and her style much less flamboyant.

During this past summer, the demon had taken control of Maggie in an attempt to infiltrate the coven and steal their magic. Her powers were simple and straightforward when compared to the rest of the young Connellys, and Maggie was sensitive to being a weak link.

She worked at the shop part-time, but her real contribution was a special gift for blending herbs and dried flowers. Her potpourri and scented candles were among their best sellers along with lotions and essential oils.

Eva Grace pointed to the cardboard box Maggie carried. "Is that the last of the autumn harvest?"

Maggie nodded as she headed toward the potpourri display. "I'm really pleased with these new mixes. There's one I called Autumn Breeze that's clean and fresh, like a cool, fall morning in the mountains."

"Get me the names and descriptions for the website," Lauren said. "These will be hot sellers through Thanksgiving. Do you have an inventory list?"

"Of course not," Maggie retorted. Her skills at organization were not as keen as her creativity and talent with plants.

Fussing, Lauren made her list while Maggie arranged the small, colorful bags on a front display.

Eva Grace let the chatter of the other witches swirl around her. This was all so normal. Just another day at the shop. How could they be standing here when danger lurked so close?

"Eva Grace?"

With a start, she realized Maggie had been trying to get her attention.

"Sorry. I was daydreaming," she said and blinked to clear her mind.

"I was wondering if the new diffusers I ordered came in."

"I'll check that box on the work table in the storeroom," Lauren said. "Maybe that's it."

Maggie studied Eva Grace, then handed her a small, pink floral bag of potpourri. "Take this in for a moment. You look like you could use it."

Eva Grace breathed deeply. Soothing lemon balm filled her senses and eased her anxiety. "This is wonderful. These should sell well."

"I hope so. I bought Ian a camera for our anniversary, and I need to pay it off next month. He's really gotten into photography lately, and I love that he has a hobby." Maggie turned as Lauren came out with another box.

"Your diffusers are here and so is my dagger," Lauren said.

"Dagger?" Eva Grace said.

"I saw it on one of our vendor's websites and had to have it." Lauren displayed a leather sheath and a knife with a silver handle shaped like a dragon. "It's only about five inches long, but I bet it could do some damage."

"Of course it could." Maggie backed away. "It's a knife."

"Don't be such a wimp. What do you think of this?" Lauren raised the hem of her crimson skirt, revealing a black leather strap around one shapely thigh. With a flourish, she secured the sheathed knife in the strap. "Isn't that cool?"

Eva Grace had to admit the dagger was sexy.

Maggie didn't. "Why are you arming yourself? You're a witch."

"Just a little extra protection. I ordered several for the shop. I think they'll be popular with some of our regular customers."

Maggie turned to Eva Grace, fear in her eyes. "Sarah and the elder aunts are convinced we're not in danger any longer. Do you think I need a weapon?"

"Not necessarily." Eva Grace was hesitant to fan Maggie's fears, but she wasn't going to lie. "We all need to be on guard and keep our wards against evil strong. The Woman isn't done with us, and the demon is her footman."

They grew silent as Lauren directed a wary glance at the windows. Maggie moved closer to Eva Grace and clasped her hand. They jumped when the bell on the front door sounded.

Maggie gasped in relief when Brenna and Fiona entered the store.

"What's wrong?" Brenna asked immediately. "You all look funny."

"Eva Grace and Lauren think we should be armed," Maggie said.

"What do you mean?" Fiona said, obviously startled at the declaration.

The four cousins began talking at once, arguing over the need for weapons and how magic could be used to wield them. Lauren raised her skirt to display her new dagger.

Annoyed, Eva Grace snapped, "Would you all just shut up?"

Four gaping mouths greeted her outburst.

Brenna recovered first and went to Eva Grace's side. "There's something very wrong, isn't there?"

To Eva Grace's horror, tears gathered in her eyes.

Fiona was quickly on her other side. "Let us help you."

Eva Grace used all of her will to keep from crying. She'd had enough tears in the months since Garth's death and more than enough of her family's sympathy.

"It's your baby," she said, turning to Brenna. "Your wonderful news made me even more aware of the curse. No matter what happens to us…" She paused to look at each of the witches. "We have to stop this for the children."

Brenna looked stricken, a protective hand curving around her stomach.

Maggie struggled not to cry. Her daughter and her brother's little girl were the witches of the next generation. "Couldn't the elders be right about the

Woman being defeated?"

"I don't think so," Eva Grace countered. She told them about Rodric's skirmish with the demon this morning.

"And he chased the demon away?" Brenna asked, her eyes narrowing. "That's…amazing, isn't it?"

Eva Grace shrugged. "Rodric said the demon was mainly taunting him."

"Hmmm." Brenna and Fiona exchanged a look that Eva Grace couldn't read.

"Are you saying that Rodric is lying?" Eva Grace asked.

"Of course not," Brenna retorted. "Rodric's as solid as they come. Jake would trust him with my life. But there's more to him than meets the eye."

Eva Grace felt the need to defend him. "He's been so good to me."

"Yes, we've noticed," Lauren drawled.

The inflection in her voice angered Eva Grace all over again, complicated by her guilt over the memory of Rodric's kiss. "You just can't imagine a man and a woman being friends. Not everyone is out casting love spells on every available male."

"It doesn't appear to me that Rodric needs a love spell," Lauren said.

Fiona stepped between them. "Let's not fight. The demon has shown himself twice in two days. Could the Woman be gathering her power to take the next step?"

"We have to keep searching for answers," Eva Grace said. "We have almost all of the missing pieces to the Woman's story."

"But how will that really help?" Maggie protested. "She's a nasty, vicious spirit."

"Who has yet to claim her tribute," Fiona said. "We can't forget that. There's nothing in the family story about the Woman appearing so many times in the past."

"Probably because of the Remember Not spell," Lauren said thoughtfully. "Something about that really bothers me."

The old spell had been used by previous generations to ease the pain of the loss of the young witches. With that in place, coven members couldn't recall what happened when the Woman came for her tribute each generation.

"You may be right," Eva Grace said. "Forgetting helps, but it doesn't change the circumstances."

"That's why we can hope it's over," Brenna said. "Both times the demon was defeated."

Eva Grace was startled. Fighting the Woman and ending the curse had been Brenna's obsession this summer. She'd even offered herself to the Woman, had battled the demon in a one-on-one magical battle, and fought with Sarah and the elders over it. Falling in love and becoming pregnant may have lulled her into a false sense of security.

"It isn't over," Eva Grace insisted.

Brenna sighed. For the first time, Eva Grace noted the deep shadows beneath her cousin's eyes and the loose fit of her sweater. She had lost weight, and Eva Grace was sure it wasn't from Brenna's compulsive dieting.

The healer's protective instincts heightened. "You need to sit down," she admonished Brenna.

"Don't be silly—"

Eva Grace raised her hand and drew a chair from the corner. Brenna sat. Fiona rubbed her sister's shoulders;

Lauren lit a lavender candle while Maggie studied a display of essential oils.

Eva Grace knelt beside Brenna. "Are you in pain?"

Though she hesitated, Brenna finally said, "I'm just so tired. I've never felt so drained in my life. That was the first signal that I might be pregnant, even before I missed my period."

"It's normal to be tired early in pregnancy."

"But this tired?" Anxiety strained Brenna's voice. "Do you think this could be unnatural? Has the curse somehow affected my baby?"

"Calm yourself," Eva Grace said as the other witches drew close. The lavender scent from the candle drifted toward them. "Take a deep breath."

Slowly, Brenna relaxed, but her worry was still evident. "I'm afraid for my baby."

"Can you get up?" Eva Grace asked.

"Of course." Brenna stood with Lauren and Fiona on either side.

Eva Grace placed her hands on Brenna's stomach. She had divined the health of babies in the womb many times. The living essence she felt from Brenna was strong. And startling. She stifled her gasp.

Brenna turned white, and the witches flanking her took hold of her arms. Beside Eva Grace, Maggie murmured, "Sweet goddess, what's wrong?"

"Nothing," Eva Grace said, wonder growing inside her. Her close connection to her cousin gave her insight she'd never experienced before. "There's nothing wrong."

She smiled as she looked into Brenna's eyes. "There are two. Twins. Just as our mothers were twins. Just as you and I were born to them at the same stroke of the clock."

Cries of happiness came from all the witches as Brenna fell into Eva Grace's arms. Tears streamed down Eva Grace's face, and genuine joy filled her heart. "You're having two babies, Brenna," she murmured. "I'm so happy."

"Thank you. This will happen for you as well, I'm sure."

Eva Grace started to say more about the very real possibility that she wouldn't live long enough to have a child. But she couldn't go there right now, not when her cousins were all filled with euphoric hope. The color was back in Brenna cheeks, and the strength of her magic shone around her again.

A breeze moved through the shop, coaxing musical notes from an array of wind chimes. Eva Grace recognized the sweet scent of their resident ghost, Minnie.

Fiona cocked her head to the side, listening and smiling. "Minnie is so happy. She wants to see these babies grow up."

"We need a party," Maggie said. "We haven't really celebrated Fiona's engagement. Now there's Jake and Brenna's wedding and the twins to get ready for."

"And you and Ian have an anniversary coming," Lauren noted.

"We'll do it at the home place, of course," Brenna said.

Lauren's eyes flashed. "I think I'll ask James Wolff. He's been sniffing around like he wants to go out with me."

"And isn't he the only unmated werewolf in town that you haven't dated?" Fiona asked.

"There is that," Lauren replied with a flip of her long, auburn hair.

Plans for a gathering on Friday night ensued. Food was recommended. Calls were made to the elder aunts and other relatives and close friends.

With arrangements well underway, Maggie departed and Lauren went to the storeroom to pack online orders.

Brenna turned to Eva Grace. "I want to know what's going on between you and Rodric."

Eva Grace's cheeks flamed. "What do you mean?"

Fiona laughed. "You should have seen your face when you were defending him earlier. If Lauren, the most self-involved person I know, has noticed the way you and Rodric are dancing around each other, then surely you realize Brenna and I can tell."

"Spill it," Brenna demanded.

It was as if they were twelve again, and Brenna was digging for information on Eva Grace's latest crush. Eva Grace was convinced Brenna used magic to find her secrets, but she could never prove it.

And a confession was torn from her. "We...we kissed."

Laughing, both cousins hugged Eva Grace. "That's terrific!"

"No, it isn't." In a rush, Eva Grace told them about all of her complicated feelings of guilt and anger. "I'm still in love with Garth. How could I have forgotten that?"

Fiona squeezed Eva Grace's arm. "You have to keep living."

Brenna's voice was gentle. "He would want you to love again."

"I'm not in love with Rodric," Eva Grace protested. "There's just this...pull between us."

"Don't resist it." Brenna pressed a hand to her stomach. "That pull could lead to something wonderful."

"Or ruin a perfectly wonderful friendship."

Fiona groaned. "Don't think that way."

"Rodric is so different from Garth," Eva Grace said. Her shifter fiancé had been a big and brawny ex-soldier. Rodric was a professor, a man of ideas and philosophies. "Why am I so attracted to him?"

"Because he chases demons away?" Brenna suggested.

Fiona nodded. "In a lot of ways that's just like Garth—a protector."

"And he's not quite human." Eva Grace was certain of that. "Does Jake know what he is?"

Brenna shook her head. "It's enough for him that Rodric is a fiercely loyal friend."

"And that should be enough for me, too," Eva Grace said.

Her cousins protested, but before more could be said, a customer walked into the shop.

Eva Grace helped the woman find a dreamcatcher and a pair of Sarah's intricately crafted wood and agate candlesticks. By then her cousins were gone. She helped box orders and load them as Lauren headed to the post office.

Alone, Eva Grace thought of Garth and of Rodric. Wind chimes tinkled again. A widow most of her life, Minnie might understand how Eva Grace felt.

"Did you ever love another after your husband died?" she whispered to the air.

The only answer was a gentle brush on Eva Grace's cheek. Minnie couldn't help. It was all up to Eva Grace.

Chapter 6

Eva Grace eyed her oven with unusual reluctance.
She was supposed to bake a sheet cake for the celebration
at Sarah's tomorrow night. Though she had aventurine,
hematite, and green moss agate crystals in her pocket,
she wasn't feeling any motivation. Probably because her
subconscious was blocking any positive energy.

*Why would anybody think she would enjoy a
gathering like this?*

She'd asked herself that question again and again.
She had no desire to make a cake and decorate it with
"Congratulations" for happy couples.

Jake and Brenna. Fiona and Bailey. Maggie and Ian.
Lauren and her latest conquest. Couples, couples,
couples.

Damn! She just couldn't do it.

Her phone buzzed, and she read a text from Aunt
Frances asking if she'd bring cupcakes, too. The elder
aunts were intent on massive amounts of food. By the
goddess, no one would dare leave hungry. And of course
Eva Grace was supposed to do her part. Good little Eva
Grace. The sweet girl.

A woman who was sick and tired of it all.

Eva Grace texted an affirmative to her elder aunt and
looked up a phone number in her contacts. A sweet voice
answered after the first ring, "Bitta's Bakery."

Five minutes later, feeling satisfied in a way she

hadn't in a while, Eva Grace sat down to read the latest research Rodric had gathered from Coven Glan, the internet used by the supernatural.

He'd been able to link the Woman in White's father to a cult of devil worshipers in the 1700s in Scotland. That reinforced what they knew about the Woman and her demon.

Catriona MacCuindliss had come to America with her parents. Her father was masquerading as a missionary, hiding that he was an evil sorcerer. Catriona's mother died soon after the family arrived in Savannah, Georgia. Catriona was left to travel across uninhabited land with her father and a small band of men on a quest to minister to the savages.

Rodric discovered in his research a group of sorcerers who called themselves MacCuindliss. He theorized they might be descendants of the sorcerer's apprentices. He found no definitive proof this was Catriona's father, but the coincidence was too big to ignore.

Thinking of Catriona living in such an atmosphere saddened Eva Grace. "She was so young," she murmured. She scanned the records Rodric and her Uncle Aiden tracked down through a historical society in Savannah. A list of ship passengers included two entries for "MacCuindliss, Female."

Sometime after arriving in the mountains, Catriona had fallen in love with a Cherokee brave and they had a child. What happened to her after her man and child were gone?

Eva Grace thought that answer might enable the coven to reach the Woman, appeal to the side of her who had loved a man and a child. Healing her wounds might free them all.

"But how?"

Closing her laptop, she sighed. She was tempted to call Rodric. But what would they do but rehash all of this?

There was also the matter of what she *really* wanted to do with Rodric.

Dishes rattled in the breakfront, and sparks flew from the fireplace.

Shocked, she demanded, "Be still," and was thankful when her house obeyed.

What was going on? She wasn't an elemental witch like Brenna. She didn't usually send foundations rattling with her emotions. Yet it was somehow pleasing to realize she had that power.

After taking three deep breaths, she decided to do something ordinary. Gathering calm with every step, she went upstairs to put the finishing touches on her guest bedroom. Decorating her new home was almost complete.

The cold autumn day was fading fast, and she turned on the overhead light. The French provincial furniture made her smile. She finally had a part of her mother in her home. After Celia Connelly was taken by the Woman, Sarah had removed the bed, dresser and chest from her house but hadn't been able to part with it. She'd stored it in the barn behind the home place. So, it had sat, covered in tarps and dust, until Eva Grace asked for it. Marcus refinished it exactly as it had been when Celia used it—white with flourishes of gold trim.

Eva Grace had painted the room's walls a deeper gold and decorated with botanical prints and photographs of the Connelly women. Filmy white curtains framed the windows, and a funky but comfortable deep purple chair anchored one corner. It was the perfect guest retreat.

She made up the bed with new linens washed with lavender. On top, she unfolded a quilt the elder aunts had stitched by hand. Vibrant colors of green, purple, blue and gold gleamed from the cats that decorated four squares. One gazed serenely at the moon. Another sniffed a colorful vase of flowers. The third sat beside a cauldron. The fourth chased butterflies.

This had been her mother's favorite quilt as a child. Aunt Doris had stored it in her cedar chest all these years.

Eva Grace took in the faint scent of cedar. "Welcome home, Mama."

How she wished for Fiona's gifts as a medium. She listened to the silence for a moment. Was her mother here with her?

She received no sign and turned to the closet to retrieve the colorful pillows that would complete the bed's appeal. As she pulled the bag out, she noticed a box in the corner. Puzzled, she tossed the pillows on the bed and dragged the box out into the light. It was dusty and dirty and sealed with cracking masking tape.

She didn't remember seeing this box when the family helped her move into the house. Could it be her mother's?

All of her life, she had been hungry for information about her mother. What would she find here? Journals? Love letters? Perhaps a clue to her father's identity?

She pulled eagerly at the rotted tape, and the top came off. The first thing she saw was a plastic football pinned to a "Homecoming" ribbon.

Tears sprang to her eyes. She could see a teenaged

Celia going to school, on dates, hanging out with friends and the hundreds of other things high school girls did. Ordinary things like trying makeup, gossiping with friends and talking about boys.

And coming into her full powers as a witch.

Eva Grace lifted out pieces of her mother's memories. There were certificates, report cards and sheets of notebook paper with neat cursive writing. Some were school essays, others were poetry. She found photos, ticket stubs and Valentines. Three cards were signed "Romeo." Was Romeo her father? Did he use this name because he knew her family would never accept him, just like Shakespeare's young hero?

As a child, she'd wished she could be a part of an "ordinary" family—a mother, a father, and her—but that was never to be, and even now that made her heart hurt.

Near the bottom of the box, she found a list of Wiccan quotes in her mother's handwriting. Just holding the paper brought her warmth and a surge of power.

She laid it down, sat cross legged on the floor and took a moment to center herself and clear her mind. From the list, she read aloud, "Breathe in the magic."

Magic flowed through her body like a healing balm. She felt steady and strong.

She looked at the paper again. "There is not one path. There is not even the right path. There is only your path."

The words resonated with her. Eva Grace had walked in Brenna's shadow for a long time, her own abilities overpowered by her cousin's strength. Had her mother felt the same way about her twin sister Delia?

The next words filled her with joy. "Walk barefoot. Listen to the wind. Drink in the moon. Be magic."

Eva Grace was very seldom barefoot. Probably only when she did a ritual skyclad did her feet touch the grass. However, it was easy to picture her mother, young and free-spirited, relishing the cool green blades between her toes. Maybe when the weather was a little warmer, she would do the same.

There was one last quote on the tattered piece of notebook paper, and Eva Grace read it with confidence. "Sky above me, earth below me, fire within me."

She gasped as the sides of the dilapidated old box collapsed in a puff of dust and dirt. In the center sat another box. This one was smooth cedar, curiously clean and intricately carved with Celtic knots and circles on top.

Conscious of how easily supernatural forces could be loosed on the world, she opened the wooden box with caution. Inside was a bundle of spotless white silk that showed no sign of storage in a barn for nearly three decades.

"A puzzle within a puzzle," she murmured. At her light touch the silk slipped away to reveal a glossy black surface framed in antique silver—a scrying mirror. The setting sun broke through the window and touched the mirror with a blinding flash that almost caused her to drop it.

This was her mother's. She was sure.

Her vision cleared, and she studied the mirror in detail. At each corner of the delicate silver filigree frame was a symbol—earth, fire, wind, water—the elements of magic.

She stood, her first thought to call Brenna and Fiona and the other cousins. Together, their magic might force the mirror to yield the secrets they needed to end their curse.

But did she need them? Maybe this box and this mirror were meant just for her. Spirits were generally attracted to scrying mirrors, and maybe she could even find a way to connect with her mother.

Spurred to action, she stored the mementos from the box in the dresser and took the mirror downstairs. On the coffee table in the living room, she placed the mirror in the center and draped it with the white silk. She dimmed the lights to a soft glow and turned to the kitchen to find sage.

She stopped as she heard scratching at the back door. She peered out the window over the sink but could see nothing in the deepening dusk. The sound came again, scratching and a faint whimper.

Alarmed to think someone was hurt, she called out, "Who is it?"

There was no response, just more scratching. Eva Grace sensed nothing troubling in the air, and her skin prickled with pleasant anticipation.

She chanted a quick protection spell and opened the door. A sleek black Labrador sat at the base of the steps. He was so black he looked blue in the early evening gloom.

How did she know he was male? She had no idea, but he looked friendly. She wasn't afraid when he came up the steps.

She also knew this was the dog they'd seen by the roadside when they went to the RV camp. Lauren had seen him hanging out at Siren's Call yesterday.

His tail wagged, and she was sure he was smiling. She offered him the back of her hand to sniff. Instead, he licked it, and then sat again in the threshold. As they looked at each other, a name came to her.

"Lorcan," she said, and the dog obediently stood as if awaiting a command. "I know it means strong and silent and is attributed to a warrior."

Once again, the strong tail wagged. Eva Grace felt a wave of warmth move through her and she knew—her familiar had found her. She stepped back. "Come in, Lorcan, and welcome home."

The dog didn't stop until he sat on the rug in front of the hearth. As if he had always lived here. As if he belonged.

"Are you hungry?" she asked.

He lay his head across his front paws and closed his eyes.

"I guess not."

Feeling even more energized and strong, Eva Grace prepared herself for the scrying session. She went upstairs and bathed with soap made from lemon balm and passion flower—herbs known for their calming properties. She pulled her hair into a loose bun and dressed in the emerald cape she wore for rituals. The silky fabric connected her to her family, and their love buoyed her. She was relaxed when she went back downstairs where Lorcan waited beside the coffee table.

He gave her the courage she needed. Brenna had her cat. Fiona had her spirit guide. Now Eva Grace had Lorcan.

She sat on the couch and cleared her mind. She carried her favorite moonstone for heightened sensitivity, a selenite to remove the energy blocks from the room and a tiger eye to have clear perception and insight.

The mirror was set at an angle so she couldn't see

her own reflection. She focused on it. She wanted answers, something that would give her insight into the Woman.

Gray and white swirled in the mirror. Then there was color—a forest, thick with foliage and wildflowers along the base of the trees. A young woman came into view. She ran faster and faster, the background blurring. Strands of blond hair streamed behind her, and she kept glancing over her shoulder, as if being chased.

Eva Grace's breath quickened as she absorbed the woman's fear. The scene sharpened and she saw the splash of red that marred the plain white apron over the woman's gray dress, the crimson that stained her arms, hands and face.

Blood, Eva Grace realized in horror. This was the Woman in White. And she was drenched in blood.

The Woman came to an abrupt halt, turned and looked through the mirror.

Eva Grace fought her fear. Every instinct strained toward the coven, but she would not call them. She would not turn away, no matter what. She was a healer. She could take what others couldn't and release them from suffering. She felt the Woman's rage and panic. And something more. Shame?

The face in the mirror morphed into Eva Grace's own.

She screamed, and the image shattered.

Lorcan howled.

The front door blew open, and Rodric ran inside.

Eyes wild, covered with sweat and shaking, he hauled her against him. "What in the hell have you done? What have you done?"

Chapter 7

Eva Grace walked into Bitta's Bakery while Rodric watched from the warmth of his rented SUV. Watching her was pretty much all he'd done since last night.

Some fast talking was needed to explain how he knew she was in trouble and had burst into her house. He claimed he'd come by, heard her scream and the front door was unlocked. Eva Grace was shaken by the scrying session and easily distracted. So, he didn't have to tell her how he had sensed her distress or how magic had transported him to her door and inside.

She believed the Woman tried to pull her through the mirror. Rodric thought she could be right. Over her objections, he had stayed with her last night. She thought he had slept in her guest room. But he had stood guard.

He and the dog.

Rodric turned to the black lab in the back seat. Intelligence gleamed in Lorcan's amber eyes before he lowered his head. From the start, he'd shown Rodric the respect an alpha would receive.

"You and I have to stick together for her sake," Rodric said.

Lorcan's ears cocked forward.

Rodric smiled. To be honest, he was surprised a familiar hadn't attached to Eva Grace after Garth died and the Woman's threat became real.

But Lorcan was here now, and Rodric trusted him to

guard Eva Grace during the day at the shop. Now they were headed to the Connelly home place for the big party.

Lorcan barked, and Rodric turned as Eva Grace came out of the bakery. The sun hit her glorious red hair. She smiled, and his heart quickened. Lorcan made a low, sympathetic sound.

"I'm pathetic, I know." Rodric hit a button to open the back and hurried into the cold to help her with three large white boxes.

"I should have come in to help you." They stowed the boxes next to the wire contraptions they'd picked up at her house. She said they were cupcake holders. "I didn't know you were getting so much."

"There are a lot of Connellys to feed, and this is going to be a big surprise." She laughed, her eyes alive with humor and mischief. It took great effort not to take that beautiful face in his hands and kiss it.

He remembered the glimpse of pale, naked flesh under her robe last night. He was no less aroused by her in snug black leggings, a burnt orange sweater and thigh high leather boots with stiletto heels.

He took a few moments to close the hatch and steady himself.

At the Connelly home place, Rodric pulled in behind Fiona's new van. He was pleased Bailey had forced the young medium to upgrade from the battered cargo van she'd had before. New Mourne was now Bailey's home base. His family's production company had laid the groundwork to take Fiona's ghost hunting webcast to a full-fledged cable show. Despite the threat of the Woman and the curse, they were moving on with their plans.

"I hope you're prepared for a little chaos." Eva

Grace carried the cupcake trees while Rodric hefted the boxes up the front steps. Lorcan was close on their heels.

"There's never a Connelly gathering without some chaos," he replied.

Maggie came hurrying out as they stepped up on the porch. "Everyone's here. We left plenty of room for your desserts." She frowned as she surveyed the bakery boxes.

"Have you noticed my dog?" Eva Grace said as they walked inside.

Maggie closed the front door behind them and looked at Lorcan. "My goodness, he's beautiful."

"He joined me last night. Quite a surprise."

Kneeling in front of the dog, Maggie put out a hand for him to sniff, then stroked his head. "The kids are going to love him. Rose has been begging for a puppy."

"I always wanted a dog," Rodric commented. He'd yearned for companionship in his lonely childhood at his family's Scottish estate.

"And now you have one," Maggie said with a pert glance between Rodric and Eva Grace.

He should have known the witches were aware of his feelings. But what did they think about it? Maggie just smiled as Eva Grace ignored her and headed to the dining room.

The Connellys' oldest cousin Inez sat near the crackling fire in her wheelchair. She wasn't a witch, but Rodric thought the kind older woman was still magical. By selling her home to Eva Grace, Inez had lifted the younger woman from the depression of living in the house Garth had built for her.

Lorcan immediately went to Inez, proving once again he was a smart dog. Rodric could hear football on the television and cheers from the living room. He was getting used to America's obsession with what should have been Rugby but was vastly different.

Lauren came out of the kitchen with a plate of raw vegetables and dip. The Connelly witches Rodric thought of as the middle aunts–Diane, Estelle and Delia–followed with more platters of finger foods. He spied a cheese board, a variety of sliced sausages and meatballs.

"Party food on parade," Brenna said as she walked out of the kitchen with a bowl of mixed nuts. "I'm eating for three now, and I'm starving."

"You've always eaten enough for three." Fiona came out of the kitchen and avoided Brenna's teasing slap as she placed a bowl of chips and a basket of crackers on the table.

Rodric set the three boxes on the sideboard where Eva Grace placed her cupcake trees.

"Where's the cake?" Lauren asked as Eva Grace opened the first box.

"I didn't make one." Eva Grace began loading the tree with cupcakes decorated with gold glitter and tiny flags that read 'She said yes!'

The stunned silence amused Rodric. Without pause, Eva Grace opened the second box and blithely filled in branches of the tree with chocolate cupcakes sporting gold bands entwined on top.

A low murmur chased round the room, and Rodric's jaw ached from the effort it took not to smile. He knew the pride the Connelly women took in their home-baked goods. Eva Grace was an amazing cook, and this was a major departure.

The third box contained white cupcakes decorated with pink and blue booties. Rodric turned as Sarah and the elder aunts came into the room bearing ham and turkey for sandwiches and a bowl of the Southern potato salad he'd learned to love.

Eva Grace turned to her sister witches and presented the desserts with a sweeping gesture. "Happy engagement, happy pregnancy, and happy anniversary. Aunt Frances, you asked me to bring cupcakes. Enjoy!"

"These cupcakes are from a bakery," Frances sputtered.

Doris chimed in, "By the goddess, we've never had store-bought desserts at a family gathering."

There was laughter from Inez. "You're forgetting my son's third wife. She never made a single thing. She brought those awful snack cakes. Bitta's will be much better, we know."

"Bitta?" Bailey said from the doorway. The males had abandoned the football game and were massed in the dining room.

Bitta, the town's pretty kitchen witch, spiced her baked goods with a little magic that was particularly appealing to men.

Jake walked over to the display. "They have pink and blue feet for our babies. That's a little creepy." He unwrapped a cake, took a bite. "But delicious." He offered a bite to Brenna, and they shared the cake.

Rodric felt Eva Grace stiffen beside him. This was hard for her. He put his hand at the small of her back and gave her an encouraging look.

Obviously puzzled, Sarah's smile was forced. "Are we ready to eat?"

Lauren took photos of each couple. Toasts were offered with apple cider or wine. Then they dove into the food in true Connelly style. Rodric hung back with Eva Grace and the elder aunts.

She said to them, "I don't think the goddess will be too upset over the cupcakes, do you?"

The elder aunts did not agree.

"It's not a small thing," Doris said.

"We don't like traditions to end," Frances added. "You took over making the cakes for special occasions from me years ago. I thought you'd continue."

Sarah entered the conversation. "I'm sure Eva Grace just didn't have time."

"No," she retorted. "I didn't want to make a cake."

"But why?" Doris sputtered. "You always—"

"I didn't even want to be here." Eva Grace's voice rose, and the room fell quiet.

"Now see here—" Frances began.

Eva Grace swung her arms up, and every plate on the table jumped.

"Don't hurt the cupcakes," Bailey said in an attempt at humor.

No one laughed. Even the children were still. Only Lorcan moved, navigating his way to Eva Grace's side.

"My fiancé died just months ago on the day before our wedding," she said. "Many of you were with him that morning, helping to cart tables and chairs into my garden so we could celebrate our marriage." Her voice faltered, then she lifted her chin. "And then he was gone. Just gone. How can I celebrate anything?"

The boisterous Connellys were at a loss for words. Eva Grace didn't have outbursts. She was the calm one.

"And for all I know…" She stopped as a small sob escaped. "He was taken in my place."

"But that's not true," Brenna protested. "The demon killed Garth."

"Because of the Woman." Eva Grace was pale and

trembling, as she'd been last night after the scrying session. He could tell she was more convinced than ever that she was the next tribute.

The coven offered reassurances, but she would have none of them. To Brenna, she said, "You obviously weren't her choice. The demon wanted your power. The Woman said she wasn't ready. She didn't take Fiona. Again, she wasn't ready. But she's ready now. She's coming for me."

Tears streamed down her face now, and the witches of her generation moved in. Rodric remained steadfast at her side.

"We should have been more sensitive to your feelings," Fiona murmured.

Brenna hugged her hard. "We're still fighting the Woman. We're going to beat her once and for all. I won't let her take you. Or any of us." Her hand rested on her belly.

"Yes," Maggie agreed, showing strength Rodric hadn't glimpsed until now. "I'm sick of these threats to all of us. It has to end."

"It will." Lauren, who often seemed so frivolous, had a new resolve about her. "She's going down."

"But how?" Eva Grace's expression was bleak.

Sarah took her in her arms. "My sweet girl, I'm going to do everything in my power to protect you."

Rodric knew her power was considerable, but he sensed fatigue in the coven leader. The impending curse had taken a toll.

Eva Grace pulled herself together and wiped tears away. "I'm sorry," she said to her family. "So sorry."

Maggie's young daughter stepped forward and wrapped her arms around Eva Grace's knees. "Don't cry,

Evie. Please don't cry."

A laugh burst out of Eva Grace as she knelt to hug the little witch.

The tension in the room eased. Doris and Frances offered tearful apologies. The Connelly men and Connelly mates hugged Eva Grace.

Even Lauren's latest conquest, a tall, rugged-looking werewolf named James, came over. Like all the supernaturals in New Mourne, he knew the sacrifices the coven made to protect his kind. "Anything for you," he said.

As the assault on the food resumed, Rodric was able to claim Eva Grace's attention and whisper, "Do you want to leave?"

She released a deep breath. "No, but I could use a minute."

"This way." He took her hand and pulled her into the deserted kitchen with Lorcan padding after them.

He handed her a monogrammed handkerchief. The nanny who raised him had insisted no man should be without one, and her rules still played through his mind.

Eva Grace took it with a rueful smile and blew her nose.

He touched her cheek. "Feeling better?"

"I'm fine. Frankly, it felt good to tell them how angry I am about everything."

She tucked the handkerchief in her own pocket and leaned against the counter. "Our main goal is harm to no one, but it seems harmful to me to not face reality head on."

"Are you going to tell them what you saw in the mirror last night?"

"Tomorrow." Lorcan nuzzled her hand, and she

rubbed his head. "There's been enough drama tonight."

"Then more drama is coming for sure." They shared a laugh.

The door from the dining room opened to admit Inez's daughter. "Excuse me, but Mother wants to speak with you," she said to Eva Grace.

They followed her to the dining room where Inez was still by the fireplace chatting with Brenna and Fiona. Some discussion ensued about Lorcan before the sisters drifted away.

Inez patted the arm of the chair. "Sit next to me, Eva Grace."

"I'll go so you can visit," Rodric said.

"You should stay." Inez pointed to the chair on her other side.

"Are you feeling okay?" Eva Grace asked her.

"Other than this, I'm fine." She pointed to the oxygen tube in her nose.

Eva Grace put her hand against the elderly woman's chest and chanted quietly.

Rodric watched Inez's color improve.

"Better?" Eva Grace asked.

"Yes, thank you. Now I have something for you." From the pouch that hung over one arm of her wheelchair, Inez produced a little velvet bag. "This belonged to my husband. I showed it to Fiona and Brenna once, but what I didn't tell them was that the fae helped him find it."

Her hands trembling, Inez opened the bag. "This was one of his treasures. When he died, he asked me to be sure it got to the right person. I always thought you should have it, and today, I realized it was time."

The arrowhead Inez held out was of creamy stone

and perfectly shaped. Rodric judged it to be about two inches long and half as wide at its base. The tip was honed to a fine point.

"Did he sharpen it?" he asked Inez.

"Oh, he would never do that." She turned the arrowhead over and over. "Craig had many arrowheads, most of them broken in some way. He used to tell me how rare it was to find one like this. He kept it in a box with other things he'd found when he was a boy plowing the farm, and he told me they were important."

Rodric didn't think the old woman was aware of the tears that rolled down her wrinkled cheeks.

"He was my beloved and such a good man." She took Eva Grace's hand and placed the arrowhead in her palm. "The day your mother was taken by the Woman, Craig got out this arrowhead. He held it and cried like a baby. He wouldn't tell me why. But he was a Connelly, and he had a good sense of magic and of danger. He put it away and told me to guard it until I knew it was time to share the power."

Eva Grace stared down at the arrowhead.

"It's time," Inez whispered. "Only you can find the answers."

The arrowhead glowed, becoming almost translucent. Eva Grace closed her fingers around it and swayed.

Alarmed, Rodric went to her and placed his hand on her shoulder. He felt a ripple of magic. She looked up at him, her face alight with beauty and strength.

Sarah and Brenna came in, looking concerned.

The front door banged open, followed by a burst of cold wind that extinguished the fire.

Lorcan growled.

Rodric was instantly alert, the blood of his ancestors surging through his veins. He pulled his glamour tight around him.

"Hide it," Inez warned Eva Grace. "Now."

She stuffed the arrowhead in the top of her boot.

The tiny old woman who ruled the fae of New Mourne appeared in the doorway. Her manservant, tall and angular and almost as ancient as she, loomed behind her.

"Where is it?" Willow demanded.

The family wand had appeared in Sarah's hand. "See here, Willow. I've told you before that you can't just burst into my home. You used to show some courtesy."

"There's no time for courtesy, you fool." Willow advanced toward Eva Grace. "Where is it?"

Rodric faced her, his hand going to the knife sheath he wanted to summon. Should he show himself for what he was? Anything to protect Eva Grace. "You need to back up," he told Willow.

She cackled, eyes narrowing as she studied him. "I know you, Scotsman." Her gaze flickered to Eva Grace. "I know your weaknesses. Stand aside."

Eva Grace stepped around him, chin raised. Lorcan was at full alert beside her.

Willow sniffed the air. "I smell fae magic. What have the Connellys been keeping from me? Do you know something I should know?"

"We know so much more than you," Inez said, her voice calm.

Willow glared at her. "What do you have to do with this?"

Sarah interrupted, "Willow, you are in my house.

There are rules about this."

"I make my own rules when you're in my business." Thumping her stag-head staff on the floor, Willow made the sturdy house rumble and glared at Eva Grace. "What did this human tell you, witch?"

"That only I can find the answers."

Eva Grace's challenging tone startled Rodric.

"So, it's on you, now." Willow pointed a boney finger at her. "This is it for the Connellys. You'd better not be meddling in what's fae."

Sarah stepped forward. Willow glanced at the older witch as she walked back out the front door. It slammed behind her.

Everyone was frozen in place until Rodric said, "What did that mean?"

Eva Grace looked at the arrowhead, which looked like an unassuming rock now. "I have no idea, but I'm pretty sure we'll hear from her about this again."

Chapter 8

"I had no idea there were fae in New Mourne that weren't under Willow's rule," Eva Grace said as they pulled into her driveway after the party. "I thought she was, for lack of a better word, the supreme ruler."

"Actually, pixies have their own monarchy," Rodric said.

Eva Grace gave him a sidelong glance. "You're kidding."

"They have a king, queen, and a complete royal court. If there are fae in New Mourne not sworn to Willow, they may well be pixies."

Intrigued, she said, "Come in and tell me about them."

This was a good excuse to ask Rodric to remain with her for a while. Tonight's events, coming on top of the scrying session, had rattled her more than she liked to admit, and she wasn't anxious to be alone. Even now she could feel heat and vibration from the arrowhead still tucked at the top of her boot.

The coven wasn't sure what to make of the arrowhead or Inez's story that it came from fae. After Willow's departure, they had all passed it around. It glowed only for Eva Grace.

The elder witches were concerned with Willow's anger, but Brenna dismissed it. She and Fiona had both dealt with the ancient one when the demon and Woman threatened them in the summer. They felt Willow would support anything that would protect all supernaturals in New Mourne.

Eva Grace wasn't as certain as her cousins. The wind from earlier had died, and the night was as clear and cold as January as they headed to her house. A hard freeze was predicted. The house was chilly, and Rodric built up the fire while she poured glasses of blueberry wine that Doris' son-in-law had made last spring. Lorcan lay near the hearth and Rodric and Eva Grace settled on the couch.

Rodric sipped his wine. "This is very good."

"Uncle Bill has raised blueberries for years, and the aunts make preserves and freeze them for muffins and pies. His is some of the best wine in the mountains." She took a drink from her own glass. "Now what were you saying about pixies?"

"I've studied pixies since I was a child. My nanny introduced me to them."

"You've mentioned her before. She must have been special to you."

"She was the only person who cared about me after my parents died," he said quietly. "I adored her."

He'd been an orphan like her, she remembered. His father had been Irish, his mother Scottish. He'd grown up with his maternal uncle, a laird named Ferguson. She imagined it was a lonely childhood.

"I'm lucky I had a big family," she observed. "As annoying as they can all be, there were so many people loving me and Brenna and Fiona. We felt like we had mothers, fathers and brothers and sisters all over town."

"I do envy that," he said. "There was no one except Uncle Boyd and me. Thankfully he was gone most of the time. I had Nanny as well as the rest of a small staff who had loved my mother. They soon fell in with Nanny and helped raise me."

"So they forgave your mother for marrying Irish?"

"They would have forgiven her anything. The cook, the maid and the gardener—all of them kept her memory alive for me."

"And Nanny?"

"Her name was Siobhan O'Hara," Rodric continued. "She had been my father's nanny. My parents died in a car crash while on a visit to my uncle's. Nanny showed up a few days later and refused to leave. I stayed in the kitchen with Cook while she met with Uncle. I have no idea what she said to him, but when they came out, he said Nanny would live with us to take care of me."

"Why wouldn't he have wanted that anyway? You needed someone familiar after such a traumatic event."

"He hated the Irish, and you couldn't get more Irish than Nanny. She was from Belfast and proud of it."

"Did you ever ask her what was said in that meeting?"

"No, I was so relieved she wasn't going to leave me in that big, cold castle with all those people I didn't know. When I was older, I did wonder, but I never asked her. Nanny had some kind of power over my uncle. She was the only member of the staff that didn't visibly tense when he was around."

Eva Grace laughed. "Not much puts fear in a strong Irish matron."

"Exactly. I also believe there was some magic in her blood. That's why she was so insistent I learn everything I could about Irish culture and beliefs. She was also a devout Catholic, and we went to mass several times a week."

"And introduced you to pixies." Eva Grace pulled her legs under her and turned to face him on the sofa. "Tell me about them."

"The legends of the pixies are very old. They're thought to predate Christianity. Christians tried to use them, saying they were the souls of unbaptized children. But they're associated with the myths and stories of Devon and Cornwall, so decidedly Celtic."

He set his glass on the end table. Lorcan got up to sniff it and then put his head on Rodric's knee. He gave the dog an absent stroke. "I think your garden here would be a haven for pixies since Inez lived here with her husband. And she and her family are so open and loving, the pixies would most likely be happy here."

"I've never seen a pixie," Eva Grace said. "In fact, there are only a few fae in New Mourne that I can name definitively—a farmer out to the west, the hardware store owner whose son was in my class at school. It's always sounded as if Willow commands an army, but I'm not sure of all the soldiers."

"They're a secretive lot, but I'm sure the elder aunts are aware of most of them."

Eva Grace drank the last of her wine. "They need to share all of their knowledge with us."

"I have to agree," Rodric said. "Let's put some treats in the garden tonight and see if the pixies respond. I'm sure word of Willow's anger has already spread. It will be interesting to see how the pixies might react."

"What do they like?"

"Sweet food—honey, pears, sweetbreads. Nanny and I used to put the food out on a colorful plate. We'd go out at dawn to see the pixies gather their treats. I used to play tag with a couple of them who were less shy than the others."

Eva Grace laughed, delighted with the thought of him as a small boy playing with fae at sunrise.

"We can do the same and see what happens," he suggested, a hint of that boy in his eyes.

Eva Grace jumped up and headed to the kitchen. "I have some canned pears. Is canned OK? I also have some of Bitta's bread. They should love that." She turned on the stove and set her kettle on the flame, then opened her pantry.

She turned to find Rodric in the doorway, smiling at her with heat in his gaze. Her body responded in kind.

Suddenly nervous, she shifted jars in her pantry. "What about preserves? I mentioned I have blueberry—"

"That should be fine." He stepped over and reached around her. "Don't forget the honey."

Eva Grace breathed in the clean scent of him, a mixture of sandalwood and musk. Yearning spread through her. It was lust, she realized. Full-on lust. She'd fought this feeling for weeks, shamed that she could feel this for anyone but Garth. But here it was—a deep, aching need for a man. This man.

She stepped back as he pulled down a plastic bottle of honey shaped like a bear. Images clicked through her head. Rodric's lips on hers, tasting of honey. His hands on her breasts, her hips. Her body naked under his.

Her heart pounded, blood rushed in her ears. It took her a moment to realize he had spoken to her. "Excuse me?"

"Where's the bread?"

She swallowed hard, forcing herself to be normal.

"In the bread box."

"You have a bread box?"

"Sarah always said it keeps bread and chips from cluttering the counter."

"I haven't seen one of these since I was a child," he said and turned to the antique breadbox.

The exchange was banal. Couldn't he see what she wanted, how she felt?

He looked at her with a smile. "What can we put all of this food on?"

She forced herself to concentrate on something other than how he made her heart flutter. "I have just the thing."

Going to the dining room, she paused to press icy hands against her burning cheeks. She called on the goddess for calm and retrieved a miniature tea set.

She managed to help him load pears, bread and jam on the saucers and tea with honey in the little pot. She set all of them on a small tray that he carried out into a night brightened by the moon. She and Lorcan followed, crunching through dried leaves.

Rodric stopped at the base of the biggest maple tree, its prematurely bare branches reaching out like tentacles. He set the tray on the ground.

"You're sure they'll like this?" she asked.

"Positive. Now all you need to do is chant to invite them to eat."

She folded her hands at her waist and closed her eyes. When she spoke, her power pushed through her voice. "Come visit us, fae; we invite you to stay. To eat, to drink, to laugh and play. My garden is yours until the light of day."

Neither of them spoke until he took her hand. "That

was perfect. Let's go back in. You're getting cold."

She followed him and the dog inside, but couldn't resist looking back at the little tea set just before she closed the door.

She turned and was in Rodric's arms. She thought at first he was just going to warm her from the chill. Instead, his lips touched hers, soft but insistent. He knew how much she wanted him. Because he wanted her, too.

Her eyes fluttered closed as he drew away. "I know you loved Garth with everything in you. He was my friend, my brother, and I don't say that lightly. But this, between us. It's…"

She waited, barely breathing, then opened her eyes to gaze into his. "It's ours."

Chapter 9

Rodric wasn't sure he'd heard her correctly. He hadn't planned to kiss her and didn't know what he thought would happen if he did.

As if she read his mind, she smiled. "Not what you were expecting?"

He answered with another kiss. Gentle at first, it deepened fast. Eva Grace's hands fisted in his shirt, pulling him closer. Her curves pressed against him, her yearning clear.

It was every fantasy he'd ever had about her. Her hair so soft. Her scent so sweet. Her magic swirling and dancing around them. Try as he might, he couldn't rein in his own magic-laced desire. The heat was instantaneous. The very air around them sparked and fell in colorful ashes that disappeared before hitting the floor.

She pulled away. "And what is this?"

"It's what you do to me."

"How does an academic make magical fire?"

"I can show you." He kissed her once more and the room exploded in the colors of flames—red, gold, orange and white.

"I like that." She laughed and kissed him again, tugging him forward until her back was against the cabinets.

He lifted her onto the counter and came perilously

close to losing control of his fire. She arched her back, and he pressed his mouth to her throat. Because of who and what he was, he could hear the blood rushing in her veins. It thundered around him, and his ancestors sang her name in his head.

He was astounded. He'd been taught they only sang the truth.

Her legs curved around him, and she drew his hands to breasts full and firm beneath her soft sweater. He pictured her naked, and the part of him that was human almost exploded.

"Wait," he said, stilling her hands. "Wait a minute."

"I don't want to wait." A thin line of perspiration beaded on her forehead, and her eyes were bright, fevered.

He backed away. "I've always thought of you as small and delicate, as fragile as a rose petal."

"If you dry rose petals, they can last for years. Never think of a rose as just something pretty that dies too quickly."

She flicked her hand, and his arms were around her again although he couldn't remember moving. She put both her hands on his face and kissed him. "Take me to bed, Rodric."

"I promised to never risk our friendship."

"I accept the risk." She traced his lips with her fingertip. "I want you tonight, and I know you'll be my friend in the morning."

"You're very sure of yourself."

Boldly, she cupped his erection. "And you're very hard. Please make love to me."

That was his undoing.

Lorcan had the manners to settle by the fire as

Rodric took Eva Grace up to her room. Candles lit when they walked in. The scent of lavender mixed with vanilla and it all blended into her.

She was rose gold, shimmering with light from within. They were naked in moments, tangled in soft, creamy sheets the next. Her breasts were as lush as he'd imagined, her bones delicate but strong, and the heat at her center was intoxicating. One touch and she quivered to completion.

Then he was in her, and she met him stroke for stroke until he came.

When they could breathe again, he fell to her side.

A line of fire crossed the ceiling above them before settling into a sweet, violet haze.

She put her head back and laughed, her long, red hair spilling across the pillows. "Sweet goddess, what are you, Rodric McGuire?"

"Yours," he answered, not laughing.

She said nothing, but slowly, tenderly, she drew him to her again.

****

Dawn was turning the frost to diamonds as Rodric spread a towel on the old-fashioned glider in Eva Grace's backyard. She was still asleep, Lorcan curled on the floor beside her bed.

Waking with her in his arms had been heaven. He could have stayed there the entire day, but there was work to be done, a curse to be broken so that his beautiful, flame-haired love would survive.

So he drank hot tea and waited in the cold. The tribute they'd left for the pixies last night was untouched. Would they come? He wanted to know the connection between the wee folk and the arrowhead Inez had given

Eva Grace.

The air around him changed, and he set his cup aside. Leaning forward, with his hands clasped between his knees, he focused on the base of the maple tree. A twinkle of light caught his eye. The sky above brightened from purple to violet, and he saw the first flutter of wings.

They came one by one and hovered above the food. Though they didn't physically consume it, he saw the consistency change as it had when he was a little boy visited by the pixies.

"Hello," he greeted them.

One of the pixies whipped up near him like a hummingbird. He was motionless as she studied him. The others joined her, and they moved around him.

"I'm a friend," he said. "Yours and Eva Grace's. I'm here to protect her."

The pixies stilled.

"Can you help me?" he asked. "It's for her."

A sound behind him sent the pixies flying. He turned as Eva Grace came out with Lorcan at her side. She watched in silent awe as the pixies swooshed up, flew in a bright circle, and disappeared as fairy dust fell to the earth like sparkling snow.

He stood and looked at Eva Grace, feeling a bit of awe himself. She wore a soft white nightgown, her hair loose on her shoulders, the lines of her body outlined in the awakening light.

"Did they tell you anything?" she asked as he crossed the yard to her side.

"Not yet, but this was our first contact. We'll leave them more treats and talk with them again."

"Look at this." She held out her hand. The

arrowhead pulsated and glowed in her palm. As the sun rose, it pulsed one more time and went still.

"It woke me," Eva Grace said. "I came looking for you."

"They'll be back. I'm sure of it." He took the hand that held the arrowhead, his thumb rubbing her wrist as he studied it. She looked up at him and smiled while his heart melted.

His hands moved up to her face as he kissed her, drinking her in like a rare, fine wine. She was still warm from the bed they'd shared.

"By the goddess," she whispered against his lips. "I thought everything inside me was dead."

"No way. You're alive and I'm alive. In fact, I'm very much alive."

"If you were human, you'd be exhausted," she retorted, eyes narrowing as she studied him. "But I don't think you're human."

"We could test that theory." He glanced up at her bedroom window. "Inside."

Lorcan barked, and Eva Grace laughed. "I think someone wants to be fed."

"Okay," Rodric said to the dog. "You win."

He followed her and Lorcan inside, glancing one last time at the garden. The clear morning sky was suddenly blanketed with clouds, and cold, dry wind picked up from the east. The warrior inside Rodric felt the threat in the air.

Trouble was moving in fast.

Chapter 10

The figures on the monthly sales report swam in
front of Eva Grace's eyes. Sunday afternoon had been
quiet in the shop, and she settled at the counter with her
laptop. Lorcan slept at her feet. And all she could do was
think about Rodric.

His lips, his touch, the thrill of his lovemaking.

She gave up on the spreadsheet and sat back in her
chair. She'd known passion with Garth. He was her only
lover until last night. He was always tender and
generous, intent on her satisfaction. But last night
was...explosive.

Once Rodric's initial hesitation ended, he aroused
something new inside her. He had challenged her to see
how high they could go.

She chuckled, thinking about how far they'd gone.
Just what kind of supernatural was the scholarly Rodric
McGuire, Ph.D.? He was all male, but he was also magic
and unlike anyone she'd ever met before.

She'd tried to ask him about it after they went back
inside this morning. Instead of answering, he carried her
to the shower where they made hot, steamy love. They'd
spent the morning in bed. The memory made her shiver,
and she contemplated calling him now. Maybe she could
just go over to the inn, surprise him, take off all his
clothes and hers...

Lorcan's bark pulled her from her daydream. Eva

Grace blinked up at Brenna and Fiona.

"Are you okay?" Brenna asked, looking concerned. "Didn't you hear the bell ring?"

"I was just thinking about sales for the month." She avoided her cousin's gaze and stood.

"You should be more careful when you're here alone," Fiona said.

"Lorcan's here to protect me." Eva Grace stood and walked toward the kitchen in the back. "How about some tea?"

"Coffee for me." Fiona stopped to pet the dog. "With that pumpkin spice creamer."

Brenna trailed Eva Grace. "We just wanted to see how you were. Last night was pretty intense."

"Yes, definitely." Suppressing a smile, Eva Grace filled the electric tea kettle and plugged it in. "I have a special herbal blend I made up for you yesterday. It will be soothing for the twins."

"I think I'll just have what you've been having," Brenna replied, a sly look in her eyes.

From the doorway, Fiona said, "Oh, wow. You and the good doctor finally got it on."

Eva Grace flushed. There were many benefits to the bond she shared with her sister witches. The downside was how well they could read her.

Brenna laughed. "Spill it, missy, we want all the deets."

"All I'm serving is coffee or tea, you silly witches."

Despite their protests, she held fast to her resolve as she fixed their drinks. They went back into the shop.

"Okay, I'll stay out of your personal biz," Fiona said as she fed Lorcan some of her muffin. "But I'm glad this happened. Rodric's a good man, and it's time to move ahead with your life."

"A good man," Eva Grace mused.

"What do you mean?" Brenna demanded.

Eva Grace changed the subject before they could go down a rabbit hole she didn't want to explore. "I'm sorry about my little tantrum at the party before the Willow drama."

"No need to apologize," Brenna assured her. "We were a little insensitive about the entire party."

"Rodric was right by your side last night," Fiona added. "I like the way he treats you."

Eva Grace smiled and looked up as the bell over the front door rang. Jake called out.

He grinned as he greeted them and kissed his wife. "I saw your car and decided to check on the little bump." His hand covered her stomach. "How are they doing?"

"I fed them leftover cupcakes for breakfast, and a hamburger for lunch," she replied. "So they're happy."

They all laughed. Jake said, "You look great, Eva Grace. I was worried last night after Willow's intrusion."

"Oh, she's fine," Brenna answered. "She got some last night."

Eva Grace almost spilled her tea, and Jake's face flamed red. It wasn't often the lawman and shifter looked unsure of himself, but she was certain he wished he could assume his tiger shape and run.

"You are impossible," she told Brenna. "Can't you keep your mouth shut for one moment?" She would have preferred Jake find out about her and Rodric another way. Jake had been Garth's closest friend. This could be awkward.

Before she could say anything more, the shop bell rang again. Sarah and Marcus arrived with Aidan and

Delia in tow.

"By the goddess," Eva Grace said, truly annoyed. "Is the whole family coming by to see if I'm okay?"

Oblivious to any undercurrents, Sarah sailed in, wrapped in a cheerful red wool shawl, a long gray braid looped over one shoulder. She crossed straight to Eva Grace and pulled her into her arms.

Her cheek was cold from outdoors, but her embrace was warm and familiar. Eva Grace sank into it. "I'm okay, Grandmother." It was rare to call her that, but it seemed right. "There's nothing to worry about."

"I don't want that old fae coming after you to get that arrowhead," Sarah said as she pulled away. "Willow always pretends she wants to help us, but she usually just makes trouble."

Marcus came over and touched Eva Grace's cheek. She pressed her face against his hand for a moment.

"Inez gave us all a lecture after you left," Sarah said. "She doesn't want us to take any of this lightly. But for the life of me I can't understand why she didn't tell us about the connection to the faeries before."

Aiden shook his head and seemed worried. "Fae matters are always serious."

"I'm fine," Eva Grace insisted.

In the pocket of her gray slacks the arrowhead was safe and secure. She was about to tell everyone about the pixies and how she and Rodric planned to get information from them. But the bell signaled still another arrival. Lorcan barked again and headed for the door.

"There haven't been this many people in here at once in a month," Eva Grace said as she followed him.

To her surprise, she found Mick and Randi at the entrance. Lorcan was on his haunches, not growling, but also not allowing them to pass.

"It's okay," she told him before greeting them. Lorcan sniffed at Mick's boots and whined but fell back.

Once again Eva Grace thought that Randi seemed familiar. "You're looking much better."

"Grandfather told me how you helped me," she said. "I wanted to say thank you."

"And I want to arrange payment," Mick added.

"There's no need—"

"I insist," he said. "I'm sure there's something I could do for you."

"Come and meet my family," Eva Grace invited. They rounded a row of shelves, and the group at the back turned.

Sarah gasped, and her eyes glazed with shock. "Ah, goddess, help me," she said and clutched at Marcus's arm.

"What is it, love?" he asked.

Brenna went to her other side. "What's wrong?"

"Hello, Sarah."

Mick looked at Sarah in a way that made Eva Grace uncomfortable. Lorcan bumped against her leg.

"I think I know the problem," Mick said. "Sarah, I never thought to see you again. We may have a few more years behind us, but you're as beautiful as ever." He moved forward, his hands outstretched.

Marcus stepped in front of her. "Who in the hell are you?"

"An old friend of hers." Mick's voice deepened, his black eyes gleaming. "We were close once."

Marcus put a hand on Mick's chest. "You need to step back."

Mick didn't retreat. Lorcan growled and bared his

teeth, and Eva Grace knelt to soothe him.

"Grandfather," Randi warned, her arm twining with his.

Jake stepped up. "Okay, everyone cool off." He put a hand on each man's shoulder.

Sarah seemed to come to herself and took her husband's arm. "Marcus, please, I'm fine now. I'm all right. I haven't seen Mick since I was young. I was stunned."

"And I didn't expect to see you, either." Mick patted his granddaughter's hand on his arm.

"Who are you?" Delia said as she aligned herself next to Brenna. The three generations of witches clasped hands.

Mick just looked at Sarah.

She closed her eyes and sighed. She turned to Marcus. "Mick and I were lovers once."

"Okay." Marcus was once again calm and steady, the man Eva Grace had looked at as a father for half of her life. He certainly knew about Sarah's colorful, free-spirited past, just as he knew she'd never looked at another since he came into her life.

"There's more," Sarah said as her gaze moved to Delia. "Mick is the gypsy my sisters always harped about. He's your father."

The words reverberate in Eva Grace's head. Even Lorcan was quiet.

Silence deepened until Fiona said, "Holy shit."

And Eva Grace realized why Randi seemed so familiar. She looked like Fiona.

Aiden put his arm around Delia's shoulders. "This is unexpected."

"For us all," Mick agreed.

"But you knew she lived here." A white line rimmed Delia's lips. "Didn't you think about that?"

"It was long ago," Mick replied. "I didn't think to see her. Or you." He smiled at Delia, and she glared back.

He turned to Sarah. "Why didn't you tell me about her?"

"I told you I was pregnant," Sarah replied. "You left in the middle of the night, and it's difficult to contact someone who has no permanent address. We didn't have the internet back then, so how would I find you?"

"I was young and restless, and I didn't want to settle here."

"Then why are you back?" Marcus asked, his voice tight with anger.

Eva Grace thought they all needed to calm down. "Why don't I close the store so we can talk undisturbed?"

"Let's not," Delia said bluntly. "I have nothing to say to this man. Being a father is more than just getting a woman pregnant. A father is there for his children."

Eva Grace saw Brenna's bitter smile. For years she had said the same sort of thing about her own parents who left her and Fiona to be raised by Sarah.

As if sensing her sister's thoughts, Fiona said, "Maybe Mother is right. We don't have to talk about this now."

"Mick and his granddaughter should leave," Sarah said. "I've nothing to say to him. He made his choice all those years ago, and so did I."

"Do I get any say in this?" Mick asked.

"He has a right—" Randi started.

"He has no rights," Sarah retorted. "And to be

truthful, I'm glad he left me in peace to raise my daughters."

"Daughters?" Mick repeated.

"I had a twin." Delia's voice had a belligerent edge.

Green eyes stone cold, Sarah said, "She's dead."

"Our child died?" Mick asked.

"She was my child," Sarah corrected him. "Eva Grace's mother."

Mick's gaze skipped to Eva Grace, and she thought she saw regret. "I'd like to know more about all of this."

Jake cleared his throat. "It's best if you go." He gestured to the door in a way that brooked no argument.

Mick took Randi's hand. "I'm at the campground if any of you want to see me."

"If you don't leave in the middle of the night," Delia said.

Eva Grace followed them to the door, Lorcan close by her side. She wanted to say something to Mick. Her family didn't agree, but this felt wrong to her. Obviously, no one wanted to welcome Mick with open arms. But should they just throw him out on the street?

Maybe Sarah had nothing to say to him, but Eva Grace might. Her mother died when she was days old, and she didn't even know her father's name. Now her missing grandfather was here, and everyone wanted her to turn her back on him. Maybe they could all be cavalier about another member of their family leaving, but she couldn't.

"I'm sorry," she murmured as she opened the door for them. "We will talk."

Mick and Randi nodded and left.

"Why did you do that?"

Eva Grace wheeled to face Brenna. "I don't want to

burn any bridges."

"He's not a bridge. He abandoned Sarah."

"Does that mean I can't be curious about him? Remember the stories we made up about the dark gypsy coming to see us? He's our grandfather."

The rest of the family clustered around Brenna as she said, "We were children. There's nothing romantic about what he did to Sarah."

Normally, if there was an argument, Eva Grace was the peacemaker, but things were changing. She was changing. That's not what she wanted now. "I want to know more about him."

Protests rang out until Sarah said, "Enough!"

She took Eva Grace's hands in her own. "Stay away from him. Please. I don't like this. We have enough turmoil to deal with."

Eva Grace said nothing. She'd always trusted her grandmother, but Sarah had been wrong about many things since the Woman and her demon were threatening their family again.

"I don't trust him," Sarah said. "In all honesty, I never did. I was young and foolish when we met, a ripe target for his charming ways and good looks. But I wasn't stupid, and I should have followed my gut. It was better all the way around that he left me."

"Better for you, but what about all of us?"

The older woman looked pained, and Eva Grace instantly regretted her careless comment.

"I'm sorry, Sarah, that was horrible, but at the same time, I just want to talk to the man who is my grandfather. Don't you have any questions for him?" Eva Grace looked to the rest of the family. "Don't any of you?"

"Sarah's right," Delia said. "He came to you late at night, out of nowhere. You sensed black magic in his camp. His granddaughter gave you a prophecy that evil was coming."

"Maybe Randi is a target of the Woman because of us," Eva Grace suggested.

"She's his, not ours." Brenna said. "If she's being used, it's against us."

Before Eva Grace could protest again, Jake said, "Let me do some checking on him."

"That sounds good," Brenna said. "We'll stay away from him until Jake does some research. Agreed?"

Eva Grace wanted to stomp her foot, but knowing that was childish, she held her silence. She wasn't agreeing to anything yet.

Delia seemed to realize there was no reason to keep arguing. "Let's cool down. We'll discuss this later."

Brenna started to protest, but Jake took her by the arm. "Delia's right. This was a shock for everyone. You should all process this and talk later. In the meantime, I'll try to find out what he's been up to for the past five decades."

Most of them left with little more than goodbyes. Clearly, they were uncomfortable with Eva Grace in the role of a rebel.

"It's not like you to be hasty." Delia stopped Eva Grace's protest. "Listen to me, please. I know you've spent your entire life wondering about your mother and your father, and then you lost Garth as well. Meeting your grandfather might seem like a great adventure. But this is not the time for adventures. The curse is upon us. We must be suspicious of everyone."

She didn't wait for a reply, just gave Eva Grace a

hug and followed Aiden out the door.

"Damnation," Eva Grace said into the quiet that followed. All the wind chimes in the shop jangled. Her aunt had hit on all of the emotions Eva Grace was feeling, making her anger surge again. Lorcan stared up at her.

She went to one of the side windows where multi-colored glass orbs were suspended for display. Most days in October the sun would be streaming through. Today was dark, the wind blowing the last of the leaves across the parking lot. The weeks before Samhain were usually filled with color, the streets teeming with tourists. They were living in an unnatural time.

She didn't want to believe that someone whose blood flowed in her veins would be party to the evil that was threatening the sanctity of New Mourne and the coven. Surely Mick meant them no harm.

She was so tired of waiting for what would happen next. They'd had no luck with calling the Woman out, though Eva Grace clearly understood the temptation.

Instead, she boosted the volume on some soaring Rachmaninoff and busied herself on the computer again.

Lauren breezed in to fulfill some more online orders, and Eva Grace settled down at a small space she had installed under the stairs to work on her jewelry creations. It was a hobby more than anything, but she had sold a few pieces. Her talent was nothing compared to her grandmother's, but she enjoyed the work because it required her full attention and relieved stress.

She laid the arrowhead on the worktable, then tapped the wall above. It looked like an ordinary part of the house's wainscoting, but it revealed a wall safe. She dialed in the combination, then withdrew some silver filigree wire.

From around her neck, she unhooked the silver chain she had tucked under her cream-colored sweater this morning. The delicate links draped through Eva Grace's fingers. This had been her mother's, and she'd been reluctant to wear it often for fear of losing it. But now she had an idea.

She wrapped the silver wire around the top of the arrowhead in a simple pattern that cradled the stone and allowed her to attach a small hoop at the top. The chain slipped through with ease, and when she put the necklace on, the arrowhead lay just at the top of her cleavage.

It warmed and glowed against her skin, and the air around her closed in. Instantly, Eva Grace felt her mother. Celia was here.

"What do you think, Mama? Is this arrowhead going to help us find answers to end the curse?"

She didn't expect and didn't receive an answer. The moment reminded her of those times as a child when she would sneak into Sarah's bedroom and sit in the window seat. She would let her imagination take flight and dream of having a mother. She'd close her eyes and picture herself in the mother's lap as they talked about school and friends and what it meant to be a Connelly witch.

Lorcan laid his head on her knee. Smiling, she stroked it. He did make her feel less alone, and she wondered if her mother hadn't sent him to her.

"Want to go for a walk?" His ears twitched forward. Eva Grace called for Lauren to watch the shop and retrieved her coat from a hook in the back. Lorcan had already shown he didn't need or want a leash, and he bounded down the front steps and short walkway.

Rodric was waiting on the sidewalk, as if he'd been

expecting them to appear. Eva Grace's spirits brightened, and her steps quickened.

He swept her up and spun her around, his brown eyes smiling into hers. "You're so beautiful," he murmured before he kissed her.

"I'm so glad you're here."

He set her back on her feet and brushed a hand down her hair. "I thought about you all day. Is there something wrong?"

"I'll tell you about it." She linked her arm through his. "But let's walk first."

He didn't press or fuss. He was just Rodric—solid and protective but never overbearing. With him, there were no expectations of who she should be or how she should act.

Lorcan trotted ahead, tail wagging. And Eva Grace allowed herself to enjoy the moment and the man who sheltered her from the cold wind.

Chapter 11

The next day, Rodric pulled his car to the side of the road on a winding lane just north of New Mourne. The afternoon was bitter cold, the sky steel gray, more like January than October. He thought it suitable weather for demon tracking.

Danger was all around. Rodric could smell it in the frozen air and feel its oily essence on his skin. Yet it remained just beyond his reach.

He'd left Eva Grace guarded by Lorcan at her shop. Then he'd circled Mourne County, driving up and down back roads and over hills covered in leafless trees. Again and again, he challenged the demon to face him as it had before. He knew the sly one was hiding somewhere and plotting its next move against the Connellys.

On the demon's first visit in June, mayhem had reigned in town. In July, the town's ghosts were stirred to violence. Now there was just a hovering sense of doom. What the hell was that about?

He got out of his car and took a deep breath. He'd been eager to come hunting. His research into the Woman in White and her father had hit a wall, and he was stir crazy. What else did they need to discover about the unfortunate young woman and the man who ruined her life? Did he kill his daughter's child? Did she kill him?

There were no written records that could answer

those questions. Even if they knew, would that give them the key to thwarting the curse?

The thrill of the hunt made his heart race in anticipation. It reminded him of hunting the big red deer in the Highlands. The meat was quite good, but it was the hunt that gave him the greatest pleasure. And today, he would enjoy that pleasure again with a more worthy enemy.

Rodric slammed his car door and shouted toward the hills, "What do you want? What can I give you?" There were no echoes ringing back at him, just a numbing silence.

They were coming for his Eva Grace. The Woman and her demon slave would take her from him, from her family coven, from the town she was bound to protect. The loyal servants of his Scottish family had taught him he would someday defend his true love. He was ready. But how did he fight if he did not know *who or what* to fight?

He raised his open hand to the sky and closed it around the hilt of his axe. He swept the weapon backward as he pivoted, expecting to confront the demon. Nothing was there. A movement of the air made him feint to the left. And he stopped short of driving the blade into the heart of Willow Scanlan's gaunt, elderly driver.

The man didn't flinch. "Hello, Scotsman," he said in a deep and surprisingly strong voice. He lifted the very sharp axe with one finger. "You have impressive moves."

"And you're very quiet." Rodric pulled his magical armor tightly around him and kept the axe in his hand. He glanced at the long, black sedan parked behind his car. When had that arrived?

"Miss Scanlan would like to talk to you," the driver said, nodding toward the trees beyond the cars.

"Where?" Rodric scanned the deep hollow that cleaved two hills.

"Look closer."

A sparkle caught Rodric's eye, and he saw the outlines of a small, disintegrating farmhouse. The other man nodded and gestured toward the bare bushes that bordered the road.

Though reluctant to turn his back on his companion, Rodric kept a grip on his axe and walked toward the building. A crumbling stone chimney and broken window panes were the highlights.

"I can't imagine Willow here," he said over his shoulder.

The old man grinned. "Can't you?"

Rodric turned back to behold a small, crystal palace where the farmhouse had stood. All the light left in the day bled into the smooth, glass walls. The windows gleamed gold, and a crimson and gold flag flew from a shimmering turret. He'd seen many wonders as he traveled the globe hunting ghosts and testing the limits of his power. This rivaled them all.

A woman dressed in a resplendent red gown glided down the front steps. Gold and rubies shone in the crown on her head.

"Willow," Rodric said, halting in front of her.

"Welcome."

"Is this your home?"

"One of them," she replied with a proud smile. "But then you know how we like creating illusions. You know faeries, don't you?"

"A few." Rodric studied her. He suspected this was her true form—milky white skin, black hair and eyes of silver gray.

"You have fae blood." She sniffed the air. "I've caught a whiff here and there from you, but you cloaked it well beneath the armor you carry from Aife, the Scottish goddess. Your family has always been friends to the fae."

"Yes, we have. One of our matriarchs was the goddess Siofra who avenged a cruel assault on a faerie by a neighboring ruler."

Willow let her fingers lightly touch a perfect red rose on the bush beside the steps. "Your mother would have been powerful had she lived. She would have raised you well and perhaps borne a daughter to continue the prowess of the Fergusons."

"She died too young, and I'm the last of my line." Rodric felt the familiar pang in his heart every time he thought of his mother.

"Maybe not," Willow said with a sly smile. "You're in love with the good witch Eva Grace. Perhaps if she escapes the Woman, she will bless you with a child."

He gripped his axe tighter. "What do you want, Willow?"

"You have your father's Irish temper," she noted, her head tipped to the side. "That's where the fae blood comes from, too. I'm sure that's made it difficult for you to control your powers."

Blood thrummed at his temples. He barely recognized his own voice. "What. Do. You. Want?"

Her smile faded. "I'm sorry, Rodric McGuire. I didn't mean to tease you. I'm as worried about your Eva Grace as you are."

"I doubt that."

"I've been here for a long time, almost as long as the Connellys. I've watched each generation rise and fall and grieve themselves through the loss. Each time they fight this curse, we all suffer and worry. But this time, if the dark is loosed on the land, it will eat us all alive."

The flag on the turret snapped as the wind blew harder. Rodric heard a low growl behind him and whipped around to find only the driver, his features sharp and somehow canine.

"We have to fight the evil together," Willow said as Rodric turned back to her. She crushed the red rose and dusted the petals off her hand.

"What do you propose?"

"That you don't hide anything from me." She picked a thorn from her palm and the spot healed instantly.

"I don't know what you mean."

"You've been seeking some rogue fae."

"You mean the pixies?"

Her expression hardened. "They're not the sweet little creatures you think they are."

"I'm well acquainted with their abilities," Rodric said blandly.

"They're secretive and greedy, and they've never given me the respect I deserve." Her perfect, white teeth sharpened to needle-like points. Another growl sounded from her driver.

"If they're so secretive, then why would they share anything with me?" Rodric didn't move as Willow strolled toward him.

"Because you're from the outside, have fae blood and you understand them. You must agree to tell me what they know. I'm sure it's something related to the

Connellys. I might be able to use it to save them."

Willow as savior was a concept Rodric couldn't quite grasp. But this was an intriguing turn of events, and he needed to gain an advantage.

"You know I'd do anything to save Eva Grace."

Her eyes glowed silver. "Yes, you would. Promise me you'll keep me informed."

He wouldn't promise a faerie anything, especially not one as treacherous and cunning as this. To give in to the demands of a fae was inviting turmoil. "Let me give this some thought."

She pursed her lips. "I may not feel so generous later on, Scotsman."

"But I know fae, as you pointed out," he replied. "Give me some time."

Willow frowned, and the crystal palace began to crack. "We don't have much time."

On that Rodric could agree. Before he could say another word, the palace shattered to dust, leaving the broken-down farmhouse in its place. As he turned, Willow and her driver were gone, the long, black sedan already driving away.

He stood in the cold and gathering darkness, tempted by a bargain with the powerful faerie and knowing nothing could be accomplished in this place.

He headed back to town. At the inn, the front desk clerk was crying. She normally was a chipper young woman, so he stopped to ask what was wrong. She said she felt like going to bed and hiding under the covers to get away from the dread. Instead, she was crying because the heavy depression had burdened her all day.

She wasn't alone. Later, as Rodric hurried down the street to meet Eva Grace for dinner, he ran into the antique shop's proprietor sweeping the sidewalk in front of his store. Tears were streaming down his face. A woman stopped to comfort him, and she burst into tears, too.

Inside Mary's Diner, the mood was somber. The family of five at the front booth didn't break a smile as Misty the waitress served platters of burgers, fries and onion rings—three of Rodric's favorite things about America. Misty also didn't sway her hips or flirt when Rodric caught her eye. The only sound was a morose country song from the old-fashioned jukebox.

He slid into the chair across from Eva Grace. "What's wrong with everyone?"

"Lauren and I have used the crystal ball and tried working with crystals most of the day to see what we could find. We came up with nothing except the demon." She looked around in concern.

He took a moment to ask, "Do you think Willow could be showing off her power?"

"Why do you think she would do that?"

"Because she can."

Willow seemed more inclined to use fire and explosions to control humans. Should he tell her now about his encounter with the faerie?

He decided to wait. "How was your day?"

"Everyone in the coven is still upset about Mick. They'd rather talk about him than Willow, the Woman or what's wrong with every human in town. Lauren said the elder aunts were with Sarah most of the day."

She rubbed her temples, and he knew she was feeling everyone's pain.

"You've got to put up some shields or you're going to make yourself sick," he said as he took both her hands in his.

"Build shields?"

Dark circles were gathering under her eyes, and her shoulders drooped. A weak light flickered in the arrowhead she wore.

"Can you shut out what's going on around you?"

Now she rubbed her chest. "There's so much of it."

He pulled her out of the booth and let Misty know they were leaving. Eva Grace brightened a little as they stepped into the brisk air outside.

He pulled her close.

"I'm fine, Rodric," she said weakly.

"Just lean against me and close your eyes. Imagine yourself somewhere safe."

"Rod—"

He put his hand on her cheek and looked deeply into her eyes, pushing a little with his magic. "You're an empath, and it's your nature to make those who are ill feel better. The demon knows that. Why do you think there's such dread and grief in town? He's using them to drain your energy and, in his own way, take your magic away from you."

"You're right, of course."

He rubbed her arms to warm them. "Do you want to go inside?"

"No, I feel better out here. The cold air has cleared the fog I felt."

He took a deep breath. "I went demon hunting today and instead I found a faerie queen."

"Willow?"

"Yes, in all her royal finery."

"Wow, I've only seen that once," Eva Grace said. "You should feel honored."

"Do you know anything about her driver?"

"Not really." She thought for a moment. "I don't think I even know his name."

"He growled at me."

"Growled?" Her face reflected the baffled tone in her voice.

"I think he must have two natures."

"A shifter? I never thought of that, but it's not surprising. There are several shifter families in town that have been here for generations, and that old man has some years on him."

"The fae can live a long time," Rodric said. "But let's get back to the shields." He took her hand again. "Close your eyes and imagine a lovely courtyard surrounded by secure stone walls."

He could almost feel her brain slowing down and focusing on what he was saying.

"Now, make the walls higher so you're standing in the courtyard surrounded by flowers and trees, and a wall no one can penetrate," Rodric said. "You can hear nothing but your own peaceful thoughts and your own body. No one else can penetrate it."

"It's beautiful," she said quietly. "And I'm realizing it's controlled by intention."

"Like anything magical, it only works if you truly believe," he said. "You believe your special gift can help others, and it does. Now you must believe your strength can be reserved to help yourself."

"The demon wanted Brenna's magic, and he used Albert to try to drain Fiona. It makes sense he would use my empathy to bend me to his will," Eva Grace said. She stepped back and took a deep breath. "Thank you."

He raised her hand to his lips. "Would you like to go

back now and have some dinner?"

"Sounds wonderful," she said. "I didn't have an appetite, but now I'm starving."

Over a cheeseburger and fries for her and meatloaf and mashed potatoes for him, they talked about how she would need to practice to keep her defenses in place.

After Misty took their dishes away, Eva Grace asked him, "Do you agree with my family about Mick?"

He hadn't been surprised to hear of Mick's connection to the Connellys. He'd suspected the man of an ulterior motive from the start. What he couldn't understand was why Eva Grace was so hell bent on defending him.

Still, the last thing he wanted to do was argue with her. "I know your feelings about Mick. Did you try to see him today?"

She shook her head. "Although I don't hate him like everyone else, it still didn't feel right to go out there. Sarah is so upset that Brenna's worried about her."

"Sarah is strong."

"But the demon placed her in a coma in July. We thought we'd lose her."

"I know," he said. "I'm worried for all of you." He told her about his fruitless search through the surrounding area.

"What gives you the power to call and fight the demon?" She tipped her head to the side. "What are you, Dr. Rodric McGuire?"

Keeping his family's secrets was ingrained in him at a young age. He learned iron control from both sides of his family. Willow had been right about one thing today. Rodric had never fully explored the limits of his magic. His warrior's nature protected him in dangerous situations when he worked with the military. In his investigations of paranormal phenomena, he had encountered evil that threatened him, and his power came to his defense—as it had today when Willow's driver appeared.

But he didn't know if he wanted to share his legacy with Eva Grace just yet. There were aspects that weren't very pleasant. How would she react?

Before he could say anything more, she went still as stone.

He was on his feet and at her side before she could rise. The connection between them telegraphed her thoughts. "It's Sarah, isn't it?"

"I have to go to her. The coven needs me now."

He flung money on the table, and they were outside and headed down the street toward Siren's Call. Eva Grace quickly unlocked the store, called for Lorcan and they headed to her car.

Main Street seemed darker than usual to Rodric. He looked around in concern, and a figure darted in front of them. Rodric stepped up to guard Eva Grace but eased when he recognized Gladys, the sheriff department's elderly dispatcher. With surprising strength, she pushed him aside and grasped Eva Grace's arms. Tears streamed down the older woman's face.

"I can feel it," Gladys choked out. "Just like when your mother died, there's a stir in the air. I loved her because she was so kind to my daughter who was so very sick."

Eva Grace tried to calm her. "I know my mother tried to heal your daughter."

"But she died, and then your mother died, too." A sob broke from Gladys, and Rodric caught her as she swayed.

Eva Grace slipped an arm around her shoulders. "Gladys, please, why are you so upset? What is it that you feel?"

"The end." Startled, Gladys put a hand to her mouth. The tears on her cheeks dried. Lights came on in the streets and in buildings all around them. Laughter trickled out as the door of the pub opened. The town had been released from its stupor.

Rodric was alarmed. The demon was playing with them all. "We have to go," he told Gladys. "Will you be okay?"

She nodded as they hurried away, intent on getting to Sarah's side.

Chapter 12

When they arrived at the home place, Lauren was helping Aunt Doris up the front steps. Rodric hurried to lend a hand.

"What's happening to us?" Doris asked, her voice tremulous. Her weakness shocked Eva Grace.

It was a great relief to hear Sarah's voice coming from the living room when they entered the house. Eva Grace had talked to Marcus and knew her grandmother was all right, but she was worried. Lauren, Maggie and the rest of the coven arrived.

Rodric joined Jake, Aiden and Bailey on one side of the fireplace. Lorcan settled next to Sarah's chair in front of the fire.

"I'm just fine," Sarah told them all. "I didn't eat dinner, and I got a little woozy."

"It was more than that." Beside her chair, Marcus looked as if he had aged overnight. "We were in the kitchen, and she went down on her knees, as if she'd been knocked down."

"I felt it, too." Brenna sat on the arm of the chair. The rest of the coven nodded. The shock had gone through them all.

"Brenna frightened me," Jake confessed as he stoked the fire with another log. "She was reading, then she cried out and dropped her tablet. I thought something was wrong with the babies."

"They're fine." Brenna touched her stomach, then clasped Sarah's hand.

Brenna was glowing with power. Did she realize how strong she seemed next to Sarah's fragility?

The connection between them surged through Eva Grace. She wanted them all to feel the same. Together they could lock out the forces that threatened them.

"Let's join hands," she suggested.

Brenna took one outstretched hand, and Fiona took the other. The other witches took their places. The curtains billowed at the windows, and the timbers of the old house creaked.

The circle closed with Sarah still seated but at their center between Brenna and Delia. Eva Grace felt a jolt of energy and saw it move through each member of the coven. She felt more hopeful than she had in weeks.

Their voices rose in a chant that flowed among them like a balm, warm and soothing. A comfortable silence followed as they broke the circle.

"I have something I need to tell you all," Rodric said.

He told them about his encounter with Willow this afternoon. He admitted he had fae blood and magical abilities, but he didn't explain exactly what he was. She suspected he'd left many details out of the story. And that was becoming a habit.

"So, you are more than human," Brenna said. She turned to Eva Grace. "Did you know?"

Eva Grace ignored her, more intent on her own anger. Why wouldn't he share with her what his magical abilities were?

"Do you think Willow did this to Sarah?" she asked him.

"No. I'd have told you immediately if that was the case." His gaze was steady on hers.

"I hope so." Jake studied his old friend with a frown. "I never knew you were fae."

"Only some fae blood—on my father's side. From Mother…" He glanced at Eva Grace and shrugged. Her irritation went up a notch.

"That doesn't really matter, does it?" Fiona asked. "Shouldn't we be more worried about what Willow's up to?"

Sarah rose from the chair. "Don't worry about Willow."

Eva Grace and Brenna moved immediately to stand beside her. She waved them off. "Willow is vain and sometimes lacking in self-confidence."

"Willow?" Eva Grace said. "Not confident?"

"She worries that all the fae in Mourne County aren't under her thumb. My mother told me she's always been that way."

"You've never shared that with me," Brenna said.

"I'm telling you now." Sarah sounded more like herself. She looked at Rodric. "You'd best be careful with Willow. Now that she's sure you're fae, she'll think she can control you."

"Not bloody likely," Rodric said with a faint smile. "What I'm worried about is how all of this ties to the Woman and the curse. What's Willow's role?"

"She's attacked Sarah before," Brenna reminded them.

Sarah seemed unconcerned. "She was angry at us for letting our troublesome late uncle out of the prison she'd devised for him."

An angry protest rose from Marcus. "That old

creature hurt you. There's no telling what she could do." He turned to Rodric. "Perhaps you'd better stay away from us all since she's decided to use you."

As ticked off as Eva Grace was with Rodric, she jumped to his defense. "He would never play a role in hurting Sarah."

"How do you know?" Brenna demanded. Her fury showed in jagged streaks of light that appeared around her.

"Whoa, whoa," Jake said, stepping between his angry witch and his friend. "Brenna, back down a minute. If Rodric was being used, why would he tell us about today?"

"That's a good question," Fiona agreed. Around the room, the other witches nodded.

Delia reached out to her daughter. "Take a deep breath, darling. We need all of our friends." She looked at Eva Grace. "And Rodric is more than a friend, isn't he?"

Eva Grace was confused. Her instincts were that Rodric was nothing but good, but he had withheld a lot from her. And despite the evidence of his magic, he was evasive about his true nature.

Lauren, of all people, rescued her from having to answer Delia's question. "Rodric has been helpful to all of us. Let's not jump to conclusions."

Delia added, "There's someone else we need to consider. Mick." She spat out her father's name like it was sour fruit. "I don't trust that he just happened to come to New Mourne."

"We don't either," Frances said with a sniff and a glance at her twin.

Marcus folded his arms. "He could be in league with

Willow or the Woman and her demon."

Eva Grace wondered if she had misjudged her newly-found grandfather. She was off-balance and questioning a lot of decisions. Lorcan got up and came to her side, bumping his head against her leg in comfort and looking up at her with concerned, dark eyes.

"Mick means nothing," Sarah said. "I am concerned about the malaise you all saw in town today."

"It seemed to end suddenly," Eva Grace said and explained how the town appeared to wake up after she and Rodric talked to Gladys.

"I suspect the demon had a hand in that," Aiden remarked. "We know how it loves to torture the town."

"But to what end?" Eva Grace was frustrated. They had all kinds of clues but no cohesive answers.

"Let's set this aside for now," Sarah said. She looked weary and drawn. Brenna and Eva Grace exchanged a look of agreement.

As was usual, the coven brewed lemon balm tea and served food on the spur of the moment. But Brenna and Eva Grace stayed near Sarah by the fire. One by one, coven members hugged her and left. Until there was only Delia, Eva Grace, Brenna, Fiona and their men.

"I'm staying here tonight," Brenna said.

"Nonsense." Sarah got up again. Though she swayed, she stood her ground. "Your mother and father and Marcus are here with me. We're all fine. Give me a day to rest, then we'll make our final plans for the Samhain celebration. It may be the time when the Woman tries to strike. We need to be prepared to fight."

Eva Grace was surprised. "You don't always talk about fighting her."

"Maybe I'm finally realizing how strong you all

113

are," Sarah replied.

"It's because you taught us well." Fiona linked her arm through her grandmother's.

Sarah pressed a hand to Fiona's cheek. "Thank you all for rushing to my side tonight. But I'm very tired. I think the tea is beginning to take effect."

She turned to Eva Grace. "I never tell you this, and I don't know why. You're so like your mother, so vibrant and inquisitive. She was a beautiful spirit, and I tried to quash that at times." She paused, her smile sad. "It's one of my biggest regrets."

She touched the arrowhead pendant that lay on Eva Grace's chest. "I'm glad you're keeping this with you." The stone warmed against Eva Grace's skin.

When Sarah smiled this time, her eyes brightened and she stood straighter. "She would have loved that— the strength it represents and the power it holds. Listen to your heart, Eva Grace, that's what Celia always said."

She hugged Brenna, Fiona and Delia. Then she and Marcus went to their room.

"That was intense," Bailey said and put his arm around Fiona's shoulders.

"I don't care what she says," Brenna replied. "I'm staying here tonight."

"The best thing you can do is take your babies home and get a good night's sleep. You know Marcus won't leave her side," Eva Grace said. "I think we've got some tough days ahead of us."

They all gathered coats, shawls and jackets, headed outside and exchanged goodbyes as they went to their respective vehicles.

Rodric said nothing as they got in her car. Lorcan settled in the back seat and bared his teeth at Rodric.

"Stop that," Eva Grace ordered the dog.

The silence deepened as they made the journey into town. In front of the inn, Eva Grace drew to a stop but didn't say a word.

He didn't open the door, and she hoped she didn't have to tell him to get out.

"We should talk," Rodric said.

"Not now."

He took her hand, and as she didn't want to be childish, she didn't resist.

"I'll see you tomorrow."

She nodded, and he got out.

He remained on the sidewalk as she drove away. Tears pricked her eyes, but not because of anger. She almost cried because she wanted to turn around, step into his arms and let him hold her all night long. How had he become so important to her, so fast?

Lorcan stuck his head between the front seats and whimpered. The bond between them, so new but so strong, wrapped around Eva Grace.

She forced out a laugh. "Okay, you'll do for the night. You're not him, but you're okay."

But for the first time, loneliness greeted her when she opened the door of the home she loved.

Chapter 13

Rodric waited until mid-morning before going to Eva Grace's. Her greeting was lukewarm at best.

"I don't have time to talk right now." At her side, Lorcan barked.

"We can't let this simmer between us," Rodric said.

"I'm not simmering." She gestured for him to come in out of the cold. "I only have a few minutes. I'm going out to the campground to talk to Mick and his granddaughter."

"What?"

She closed the door and turned to face him. "I don't feel about him the way everyone else does, but the episode last night with Sarah has me very worried. If there's a chance that he's working with Willow or the demon—"

"Then you need to stay away from him."

Her eyes blazed. "Don't tell me what to do."

He held up his hands. "You know that's not who I am. I don't order anyone around."

"But that's the point, I don't really know who or what you are."

Her words hit Rodric hard. He was in love with her. The last thing he wanted was to bring her pain.

"I'm sorry," he said. Slowly, carefully, he drew her forward and into his arms.

She was stiff but didn't pull away. Against her soft,

116

fragrant hair he murmured, "Please forgive me. I'm not used to being open with anyone. I didn't mean to hurt you. I would never do anything to endanger you or your family."

She resisted a moment longer, then relaxed against him. "Everything's just moving so fast, and I'm in such danger. Getting involved with you has only complicated things."

"Don't say that." He drew away and framed her face with his hands. "I've never lost my heart to anyone but you. I've never come this far in sharing myself. I don't feel lost. I feel as if we've found each other."

Her gaze was searching. "Share something with me, Rodric. Tell me about your magic."

He took a deep breath. "Can we sit and talk?"

"Of course. I just made tea. I'll get you a cup."

He took off his jacket and sat on the couch in front of the fire. Lorcan turned his back on him and lay down on the rug. Eva Grace came from the kitchen with steaming mugs that smelled of cinnamon and spice.

But she wasted no time on niceties as she sat beside him. "Now tell me what you are."

"I'm a warrior," he said simply.

"A faerie warrior?"

"I have fae blood, but that's not what gives me my magic. My powers come from my mother Rhona Ferguson who loved and married the bloody Irishman Finn McGuire." He paused for a dry laugh. "That's how my Uncle Boyd always referred to him. He never once just called him Finn. My God, how he hated my father."

"Your uncle hurt you, didn't he?"

"He largely ignored my existence," Rodric said, lacing his fingers through hers. "He came home twice a year. He'd call me into his study and tell me how much he hated that I was his heir and there'd be no other."

"He didn't want a family?"

"Thank God he never put any woman in that position. He had the mumps as a child, and he couldn't father children. It was up to my mother to keep our bloodline going."

"And she diluted that by marrying an Irishman?"

"Exactly." Anger rose inside Rodric. He hadn't allowed himself to feel this rage against his uncle for many years. "When I was younger, he made me cry. Nanny would comfort me, and the rest of the staff told me stories of my mother and her magic. They said my uncle was jealous of her abilities and that his own were feeble at best."

"Was she a warrior, too?"

"They said so."

"If your uncle was as weak as you described— someone who was so cruel to a child—I imagine your mother's prowess was hard for him to accept."

"Nanny believed he killed my parents." These were the words Rodric had never uttered out loud.

Eva Grace looked horrified as he told her how his parents and he came to the family home at Boyd's invitation, supposedly to make peace.

"They went out one afternoon, and their car went off the road on a steep curve. They were killed instantly."

"What did your uncle have to do with that?"

"He was also gone that afternoon. There were some skid marks that made it appear there was another car, but the police didn't pursue it. My uncle was rich and powerful. No one could imagine it was him, and the staff were all a bit afraid of him. But they closed ranks around me, a protective shield, if you will. They told Nanny they thought he killed my parents."

"But his own sister?" Eva Grace was still incredulous.

"I was also supposed to be in the car. I was left home because I had a cold."

Eva Grace gasped. "But what about your mother's power? Couldn't she have saved them?"

"One would think so." Rodric frowned. "But the demon said something to me. . ."

"The demon?

Quickly, he recounted everything that had happened during his first encounter with the demon in the woods. "It knew the Ferguson name and my lineage. It made me think about how my uncle died and what he might be capable of."

Rodric found it difficult to tell her the rest.

"Tell me… Please. No more secrets."

He pushed ahead. "Uncle Boyd died in a fire at his home in London just before I turned 13. There were whispers among the staff and at the day school I attended. Nanny told me to ignore them, but I hid myself when she met with the banker who took over as executor of the estate. He said the authorities didn't know what caused the fire. Worse, there were other bodies found in the house." He hesitated. "They were bound."

"Bound?"

"Handcuffed."

"Dear goddess," Eva Grace's hand flew to her mouth. "Who were they?"

"Apparently that was another mystery. They couldn't be identified."

"Was it all over the news?"

"His business partners kept it quiet. Uncle Boyd made a lot of people a lot of money. They didn't want to be tainted by his perversions."

Eva Grace shuddered. "How horrible for you. You were just a boy."

"It made me ill to think I shared blood with a sick bastard like that. I finally confronted Nanny with it. She told me that he was wicked, reaching for magic he would never find, and it led him down a dark road. That's when she told me he killed my parents."

Eva Grace studied Rodric for a moment. "He was dabbling in black magic?"

"Yes." Rodric took a long sip of the cooling tea. "I think that's how Nanny got him to leave me to her care. She could see his evil, and she threatened to expose him."

"And the demon knew something about this?"

"Not directly, but he knew my family. There's definitely a connection."

"What happened after your uncle died?"

"I went away to school, but I continued to practice using my weapons when I returned to the estate for holidays."

Eva Grace's eyes narrowed. "Weapons?"

"Perhaps I should show you."

Learning to control his gifts had taken Rodric a long time. He'd been taught by Nanny and the estate servants to use caution and judgement before turning to his inherited powers.

But now he stood. He gathered the magic in his veins. Lorcan whined and went to Eva Grace's side. The floor shook as a spear flashed into Rodric's right hand.

Her eyes went wide.

His axe appeared in his left hand.

The dog growled, but still she was silent.

"I can summon my armor if you wish," Rodric said.

"No, I believe you." Eva Grace stood. She touched the cool steel axe handle. Magic sung between them, and the weapon glowed. Lorcan fell to his haunches, mesmerized.

Eva Grace sat down, calm and composed, as if this was nothing if not ordinary. "Now tell me more."

Rodric allowed his magical weapons to fade before sitting beside her. "My Scottish lineage goes back to the goddess Aife. Have you ever heard of her?"

"Brenna and I read all the Celtic legends. Aife stole the alphabet from the gods so humans could have it. We thought she was Xena but better."

"That's a good way to describe her, but there was also Siofra, one of her first descendants, who warred with a god because he raped a faerie in Cullodena. Because Siofra fought for the faeries, they gave her a gift."

"A magical dirk," Eva Grace said. "Which made her able to kill the god who was so cruel."

"It was a keen weapon, for sure."

Eva Grace looked startled. "You have the dirk of Siofra?"

"I will someday." He paused, wondering if he should tell her he could only use it to defend the person he loved above all others. He settled for, "Family legend tells me it will appear at the right time."

"That's just. . ." She shook her head. "I'm stunned. Can I tell Brenna?"

"Of course." "He laughed. "I was sure no one would have ever heard this legend. I learned everything I know from Nanny and the household staff. Uncle Boyd never spoke of anything to me."

"It's interesting how different our lives are," Eva Grace said. "My family has always been proud of the craft and our heritage. Family is the reason we're fighting so hard for the future, to stop the curse and focusing on remembering instead of forgetting tragedies."

"I am the last of my mother's lineage."

"There's still hope for the future."

"There is...now," he agreed.

Her smile warmed, and a soothing balm moved through his body.

"I'm so glad you told me all of this." She lifted her hand to his cheek. "Feel better?" she asked softly.

"Yes."

He framed her beautiful face. Her lips met his with a ferociousness he was unprepared for. Desire whipped through him like a blade.

She pulled away, smiling. "Come with me to the campground."

"I'd rather stay here," he murmured.

"I promise we'll get back to this."

He sighed, knowing she would not let this go. At least she didn't protest when he asked to drive as Lorcan jumped into the back seat.

The camp was busy with women cooking at barbeque grills and young children chasing one another around in the cold, laughing and squealing.

"They're not properly dressed for this weather," Eva Grace said.

Eva Grace got out and strode toward the tiny camper they had visited before. Lorcan trailed behind and was soon surrounded by excited children who wanted to pet him. But the women and children fell silent as the trailer door opened and Mick stepped out. He smiled and welcomed Eva Grace in a self-satisfied way that made Rodric want to punch him.

She greeted him politely, but wasted little time in asking, "Why aren't these children in school?"

"We homeschool," Mick replied, unruffled. "We comply with all of the laws. We even have a certified teacher. There's so much available online, our children are missing nothing."

Eva Grace looked doubtful.

"I can show you the paperwork." Mick indicated that she should come in the trailer.

"It's true." Randi came across the yard. Rodric noted again how much she looked like Fiona.

Randi smiled. "I've been working with some of the older kids on math this morning. I left them doing fractions in another trailer."

"But these children out here are freezing," Eva Grace protested.

Randi darted a look at her grandfather. "We weren't prepared for how cold it was going to be here."

"The children aren't suffering," Mick said, remaining calm. "We're a sturdy group of people. You have that blood in you, too, Eva Grace. You're very strong and talented. Look at Randi—there's not a trace of what ailed her just a few days ago. Thanks to you."

"I am very well," Randi said. "Thank you so much."

"Eva Grace is a gifted healer," Rodric said.

"As was my own mother," Mick added.

"Really?" Eva Grace looked at him with new interest. "I never thought my abilities could come from anything but Connelly blood."

"Not much chance to know anything about this part of your gene pool," Rodric said. He kept his gaze steady on the other man's. Was Mick just a man? Rodric felt something more from him—not evil, maybe—but certainly not good.

Randi broke the charged silence. "How is your grandmother?" she asked Eva Grace.

"She's just fine." The wheels in Eva Grace's brain were clearly turning as she studied the young woman. "Why do you ask?"

"I just felt terrible for her," Randi answered with no trace of guile. "It was a shock for her to see my grandfather. And she didn't seem well."

"She's fine," Eva Graced repeated with perhaps more firmness than necessary. "We saw her just last night."

"Were you two sent out here to run me out of town?" Mick asked. "Your sheriff came by yesterday. I'm paid up through the month, and we have work to finish this week, as well. The park owners told him we've caused no trouble. There's no reason to ask us to leave."

"We'd like to stay," Randi said. She smoothed back her long, dark hair, so like Fiona's but missing the fiery strands of Connelly red. "I'd like to know you, Eva Grace."

Eva Grace touched her arm. Rodric gritted his teeth. Randi seemed sweet and innocent, but no one outside the family and closest friends could be trusted right now.

Mick looked delighted by the exchange between his granddaughters. "Come in for a cup of coffee. Randi and I will tell you more about this side of your family."

A chill moved up Rodric's spine. He didn't want this

man to be Eva Grace's family.

A horn sounded, and they all jumped. A large white van pulled in behind Rodric's SUV. "Circle of Faith Church" was painted on the side in bright blue letters. Colorful faces of happy children underscored the words ``Children's Ministry.''

"Ginny Williams," Eva Grace murmured as three women got out of the van.

Rodric recognized a tall, attractive woman as the wife of the minister of the county's mega church. Fred Williams had gone to school with Delia and Eva Grace's mother. He was sympathetic to Connellys but kept his distance from the practicing Wiccans for the public and his wife. Ginny was a singularly unpleasant person who made no secret of her hatred of the coven.

Today she wore trim black pants topped by a black fur jacket in stark contrast to her white-blonde hair. Her blue eyes glittered like ice. "Mr. Phillips," she greeted Mick. "What are you doing with this Connelly? You know she's a witch, don't you?"

The words rolled off Mick. His slick smile in place, he stepped forward with hand outstretched. "Now, Mrs. Williams. Eva Grace has been here in the same spirit as you. She's ministered to my dear Randi."

Ginny sniffed. "You'd best not allow her to touch any of your people. She'll put a hex on them for sure."

Eva Grace smothered an oath, and wind whipped through the campground. Two of the women cooking nearby smiled and whispered to each other.

"You can save your tricks." Ginny took a step toward Eva Grace.

Rodric moved forward, but Mick reached Ginny first and took her arm. "There's no need for unpleasantness."

To Rodric's amazement, the minister's wife didn't try to break away.

"We're all friends here, surely," Mick continued.

Eva Grace's chuckle was mirthless.

Ginny drew herself up, chin lifting. "I am here in the spirit of friendship."

"We thank you for that." Mick turned to smile at Eva Grace. "I'm sure there's no reason to upset the children, is there?"

"Yes, the children," Ginny exclaimed. Her smile flashed as she turned toward the van. As if on cue, the two other church women opened the side doors and started giving out coats, sweaters and jackets.

"For you, too," Ginny said, nodding to the women in the camp. "When I heard so few of you had coats, we appealed to our congregation. Look how they responded."

Delighted giggles of children filled the air, and Ginny turned back to Eva Grace. Rodric was shocked to see she wasn't gloating. "With this terrible weather, we were afraid the little ones would suffer. We can't have that in New Mourne, can we?"

"No, we can't," Eva Grace agreed though her eyes narrowed.

"We appreciate this." Mick continued to smile. "Let's go see what you've brought our babies." With a hand on Ginny's elbow, he escorted her to the van where the other two women were trying coats on a couple of little girls.

"Let's go," Rodric murmured to Eva Grace.

"You can't stay?" Randi asked in disappointment.

"Another time," Eva Grace said. "I'm sure you want

to help the older children pick out some warm coats. But I do have something for you." She reached into her bag and pulled out a small pouch. "Keep this nearby. If your fever returns, this will help."

Randi slipped the pouch in the pocket of her long sweater.

As Eva Grace and Rodric went to their car, Mick called out a goodbye. Ginny was helping him into a heavy, gray coat as if they were old friends.

Rodric resisted the urge to peel out as they left the campground. "That wasn't good, Eva Grace. Why did the two of them act so chummy?"

"It was very strange," she agreed. Lorcan thrust his head between the seats, and Eva Grace stroked him absently.

"You can't say you still trust him?"

"Ginny's very manipulative. No doubt she's heard who he is. She probably hopes to fall in league with him against the coven. She may have decided to pretend she's a pleasant person."

"It was more than that."

"Did you sense evil from him?"

Rodric sighed. "Not exactly."

"Me, either." A frown creased her brow. "I don't want to believe he's the enemy."

"But you're afraid for Randi, aren't you? What did you give her?"

"Amethyst, citrine, and hematite." She chewed on her lower lip. "I think I smelled some residual magic. I hope she hasn't been harmed."

"Don't go back there alone," Rodric told her. "Even if Randi asks you to come, please don't. Promise me."

She promised, but Rodric was still worried. At

Siren's Call, he watched Lorcan trail her inside. Then he cruised down to the town's center and parked behind the big white courthouse. He went into the sheriff's department where a young clerk waved him toward Jake's office.

"We need to talk," he told his friend. "What have you found out about Mick Phillips? Do we know where he's been for the last 48 years?"

Chapter 14

Late that afternoon, Eva Grace locked the front door of the shop and sighed. At her side, Lorcan whimpered.

Lauren joined them. "Yes, we might as well close early. This has to go down as one of the worst days in the shop's history. Not one customer. The town is dead."

"People are worried."

Lauren folded her arms and peered out at the gloom of the late afternoon. "The Samhain festival is the biggest event of the year. But the inn and the other B&B's have had nothing but cancellations."

"Samhain is coming fast. We're not preparing the way we usually do." Eva Grace leaned down to stroke Lorcan's head, thinking of the past.

By now, the coven would normally have produced hundreds of potions, always popular items. Besides the good luck potion brewed last week, there'd be others to aid insomnia and promote fertility, ease anxiety and encourage wisdom with finances.

Lauren and Maggie had spent the afternoon bundling sage and other herbs. Maggie was still working in the storeroom, but they were all worried there would be no festival this year.

"We can weather this," Lauren said. "Other businesses aren't sure. The little boutique down the street that sells woven goods is thinking of closing. The diner and the inn have laid off several employees."

"I know. Mick's group is the only one at Callie's RV Park. She's never been so empty this time of year."

Lauren gave her a sharp look at the mention of Mick's name. "Eva Grace—"

She cut her off, "I've called Brenna and Fiona. We need to talk." She turned as Brenna's SUV pulled into the small parking lot.

Lorcan padded to the back door to greet Fiona and Brenna with a happy bark. Fiona said hello to Minnie the shop ghost. Minnie was worried about the strange weather and the lack of visitors. The friendly spirit enjoyed the hustle and bustle of customers.

Maggie joined them in the area near the register.

"I hope you're all okay with leaving Sarah out of this," Eva Grace said.

"How can we bring her in?" Brenna asked. "She's not strong enough to do much. The elder aunts are so upset about her they can't focus."

"And the others aren't prepared," Lauren said, her blunt assessment taking Eva Grace by surprise. "My mother is a good, loyal witch–even talented in her own way with spells and herbs. She would do anything for us, but she doesn't know what to do about this."

"I'm not raising Rose that way," Maggie added with the same firmness. "My daughter is going to be prepared to defend herself, her family and this town."

Eva Grace realized Lauren and Maggie had changed in the past few months, becoming stronger and more focused.

"Mother was away too long," Fiona said. "Bailey and I talk about leaving, but I don't want to lose my connection to the coven."

"You shouldn't feel bound here," Brenna said. "I

never begrudged our parents their travels—just that they left us here."

Eva Grace realized they were straying from their purpose, and she was tired of going off track. She'd begun to believe the coven's inability to stay on topic was part of the Remember Not spell. "Is there anything magical we can do to bring tourists back to town?"

Brenna cocked her head to the side, eyes narrowing as she considered the question.

"It's not like there's a force field around us," Fiona observed. "Shipments come in and out."

"It's the weather that's keeping the tourists away," Maggie said. "Even those that show up leave quickly. It's freezing. The leaves went from green to brown overnight."

"Could we do something about the leaves?" Eva Grace looked at Brenna. "You can command the elements. Surely you could inject some autumn color back into the landscape."

"This is large scale," Brenna replied. "Remember the storm when Garth was murdered? I couldn't touch it."

"You're stronger now," Eva Grace told her. She could feel Brenna's magic expanding even now. She felt her own power surge in response.

"We'll help," Lauren said. "We have to try something."

"Yes," Fiona agreed. "We're sworn to protect New Mourne. Let's do it."

"The rest of the coven will probably sense what we're doing," Brenna said.

"So what?" Eva Grace was defiant. She was tired of waiting for what was to come.

Brenna looked at her long and hard before nodding in agreement. "We have to be careful. The last time we tried a spell here, the demon responded."

Eva Grace reassured her, "We're ready if it comes."

"Let's go out back," she suggested. "We can experiment with the big oak back there." Since the shop had once been a house, she maintained a little garden. Fiona said it made Minnie happy, and in warm weather customers sometimes rested on benches she had placed there.

They gathered supplies and put on coats. Lorcan followed them out into the cold. Eva Grace ignored his beseeching look. He didn't like this. Too bad.

They set a large circle around the tree, big enough to enclose them all. Then they placed red, orange, purple, violet and yellow candles at the correct intervals. Inside the circle, they clasped hands and lifted their faces to look up into the branches filled with brown leaves.

Brenna began the chant, "Goddess, goddess, hear our plea. The hues of fall have left the trees. We need them here so the town can glow. Red and orange, amber and gold. Bring them back despite the cold. Bring the leaves back to the tree. As we will so mote it be."

Magic spread from Brenna and through Eva Grace. She watched a golden glow move around the circle. The arrowhead warmed against her skin. In the deepening shadows of the day, the only sound was the faint hum of a car engine on Main Street. But the dead leaves on the tree remained limp and frozen.

"Goddess, goddess," Eva Grace murmured, closing her eyes. "Hear us now. Our town is in need. Please plant the seed. Bring back the colors and the light, break the grip of our fearful plight. Please make the darkness flee.

As we will, so mote it be."

Like wind chimes, the leaves tinkled above them as a breeze stirred. Eva Grace heard Lorcan growl.

"Goddess, goddess, hear our plea." The witches chanted again and again while the music of the leaves rose.

Eva Grace recited the words, trying to open her heart to the goddess, but alarm rose inside her. She could feel something else stirring, something she didn't like. She glanced around the circle. All were intent on the spell. Even Maggie's eyes were closed, and she seemed fully engaged.

"Oh no." Brenna's soft words broke the chant.

Like her, Eva Grace looked up into the tree. The leaves were turning black.

"It's in our circle," Brenna murmured. "How can this happen here? By the goddess, I know all of our hearts are pure."

Laughter sounded all around them. It seemed to have no source—like thunder that traveled in an unbroken line.

Eva Grace cautioned, "The leaves are an illusion."

"You're right," Brenna agreed. "It can play with our minds, but it can't penetrate the circle we set."

Eva Grace felt Brenna strike a chord in the evil entity surrounding them. The laughter turned to a roar, and the wind blew harder.

A shadowy figure moved out of the corner of Eva Grace's eye. She sensed fury and evil as it stalked them just beyond the circle.

Her own ire rose. "Yes, be angry," she jeered. "We're not like the others you've fought. We won't back down."

Brenna's appreciative look made Eva Grace smile. "We won't bow and scrape to this thing and wait for the Woman to subdue it."

"Focus on defeating it," Brenna exhorted the witches. "Concentrate."

Their appeal to the goddess rose again. The demon continued to roar.

Another, very different, roar sounded, and Brenna sucked in a breath. "Shit, it's Jake."

Eva Grace looked to the right just as a huge white tiger leapt into the yard. Jake wore his second nature. He reared on his back legs, his powerful claws raking at the column of darkness close to the circle. He was fighting the demon's physical manifestation, she realized. But the thing appeared to be only smoke this time. She could see the outline of horns and the flash of a tail, but it wasn't solid.

"Be careful," Brenna shouted to Jake.

Eva Grace sensed her cousin's struggle not to go to her mate's aid.

"Goddess, goddess, hear our plea," Fiona chanted again. The others took it up, and the witches began to circle the tree. Immediately the wind blew from the south, somewhat warmer. Water dripped from melting ice on the tree, and Eva Grace saw the demon's misty form stagger as Jake's claws swiped through him.

They were getting to him, she realized. The goddess was aiding them.

"Be gone!" The command came from the left, and Eva Grace almost dropped Brenna's hand as Rodric strode into the garden, Lorcan at his heels. Rodric was his normal self, but in his hand, he clenched the axe he'd shown her earlier.

"Stand down," he shouted at Jake who retreated a few feet.

The demon's laughter rang out again as it advanced on Rodric. "So you come again, spawn of Aife, nephew of the Ferguson, who worshiped my kind."

"I said, be gone!" Rodric raised the axe over his head and brought it down and through the figure of smoke and evil, cleaving it in two.

The demon's scream was how Eva Grace imagined doomed souls sounded when they realized their fates. For a moment, her heart felt free. The demon was gone. It had to be gone.

But her heart sank as the two columns of evil melded. Rodric swung out again, but the demon shot into the air, disappearing as laughter filled the valley that cradled New Mourne.

Eva Grace felt her power drop. Like her sister witches, she crumpled to the ground and struggled for breath. Seconds later Brenna was up and running toward Jake who was morphing into his human form.

Then Rodric was beside Eva Grace, pulling her up into his arms. "Oh, my sweet love. I thought he had you all. I didn't think I'd make it in time."

"How did you know?" she whispered, pulling back to study him in wonder. "What told you we were in trouble?"

"My heart and soul," he murmured before he kissed her and drew away.

He pushed his hand through her hair and gazed at her with brown eyes that could have melted stronger women than she. "I started to ache, all over my body. I knew something was wrong, so I ran this way from the inn. Lorcan met me halfway, and I knew you needed me.

Jake must have seen us. He streaked by me."

Eva Grace looked down as Lorcan licked her hand. "You really are my protector, aren't you?"

She looked around. The automatic lights on the back of the shop had come on, illuminating the scene.

"Is Jake all right? Did it hurt him?"

"Brenna's got him. He's fine," Rodric said, standing.

Eva Grace saw Brenna with Jake, who was fully restored to his human form. Lauren was helping Maggie up.

"We're okay," Lauren said, waving her off. "See to Fiona."

The youngest cousin was still on the ground, though her eyes were open, and she was staring up into the tree. Eva Grace and Rodric dropped down on either side of her.

Eva Grace took her hand and felt her fear. "Easy now. Let it go, Fiona. Let me take it."

"No." Fiona pulled away. "I want to feel it all. I want to remember."

"What do you mean?" Eva Grace helped her sit up.

"Until this thing is destroyed, until the curse is broken, I want to feel every moment," Fiona said. "Our coven has spent too much time forgetting and comforting each other. We have to fight."

"Yes, we do," Eva Grace replied, feeling energized.

Soon they all stood near the oak tree, which was once again frozen and brown.

"Well, that didn't work," Brenna said, hands on her hips. "But we chased it off again." She turned to Rodric. "Thanks to you."

"Jake might have taken it," Rodric said.

The sheriff shook his head. "I have enough magic to give it a fight, but it's too strong. I think the Woman's allowing it a lot of power."

"But still she doesn't take one of us, and we haven't seen or heard from her," Eva Grace murmured, looking up into the dark sky where the demon had disappeared.

They knew so much about the Woman—how she had come to this land, how she had defied her father for love, had a child and lost her husband. What were they missing that might be used to reach her and end this torture forever? The answer was close. She could feel it.

"I just realized the rest of the coven hasn't contacted us," Brenna said. She pulled her phone from her coat pocket, called and soon reported Sarah was safe at home with Delia and Aiden. "Mother says Sarah seems better than she has been in days."

"Then why didn't she know what happened?" Eva Grace asked.

"I don't know," Brenna admitted. "Let's call the rest of the coven."

In moments, they confirmed no one else had sensed the struggle with the demon.

"This is very strange," Eva Grace said, looking from one to the other of her sister witches.

"It's because it's up to us," Lauren said.

No one argued with her. They agreed to regroup the next day. Soon only Rodric and Eva Grace remained.

She dimmed the lights in the shop and moved the cash register tray to the safe.

Arms crossed, he stood at the counter, watching her.

"What is it?" she asked as she came toward him.

"You're very calm," he observed. "What are you thinking?"

She leaned her back against the counter and surveyed the darkened shop that she loved so much. Then she looked into his eyes, this man she thought she could love.

"We could win," she whispered. "Tonight, I thought we could win. I don't always believe that."

He smiled and kissed her. Energy rippled around them, and desire kindled inside her. "Make love with me."

Rodric nuzzled her neck, laughing softly. "Gladly. Let's go home."

"Here," she said. "Now."

He looked surprised, but very game. "Okay."

"You were very sexy with that axe."

"So, you like the warrior type?"

"I like you—in whatever form."

Later, Eva Grace would remember it like a dream. Rodric's hands drifting down her body. His lips trailing fire up her throat to her mouth. The way they pushed the most unnecessary clothes out of the way. How she straddled him on the chair where customers sat to try on earrings in front of an antique dressing table that had belonged to Minnie.

Did the ghost peek at them when Eva Grace came not once, but twice? Did Minnie sigh in memory of her own lover?

"You are a witch," he murmured as their breathing returned to normal. His hands cupped her bottom, holding her still against him. "I'm under your spell for sure."

She laughed, feeling so alive, so free and so hopeful. It felt good to have hope. The feeling was intoxicating.

"I'm starving," she told Rodric.

He drew away, one brow lifted. "Again? That will take some magic."

"Starving for food. It's been an eventful night."

A soft whine from behind the counter echoed that thought. "Oh, my," she said. "Poor Lorcan."

"I think we embarrassed him," Rodric agreed. "He hid."

"We'll give him something special at home to make up for it."

Less than twenty minutes later, they pulled her car into the driveway. Lorcan bounded ahead of them but stopped at the bottom of the front steps barking frantically.

Eva Grace's senses sharpened. "Something's wrong." With a flick of her hand, she turned on the porch lights.

A body lay under a crepe myrtle tree. The long, gray braid told Eva Grace exactly who it was, and she raced forward.

"No." She fell to her knees beside the blood-soaked body. "Sarah. Grandmother, no." She grasped Sarah's ice-cold fingers. Her life was ebbing. Eva Grace clutched onto her pain to hold her in this realm. The pain was a shocking punch to her gut. Eva Grace reached out to the coven. She knew they were coming.

Dimly she heard Rodric call 9-1-1 as he sank to the ground on the other side of Sarah. "She's been stabbed."

"Again and again and again," Eva Grace said, sobbing. Her grandmother's denim jacket was sliced to ribbons, the cuts too numerous to count. It was a miracle she was still alive.

"Look at that," Rodric muttered and pointed at a blade that glittered in the leaves next to Sarah. "What is it?"

"A dagger," Eva Grace gasped, recognizing the small, bejeweled weapon. "From the shop. How in the world—"

Her grandmother stirred slightly, and Eva Grace felt her sliding away. "I have to help her." She pulled at Sarah's clothes, hoping to apply pressure to stem the bleeding, but there were too many wounds and too much blood.

"Help me!" she screamed at Rodric. "Help me save her!" She grabbed his hand.

His magic surged into Eva Grace, and she wrapped her free hand around Sarah's wrist. "No, no, no," Eva Grace begged her. "You can't go. Hang on."

Sirens wailed in the distance. Eva Grace called the other witches in her mind. Help was on its way from every front.

"Goddess," she whispered. "Save her, save her."

Sarah's eyes opened. She smiled. "Sweet Eva Grace. Let me go."

"I can't," Eva Grace sobbed. "Just hold on. The coven is coming. I can feel them. They'll be here soon. We'll save you."

"No."

"Grandmother, please." Tears streaming, Eva Grace laid her face against Sarah's chest. She bore down on Sarah's pain with every bit of empathic skill she possessed.

"You save your strength for the final fight," Sarah murmured. "Don't give yourself away."

And then her light winked out. Like a star plucked from the sky, Eva Grace thought, a black hole where once there was a glow. Their matriarch was gone.

Chapter 15

Eva Grace's heartbroken sobs were overridden by sirens. The fire department's rescue squad was only blocks away, so they arrived before law enforcement. Rodric had to pull her off Sarah so the paramedics could see if there was truly no hope. Eva Grace's body trembled in his arms.

The medic looked up and shook his head. Like so many in this close-knit community, he obviously knew the Connellys. "I'm sorry, Eva Grace. So sorry."

Her sobs ceased, and she pulled away from Rodric. He watched her gather her strength and calm her emotions. She turned to her house, and for the first time Rodric noticed the front door was ajar.

Eva Grace snapped her fingers, and the rest of the lights came on. All the windows stood open. Here and there curtains blew in the cold wind.

Before he could stop her, Eva Grace charged up the steps, Lorcan at her side.

"We need to wait for Jake and his deputies," Rodric said. "This is a crime scene."

"This is my home," she retorted. "Someone was going through my things. What were they looking for and what was Sarah doing here?"

Inside was turmoil. Furniture was turned over and upholstery ripped in places. Delicate collectibles lay shattered. Plants were overturned, pots broken. Every

Neely Powell

room had been touched. In her study, desk drawers hung open and papers spilled onto the floor.

"Smell it?" Eva Grace asked. "Black magic. In my home. Right in my home. I renew the wards every day. How could anything get through them?"

The faint scent of evil filled Rodric with anger. The demon had been here, he was certain, in his beloved's home. He felt the outline of a sword form in his hand. Was the evil still here? By Aife, he would protect her.

As if she sensed his thoughts, Eva Grace said, "It's gone. It killed Sarah and left." She looked around. "These papers were my mother's, poems and other things she'd written. I found them in a box upstairs last week. I moved them down here to put them in some order."

Near the desk, Lorcan growled. Rodric stepped over and saw a smear of blood on the corner. There was another on the casing of the pocket door to the hall.

"She fought it," Eva Grace murmured.

"She was Sarah Connelly," he said. "Of course, she fought it."

Rodric could see Eva Grace's thoughts taking shape in her head. "The demon left us at the shop and came here. Somehow, it got through my wards. It was searching for something here in my house when Sarah came by."

"But what?" Rodric said. "Do you see anything that's missing?"

Shouts from outside drew them back to the porch. Sheriff's cruisers were here, and bright headlights lit the entire scene like it was midday. Eva Grace's cousin, Deputy Brian Lamont took the front steps two at a time. "What happened?"

Before they could answer, Jake and Brenna arrived with the rest of the coven in quick order. Jake and Brian tried to hold the elder aunts away from Sarah's body. The petite witches that Rodric had always thought of in terms of potions and love spells called on magic to push them out of the way and hurried over to Sarah.

They knelt on either side of her body. Together, they said, "*Deirfiúr dhil.*"

"Beloved sister." Tears gathered in Rodric's eyes as the twins joined hands over their fallen sister's body and began a soft chant. Eva Grace clutched his arm.

"Mama, oh Mama." Delia's voice caught and she turned her face into Aiden's chest. The other coven members stood behind them, their sobs rising in the cold night air.

A truck screeched to a halt on the street.

"Marcus," Eva Grace breathed.

"He was in Dalton getting a load of barn wood," Aidan explained. "Sarah was fine before he left. I called and told him she'd been attacked."

"I checked on her when you called earlier," Delia told them. "She was in the window seat in their room, looking through the *Book of Magic*. She came here without us knowing she left."

Marcus ran up the sidewalk, calling his wife's name, his face a mask of horror as he saw the elder aunts near the body.

"She's gone," Frances told him in a shaky voice.

"No." The man's wail was heartrending as he fell to his knees beside Doris and reached for Sarah.

"Wait." Jake put a hand on Marcus's shoulder. "We need to process the scene."

"No, you don't," Eva Grace said. "It's obvious what

happened. Let Marcus be."

The elder aunts took over again, daring anyone to come near while Marcus grieved holding his wife's body.

"Here," Rodric pulled Jake away and offered him a bloody handkerchief. "It's a dagger we found beside Sarah." Brenna, Eva Grace and the other witches clustered around them.

Jake's eyes narrowed. "Why didn't you leave it where it was? That's evidence."

"I don't think you'll be finding any fingerprints," Rodric said. "This was the demon's work."

"She was stabbed," Jake protested. "We don't know who did this."

"No, he was right to take it," Brenna said. "We don't need the town knowing everything about coven business." She nodded toward the medics and two of Jake's other deputies who had retreated to the driveway to give the family privacy.

Before Jake could protest again, someone clutched Rodric's arm. He turned in time to catch Lauren before she collapsed.

"Oh, dear goddess," she sobbed. "It's my fault. I'm the reason Sarah was killed."

"What do you mean?" Jake asked.

Eva Grace filled in the blanks, "The dagger came from Siren's Call. Lauren ordered them."

Lauren pulled away from Rodric, sobbing anew. He tried to soothe her, but she waved him off and staggered away.

Brian caught up to Lauren and put his arm around her shoulders. "This isn't your fault. This damn demon would have found another way. The Connellys are under attack just like they always are."

While Brian and the others tried to comfort Lauren, Rodric and Eva Grace went to help the elder aunts get up. Their clothes were stained with Sarah's blood. Rodric realized he and Eva Grace were in similar shape.

"Let's go inside and clean up," he murmured.

"Aiden and I will stay here for now," Delia said. She nodded toward Marcus who still sat on the cold ground, clutching his wife's lifeless body, tears streaming down his face.

Before everyone else went in the house, Rodric heard Jake ask the other two deputies to check the perimeter of the house again. Even as they moved away, Rodric knew they would find nothing.

The witches stood in the foyer, all of them touching, a shocked and silent group. For once, no one suggested tea or moved toward the kitchen to get food.

They were simply shattered, Rodric decided. He could feel the thrum of their magic, but it wasn't unified. Brenna and Eva Grace were trying to pull themselves together, but they were hurting.

Brenna turned to Eva Grace. "Tell us everything that happened."

She complied, pointing out the blood in the office.

Jake studied the foyer and found two more smears near the front door.

"So, we believe the demon came here after we turned it back at the shop," Brenna said.

"And Sarah came here, too." Fiona looked at Eva Grace. "But why?"

"Rodric and I were at the shop for about forty-five minutes after you all left. I had no idea that Sarah was coming here."

He thought that sweet, intimate time with her seemed very long ago.

"Sarah came in and found the demon," Brenna surmised.

"Or the demon found her," Jake said. "I know you don't want to hear this, but we really do need to go through this scene, see if we can reconstruct part of what happened."

"Why didn't we know she needed us?" Frances murmured. The younger women helped her and Doris to the sofa. The strength the twins had shown earlier was gone.

"She didn't call for us," Doris agreed.

"She was weak," Eva Grace said. "We all know she wasn't herself."

"I think something has been working on her, eating at her magic." Brenna's eyes narrowed. "Maybe it was Willow."

"Is that possible?" Fiona looked at Rodric.

"A powerful faerie can do a lot of damage," Rodric said grimly. He thought of Willow's cold, blue eyes as she'd confronted him yesterday. She was capable of fighting any witch.

"Maybe she was looking for this." Eva Grace touched the arrowhead on the chain around her neck.

"She knows where that is," Brenna said. "And I don't believe she can get it."

"But what else could she want here?"

The front door opened, and Brian said, "You guys might want to come out and see what Marcus found."

They filed out, and Eva Grace took Rodric's hand. Delia and Aiden stood on either side of Marcus on the porch.

Delia held out a folded sheet of paper. "This was under Sarah. It's sealed by magic. I couldn't open it."

"Let me see." Brenna took the paper, and it immediately unfolded.

"It needed the coven leader," Eva Grace said, her voice steadier than it had been since finding Sarah.

She went to her cousin's side, as if taking her natural place, Rodric thought.

"What is it?" Lauren asked as she, Fiona and Maggie drew near.

"It's a page from the *Book of Magic*." Brenna frowned. "But it makes no sense."

"What does it say?"

"It's scripture," she said, puzzled, "from the Bible."

A gasp ran through the group.

Rodric looked at Eva Grace. "We've studied the book several times since this summer. There's no mention of scripture anywhere else."

"Maybe it's not really from the book," Fiona suggested.

"Look at the paper." Brenna held it up. "There's no doubt."

"Read it to us," Eva Grace said.

Brenna said, "'But for the cowardly and unbelieving and abominable and murderers and immoral persons and sorcerers and idolaters and all liars, their part will be in the lake that burns with fire and brimstone, which is the second death.' It's a verse from Revelations."

"A sorcerer," Rodric said quietly. "MacCuindlis. The Woman's father and his apprentices." He swallowed hard, glancing at Eva Grace and thinking of what the demon had said about his uncle. How deep was Rodric's own connection to the demon and the Woman?

Brenna paused and looked up at all of them. "There's one more thing. It's signed by Fred Williams."

"Why would something the pastor wrote be part of our family's book?" Eva Grace said. "Could he have given it to Sarah?"

"It's not our Fred," Brenna said and pointed to the signature. "It's his father, and it's dated the day the Woman in White took Aunt Celia."

"What?" Delia reached for the paper. "I don't understand."

A gust of wind blew across the porch.

"Aunt Celia?" Fiona looked around.

Rodric knew their aunt was Fiona's spirit guide, but her appearances were rather sporadic and unpredictable.

"She went right through me," Fiona said.

"Mama?" The yearning in Eva Grace's voice twisted Rodric's gut. "Do you know what happened here? We need to know what to do next."

There was silence, then Fiona sighed. "She's gone."

A choked sob tore from Marcus. "At least Sarah is with her now. She grieved for Celia every day."

The coven closed ranks around him, loving arms, gentle words and comfort only family could provide.

Rodric stood to the side with Jake. "They are magnificent."

"And they're in danger," his friend said. "The demon took Garth and their Uncle Sully. The Woman has taken witches one after the other for so long. But how is it possible that Sarah is gone? We have to protect them."

Rodric nodded in agreement. He didn't verbalize his worst fears. If Willow or the demon could now penetrate the coven's wards, what did that say about their strength?

They needed to mourn, but there wasn't much time left for this generation.

Not much time for Eva Grace.

Chapter 16

Sarah was dead. Murdered in the front yard.

It wasn't grief that overwhelmed Eva Grace as she stood at her kitchen window early the next morning. It was a roiling rage such as she'd never felt before. The teacup in her hand broke and fell in the sink.

She stared down at her hands. They were covered in blood. Sarah's blood—crimson dripping from her fingers. She blinked and the blood disappeared, but her anger remained.

She opened a cabinet door and swept all the dishes on the bottom shelf out, enjoying the crash that shattered the stillness in the house.

Lorcan barked from the doorway. She glanced over and saw understanding in his eyes.

"By the goddess," she told him. "I wish I could destroy someone, just tear them apart, piece by piece."

The dog barked in agreement.

Eva Grace started for the living room to find more things to break but stopped when she remembered most of the house was already in shambles—the work of the demon or whoever else Sarah had interrupted last night. So many of her collectibles and glass items were smashed, the cushions on the couch ripped open, pieces of her life scattered and broken.

Brenna and the rest of the coven had said they wanted to clean up her house with a restore spell, but they were all too grief-stricken to attempt it last night. And what did it matter? It was Sarah that needed restoring, and there was nothing, nothing Eva Grace could do. She was a healer, but the dead couldn't be healed.

Anger flamed through her again. She charged outside.

First, she ripped away the yellow crime scene tape. Then she fell to her knees and began digging beneath the crepe myrtle where they found Sarah. She tore plants out of the ground as fast as she could. The dirt kept turning to blood, and she dug harder.

Lorcan whined, but she kept working until she heard Rodric's voice.

"Eva Grace?" he called as he got out of his SUV. "Are you all right?" She wouldn't leave her house last night, so he had stayed. He left this morning to get his things from the inn. He said he was moving in with her and there would be no arguing about it.

She couldn't think about that now. Her breath puffed in clouds in the cold air as she threw a plant on the sidewalk. Rodric stopped just a few feet away. Lorcan got up and went to him.

"So, what are you up to?" Rodric asked, his voice measured and calm. "Did Jake say it was okay to do this?"

"I don't give a fuck what Jake says," she retorted and knew he was a bit startled by her language. "I want everything in this flower bed out. It's tainted by what happened here last night."

He hesitated. "Maybe you should—"

"No." She glared at him. "I. Want. It. Gone." She went back to clawing in the ground.

Rodric disappeared and came back with a wheelbarrow loaded with tools from her garden shed, including a small chainsaw. She grabbed a shovel and began digging up monkey grass along the edge of the sidewalk.

"You want the crepe myrtle gone, too?" Rodric asked.

That pained her. The dwarf tree bloomed rosy-pink in the spring and summer, and it was beautiful still with leaves darkened to darkest bronze due to the cold. Cousin Inez had lovingly tended it for years. But even as Eva Grace wavered, she could see the blood dripping off the leaves and down the trunk.

"Get rid of it," she told Rodric tersely. She had to lose this tree, just another loss among many.

He used the chainsaw to cut away the branches while she continued her assault on the smaller shrubs. Together, they dug around the tree's base.

"It's been here a good long while," Rodric said, huffing. "The roots are deep."

"Back up." Eva Grace held out her hands and pushed the fury inside of her toward the tree. When she could feel heat rising from the ground, she grasped her shovel again and worked at the loosened dirt. The tree gave way easily, and the roots that came out of the ground were burnt and blackened.

But she no longer saw Sarah's blood, and that was the point.

Rodric worked beside her in silence as they cleared the rest of the space. They loaded the wheelbarrow several times and took the debris to the edge of the backyard to an old barrel that Inez had always used for burning leaves.

When they filled the wheelbarrow for the last time, she turned to Rodric. "There's sage in a drawer near the refrigerator. Can you get some for me?"

He was back in moments with several bundles of the herb. Eva Grace lit them with a snap of her fingers and walked slowly back and forth as the smoke cleared and cleansed the air over the bare earth. She prayed to the goddess, "Make this land pure again. Wipe away this evil."

Sage still burning, she led the way to the backyard. Lorcan stood by, every line of his body on alert as she and Rodric filled the barrel. At her unspoken command, dog and man stepped back.

She stripped off her clothes and added them to the pile. She tossed in the sage, flipped her hand, and flames burst above her head. A shriek split the air. The smoke was black and smelled of sulfur.

Eva Grace stood without speaking until the flames smoldered and disappeared. She looked down at her hands. They were covered in dirt rather than stained with blood.

Only then did she feel the cold. She began to tremble, and Rodric pulled off his jacket and wrapped it around her.

"Is it gone?" he whispered.

"It won't truly be gone until the curse is over."

"I fear you're taking too much blame for what's happened."

"It's my home. What killed Sarah came through me, broke my magic. It's not acceptable."

Rodric hugged her closer. "Don't you want to plant something out front? Even though it's cold, your magic could make anything grow."

"It needs to stay bare to remind us of what happened. Maybe I can plant in the spring."

He brought her around to face him. "Maybe?"

"If I'm still here."

The muscles worked in his throat, and she could feel the denial he wanted to make. But he didn't insult her by saying a word. They both knew the Woman might take her at any time.

"I should go in," she said. "We all agreed to take the morning for ourselves and meet at the home place as soon as we could."

"Brenna texted me to ask if you were okay. She seemed to know what you were doing."

"With Sarah gone, I feel connected to Brenna in a whole new way. She's the head of our coven now."

"She needs you."

"We all need each other more than ever." A breeze stirred the dry leaves around them, and Eva Grace sighed. Her body ached from the hours of work, and she yearned to just hide away from the world and mourn the grandmother she loved so much.

Instead, she squared her shoulders. "Let's get cleaned up," she told Rodric. "The others are waiting for me."

Chapter 17

At the home place, Eva Grace hurried toward the door, knowing everyone was waiting for her.

Rodric seemed to always know what she was thinking. "Don't feel guilty," he said. "You needed to cleanse the ground at your house. Evil had lingered."

"Evil that breached our wards." She shivered and glanced toward the woods. She quickened her pace. What had happened to their protections? Was the Woman taking them out piece by piece?

A man in denim overalls and a crisply ironed white shirt came down the driveway. He hugged Eva Grace and offered a large, work-roughened hand to Rodric when introduced. Gordon Andersen's farm adjoined the Connelly's. He was a head taller and almost twice as broad as Rodric.

"I am so sorry," Gordon said. "Everyone is. And we're. . ." His gaze darted toward Rodric, then locked on Eva Grace. "We're worried."

"Don't be. We're here for New Mourne as we've always been." She could feel the jotnar's magic. He wore his charm very well today, but as he walked away, the tip of his tail slipped up into the leg of his overalls.

"Interesting," Rodric mused.

"Not like a troll to express such concern."

They looked at each other with growing unease and hurried toward the house. Her cousin Brian and

Maggie's husband Ian were on the porch.

"Should I wait out here?" Rodric asked.

But she wanted him with her.

"Jake and Aiden are in there," Brian said. "Brenna said they could stay. We're staying here, and others are out back."

They were on guard, she realized. The family's men were closing ranks against any intruders.

"Cousin Inez and her daughter have the children upstairs," he added.

"Where's Marcus?"

"In his shop." The young deputy looked away, his green eyes filling with tears. "He's building Sarah's coffin. Uncle Aiden is with him. What the hell, Eva Grace? What are we going to do?"

Brian looked so sad, she hugged him and absorbed some of his pain.

Inside were delicious aromas that belied the sadness. The South's traditional funeral food had appeared in full force. The buffet in the dining room was lined with pies, cakes, cookies and other desserts. The door to the kitchen was propped open to reveal a busy hive of women—in-laws, neighbors and long-time friends. Eva Grace was certain they had meats, casseroles, vegetables, biscuits, rolls and cornbread ready for lunch.

One of the women in the kitchen looked up and saw Eva Grace. She nodded and turned to the others. "She's here. Let's go."

Soon the only sounds were car engines starting and the low murmur of voices from the porch. Rodric took a seat beside Jake on the periphery of the room.

The coven was gathered around the table with the *Connelly Book of Magic* open in the middle. Eva Grace noted that the seating arrangement had shifted.

The elder aunts now sat together at the foot of the table, hands clasped and still as stone. Their daughters Diane and Estelle flanked them. Delia was staring off into space, her face puffy and eyes red. Next to her and to the left of the head chair, Fiona kept looking around the room. Ghosts, no doubt, Eva Grace thought. Even she could feel unrest in the air. Was her mother's spirit here? She wanted to believe she was.

Maggie, the one she'd expect to be in tears, looked oddly strong next to Lauren, who was a wreck—hair scooped back, face devoid of makeup and expression vulnerable.

Eva Grace sat to the right of the empty chair at the head of the table.

Brenna paced behind it, family wand in hand.

Strain showed in her voice as she faced the group. "We're all devastated, but the last thing Sarah would want us to do is take our eyes off our goal of defeating the curse."

"The pattern is repeating," Lauren murmured, not looking up from the table.

"What do you mean?" Eva Grace asked.

"The Woman and her demon distract all of us with something terrible. They beat us down until we feel defeated, then they take us." Lauren finally looked up at the women. "I finally understand how someone could just give it up, refuse to fight any longer. I feel that way today."

"You can't do that." Brenna's voice rose.

"What would it matter if I died?" Lauren demanded. "I'm not the leader like you, Brenna. Or the coven's heart like Eva Grace, gifted like Fiona or a mother like

Maggie. Maybe I'm disposable, and I should get on with it."

Brenna and Fiona responded with loud protests. Both had been on the firing line with the demon. Lauren's mother Estelle broke down in sobs.

"Stop it," Eva Grace commanded, standing. "All of you, just stop. The demon succeeds if our coven is dispirited and disconnected."

It wasn't like her to take the lead in such a way. Brenna's nod of support was a relief.

"She's right," Brenna said. "We have to pull ourselves together. It's what Sarah would tell us to do."

She lifted the wand and sparks flew. They shot around the room, up to the 12-foot ceiling and showered down like rain, every color in the rainbow and bright as fire. It warmed the air.

The head chair slid back, and Brenna stared at it, her expression caught between sorrow and yearning.

On instinct, Eva Grace held out her hand to her cousin. "Take it, Brenna. It's yours, and we need you."

The coven stood. Even Lauren's head was high as Brenna took her rightful place. Fresh energy charged through the group as they sat.

Eva Grace smiled. She was Brenna's right hand, and it felt good.

"Let's get down to it." Brenna said. "There's no record of any coven leader being murdered by the demon or the Woman. We have to figure out why she's done this."

"But how?" Fiona asked. "You tried to sacrifice yourself. I tried to help the Woman cross over. We've tried to connect her to her dead child and the man she loved. What else is there?"

"Maybe Sarah was bringing you this page from the book to help." Brenna pulled the folded paper from the pocket of her sweater and smoothed it out on the table. She read aloud the scripture they'd all heard last night.

And then she added what Sarah had written, "'Kahlil Gibran says, 'If you reveal your secrets to the wind, you should not blame the wind for revealing them to the trees.' 'For the good of all, we agree.'" She looked up at the group. "It's signed by Sarah and Fred Williams on the day the Woman took Celia."

Delia frowned. "I remembered this morning that Reverend Williams was here that day. I don't know why. He tried to comfort me, and I wanted nothing to do with him. I couldn't understand why he was here."

"He respected us, at least," Doris said. "And his son came here this summer, also offering his help."

Frances nodded. "We need to ask his son what he knows about this."

Brenna snorted. "Good luck getting past Ginny to talk to Fred."

"But I still don't understand," Eva Grace said. "Why in the world would Sarah sign something like this with him and place it in the book, like it's sacred?"

Brian stepped inside and said, "Rob Stevens is here. He says it's important."

Rob was a werewolf, and it was strange that he was here instead of his pack's alpha. The young man was tall and muscular and black-haired, his expression fierce. Eva Grace could sense his wolf close to the surface. So could Jake. He growled deep in his throat, and the two shifters glared at each other.

Rodric was instantly on his feet and at Jake's side, and the glint of a sword flashed in his hand.

Faced with Jake and Rodric, the werewolf brought himself under control. "Alpha sent me," he told the coven. "Willow is gathering the supers. She's stirring some trouble."

"That bitch," Brenna said.

Remembering the jotnar's words, Eva Grace's worry deepened. Had he known about the meeting then? As a troll, he was under Willow's control, but he had always been the Connellys' friend.

"Willow says the coven is weak," Rob continued. "She's playing on everyone's fears about what might happen."

Brenna stood with the wand in her hand. "We go on as we always have. We protect New Mourne."

Eva Grace joined her. "Brenna is our leader now."

"And she's powerful," Fiona said, going to Brenna's left.

Maggie and Lauren surprised Eva Grace and flanked them.

The wand pulsed with light and power.

Rob's eyes widened.

"Where is Willow's meeting?" Brenna demanded.

"A hollow just past her house. We've never been allowed to hunt there, but we all know it well."

"As do I." Brenna dismissed Rob with a wave. "May the goddess keep you safe."

He left, and in the ensuing silence, the coven looked to Brenna.

Eva Grace placed her hand around her cousin's and felt the wand's vibrations.

The five witches formed a circle.

A lifetime of following Brenna told Eva Grace what was about to happen. "Can we do it?" she whispered.

"Hell, yes," Brenna said as she closed her eyes.

And they flew.

Chapter 18

Though Brian drove Fiona's van as fast as he could on the winding roads, Rodric never wanted to fly more in his life. He didn't know where Eva Grace was, but he sensed she was using strong magic. He felt a desperation to be by her side.

He knew Jake was feeling the same because the shifter was sweating to hold back his tiger. He had his head down and his eyes closed.

"It's only a few more miles," Brian said.

The van skidded on the asphalt as he took a tight curve without reducing speed.

"Jesus," Bailey said. "Do we even know where we're going?"

"Here," Jake growled.

Brian braked, cut the engine and let the van roll behind a huge tree. All the doors opened at once. By the time Jake hit the ground, he was a restless white tiger. He sniffed the air and then started east.

Rodric pulled his warrior to the forefront, holding back enough to keep his human in control. Though no one was sure it would help, Brian was decked out in riot gear with a rifle. Rodric knew Bailey wore an amulet under his shirt that Eva Grace designed for him. It contained all the gems needed to provide protection in a multitude of situations. Rodric hoped this situation was one of them.

They followed the tiger until the sun filtered through a break in the trees ahead. The gathering of supernaturals in the clearing sent Jake bounding forward.

The witches were on one side, Willow on another. Behind the ancient faerie was her faithful coyote and a tall, muscular blond man. Something about the man made Rodric even more uneasy.

Shunting that aside, Rodric surveyed the other supers. There were Druids, led by Riley O'Neal from the county's Board of Commissioners, the shifters who ran the RV park, and a group of jotnar that included the farmer they had met at the Connelly home earlier. The werewolf pack's alpha stood a little apart, flanked by several of his lieutenants. To the side, pixies sat on a fallen log.

It was difficult to determine who might be on Willow's side, who was neutral, and who might support the coven.

Brenna was face to face with Willow. Though the faerie had used glamor to appear young and beautiful, there was no glittering gown today. She was in black leather head to toe, ending with wedge-heeled, thigh-high boots. Rodric thought it was no accident that she looked like a dominatrix.

Brenna looked no less formidable in her royal blue cape with the Connelly wand glowing in her hand. Behind her in a "V," the other young witches stood in their capes, Eva Grace in emerald green, Fiona in ruby red, Maggie in citrine yellow, and Lauren in the deep purple of an amethyst quartz.

Brenna stepped forward and the four other witches followed her as one. Pride surged inside Rodric at their show of unity. He was unaware Jake moved until the big tiger rubbed his head against Brenna's thigh and then sat watching Willow with silver eyes that displayed his human intelligence.

Brian moved between Maggie and Lauren, his rifle at the ready. Bailey reached Fiona, and she took his hand. Rodric stepped beside Eva Grace, who acknowledged his presence with a slight nod.

"So, you brought your men along to help with your fight?" Disdain dripped from Willow's words causing sparks to pop like water hitting hot grease.

"We're here for support, just like them," Rodric said, pointing to the coyote and the blond man. Recognition dawned, and Rodric could see the ancient, evil faerie beneath the man's facade.

He glared at Willow. "Who brings a Fachan except to wreak havoc?"

She couldn't hide her surprise.

"I've seen his kind before," Rodric continued, remembering an encounter during an investigation in France. This Fachan was disguised from his true form— one eye, one arm, one leg in the center of a furry body. Stories said Fachan were able to stop a human heart with just one look and were always angry because they couldn't fly like other faeries.

"Yearning for some wings?" he taunted the creature.

The Fachan took a step forward, sharp teeth baring as he hissed. The coyote nipped at his leg.

"Control yourselves." Willow told her minions with an icy glance. "Let's stop this nonsense and get back to why we're here."

"Fine with me," Brenna agreed, though Rodric still glared at the Fachan.

"I seek to protect New Mourne." Willow pressed a

hand to her heart—or whatever was in her chest. "With Sarah dead, it's possible we'll all be under attack."

"It appears to me the attack is coming from within," Brenna said steadily. "You know the Connelly coven has made this a sanctuary for supernatural beings. Why are you causing this stir?"

"The wards will be weaker without Sarah, and we all know there has been dissension among coven members of late," Willow said with a half-smile.

"Yet here we stand, united and ready to fight for a way of life that is essential to peace and harmony," Brenna countered.

"There is no such thing as peace and harmony," Willow said. "In case you haven't noticed, the entire world is in chaos."

Turning away from the witches to face the crowd of supernaturals, Willow said, "For years, we've depended on this coven to protect us, and in every generation we all live in fear because of *their* family curse. Does that make sense to anyone?"

"We've always made it through," a jotnar responded. Clearly, they were on the coven's side.

"But at what cost?" Willow sneered. She turned to the shifters. "Didn't your kind struggle for control this summer when evil swept through our town?"

She looked at the werewolves. "One of your pack was nearly murdered because of this coven."

A ripple of unease moved through the crowd.

"And now they have no leader. Just young, inexperienced witches," Willow said.

Rodric could tell Willow's words were enhanced by magic to impress her audience.

As he expected, Brenna sensed the same trickery.

With a wave of her wand, she revealed the dark haze of magic hovering above the crowd.

The alpha growled in protest. The pixies' wings deepened to a dark, angry purple. Jeers rang out from the rest of the crowd.

The witches locked themselves together with hands on one another's shoulders. Brenna said, "*Bloc an daiocht*," and the haze disappeared.

"Why you little—" Willow began.

"Witch?" Brenna interrupted with a smile that made her eyes glow.

Willow raised her hand and threw a ball of fire toward Brian and Bailey. Both men hit the ground, Lauren intercepted the fireball and sent it back at Willow.

The faerie ducked, and the ball dropped to the ground, sizzling out.

Rodric resisted the temptation to step in front of Eva Grace. Beside Brenna, Jake's massive white tiger roared.

"If you've come to fight, Willow, it's you and me," Brenna said. "You know you'll always win against a human. Leave them out of this."

Maggie conjured a bag of salt and poured a generous circle around Brian and Bailey. Rodric smiled at the young witch's ingenuity. The two men were safe as Maggie returned to her spot beside Lauren.

Brenna turned and spoke to the crowd for the first time. "I suggest you all move closer together. This may get a little messy." Her tone held just the right amount of menace.

The crowd backed up a bit, but the werewolves and the jotnar refused to cede much ground. The pixies rose as one, voices tinkling like bells. Rodric frowned as an eagle swept down from the trees to perch near the pixies.

"Who is that?" Rodric whispered as the eagle's hooded eyes looked around at the crowd.

"No idea," Eva Grace answered. "But the pixies have pissed Willow off."

Indeed, anger emanated from Willow as she studied the tiny creatures who flew around the bird in protective circles. "Et tu, *bloc an draiocht*?"

The pixies giggled at her Gaelic reference to them. She had no allies there, Rodric realized, puzzled.

Lightning crackled around Willow, and the air grew heavy, like a threatening storm.

Another growl drew Rodric's attention to Jake. Brenna laid her hand on her tiger's head.

Rodric gripped the axe and sword that came to his hands. The coyote howled, and the Fachan's unearthly cry split the air. Jake reared to his back legs, snarling.

Brenna's wand glowed. Eva Grace stepped closer to her. Rodric knew Brenna would not die today. Eva Grace would not allow it.

Willow never took her eyes off Brenna, who was still and quiet as Jake paced like a sentry in front of her.

"Surely you don't trust these witches," Willow said, with a look of entreaty to the group surrounding them. "Why can't you see that protection from the fae would be stronger and fiercer?"

"If that's true, why haven't you ended the curse before now?" Brenna asked. "You deem yourself all powerful, yet you've never actually confronted the Woman in White, have you?"

As she spoke, the wind picked up, and Rodric felt Brenna's magic growing.

Willow's laughter was wicked. "We've never been

in this crisis before. There's always been a smooth transfer of power from one generation to the next. But you allowed Sarah to be *murdered.*" The word cracked like thunder from the mountain.

The witches drew in a collective breath. Sparks flew from one to the other. Rodric's own magic was drawn in, summoned. The tiger hunched as if ready to spring at the coyote and Fachan.

The jotnar farmer stepped out of the crowd, holding out his hands. "Willow, please, you may be going too far."

Her head whipped toward him and for a moment everyone could see her ancient, skeletal features. The farmer was shoved back against another jotnar, and angry voices rang out.

"*I'll do as I please,*" Willow shouted. "I should have seized control long ago while the rest of you blindly followed the coven."

Rodric felt the assembly turning against Willow.

"So, this is how you convince our neighbors that you're the one who can protect them?" Brenna jeered. "You mean you've never cared about them before?"

Willow tossed a small ball of light between her hands like a tennis ball. "The time was never right." The light grew bigger.

"And you think it is now? Wrong move!" Brenna raised the wand, and Willow's ball of light went out.

"You bitch!" Willow pulled her arms back against her chest and pushed toward Brenna, who fell back several feet.

Eva Grace didn't move, but Rodric could feel her channel power to Brenna. The wand flashed in Brenna's hands again. Willow's body flew through the air and landed hard. But she jumped up quickly, racing toward Brenna, enraged.

The women met with a boom that shook the ground. A magical barrier held them apart, glowing yellow, then red, like a flame ready to quicken and burn. Their breath was labored as they struggled.

The Fachan moved forward, and Jake swiped at him. Rodric stared down the coyote who paced just beyond his mistress.

"How do you expect to protect anyone? Why didn't you kill the demon when you had a chance this summer?" Willow snarled.

"Why haven't you done something about the Woman in White?" Brenna's magic pushed Willow backward.

The old faerie struggled to keep her balance as she backed up.

Brenna advanced on her, her confidence growing with every inch. "I'll tell you why, you don't know what to do either. You just want to take over New Mourne and run it like the little dictator you are."

"I've lived here almost as long as you witches," Willow said.

"Yet you did nothing," Brenna said as the two women circled each other like boxers.

Willow threw a fireball that Brenna easily dodged and put out with a spot rain shower. Willow held out both hands and streams of magic battered Brenna to the ground.

The Fachan chuckled and Rodric nicked the man's arm with the tip of his sword. "Don't laugh too soon, beast."

As the fight continued, the magic grew stronger,

flowing back and forth with such speed it was impossible to watch at times. In minutes, the two women looked like they'd been in a brawl with a gang of sorcerers on speed. Both of them retreated, bedraggled and out of breath.

Rodric saw Eva Grace slip a small ball to Brenna.

"What was that?" Rodric muttered, keeping an uneasy eye on Willow's two cohorts.

"I conjured poppy seed extract," Eva Grace replied with a small grin.

"Smart lady." The sweet-smelling extract was stunning to faeries—literally, they couldn't move once it touched them.

Brenna broke the small ball over her wand. Magic crackled in the air as she shouted, "Enough."

Willow froze mid-stride, though Rodric could see her try to move. Brenna looked powerful as she walked around the fae waving her wand.

"It's time for you to learn, Willow, that we will not trust you as Sarah has. We know your intentions and jealous desires. New Mourne is a sanctuary, and it will continue to be just that, protected daily by the Connelly coven, not a power-crazed fae."

Willow's clothes changed to a peasant dress and canvas sneakers with socks. Her hair spun into a bun, and her fingernails shortened, leaving her looking like an ordinary old woman.

"Willow Scanlan, people often forget witches have a power faeries despise. We can banish them, get them out of our way and go on with our lives, and that's going to happen to you."

The four young witches formed their "V" behind Brenna again as the Fachan sprang forward. Rodric had been waiting just for that. The sword went through the

Fachan's body like a knife through butter. As he fell to the ground, the handsome man disappeared. In his place a hairy, one-armed cyclops writhed in the grass, meeting his slow, painful death.

At the sound of a sharp animal cry, Rodric looked over to see the coyote running into the woods while Jake calmly licked blood from a huge paw.

Rodric turned back as Brenna raised her wand, and the five witches recited the spell together, linked again with their hands on one another's shoulder.

"Betrayal, deceit, and your coup end here. Your power and magic we no longer fear. For thirty days and thirty nights, you'll live by the sea, unable to leave. No magic, no glory, no chance to be free. As we will so mote it be."

Willow vanished without a sound. The meadow was utterly silent as Brenna stepped up and faced the town's supernatural beings. They all looked at her expectantly.

"Is there anyone among you who feels the Connelly witches cannot protect New Mourne?"

"Not our kind," the alpha said.

"Nor us," the Druids proclaimed.

And so it went. One by one the supernaturals pledged to support the coven. They hurried away, while the eagle rose and flew a couple of circles around the site before heading toward the hills.

When they were all gone, Brenna plopped to the ground and rested her head in her hands. Eva Grace went to her, placing her hands on her cousin's shoulders and chanting softly.

The men gathered around. Jake was human now, and Maggie had released Brian and Bailey from their protective circle of salt. Rodric wiped his sword on the

Fachan's furry body and it disappeared.

Brenna moved away from Eva Grace. "Save some of your strength. We have more work to do."

"I'm fine," Eva Grace said. "I did a power spell while you were working. What is it we need to do?"

Brenna stood and Jake put an arm around her shoulders, and she leaned against him. "We've got to go all over town strengthening the wards. If Willow thought she could make her move, she knew there was weakness. We have to be sure everything is secure."

"And tomorrow we bury Sarah," Eva Grace whispered.

"So, we protect her town now," Brenna said, sounding stronger.

They agreed that each of them would take a different sector of the county and work their magic before they all met back at the home place for sustenance. Magic always took its price, and the men knew their women would need more than food when their job was done.

Rodric walked over to Eva Grace and pulled her into his arms. "Feeling okay?"

"I feel energized. I know Brenna did all the work, but it felt good to see Willow put in her place," Eva Grace said, and then surprised him with a long, passionate kiss.

"Thank you for being here," she said.

He leaned his forehead against hers. "Always. I love you."

She kissed him again.

The witches joined hands and rose. As they moved up into the colorful sunset, they separated and were instantly out of sight.

Rodric went with the men toward the van.

"What a night," Bailey said. "And me without a camera."

"Better that way," Jake said with a laugh. "I know people like TV shows to help them believe magic happens, but they don't need to see the truth."

"Still," Rodric said, getting into the back seat beside Jake. "Nothing says you can't write another great movie and add just enough special effects for them to believe it."

Brian laughed as he started the van. "Come on, Hollywood, let's go home."

Rodric realized as he enjoyed the good-natured laughter that this was what family felt like. For the first time in his life, he had found family.

Chapter 19

From her bedroom window, Eva Grace peered out at her frost-covered garden and pressed her hand to the cold glass. It was freezing outside, the three-quarter moon rode high in the sky and stars shone like hard, frozen crystals.

Had it been like this that first autumn for her ancestors here in New Mourne? *The Connelly Book of Magic* said they had been starving, their people were dying, and snow came before Samhain. Then the Woman saved them with her evil bargain.

The holiday—the coven's biggest celebration of the year—was only a few days away. Who might be dead by then?

At her side, Lorcan whined. He'd been subdued since they came home from Sarah's funeral.

She sighed and leaned her forehead against the window while the dog nudged her leg.

A touch on her shoulder startled her.

"Sorry," Rodric murmured. "I didn't mean to frighten you."

His arms folded around her. He had such strong arms. She felt safe when he wrapped her in them. She closed her eyes and allowed herself to lean back.

They were silent. The last two days were a blur— the confrontation with Willow yesterday, followed by the small, private funeral today. There had been so much adrenalin and so much sorrow. Eva Grace felt hollow.

"Did it surprise you that Marcus left for Atlanta?" Rodric asked.

"A little," she said. "But he seemed to take a lot of comfort from his brother and sister-in-law being here, and they wanted him to come home with them. With everything we're facing here, perhaps he needs that attention."

"Did you want to run away?"

"Today?"

"When Garth died."

They didn't often talk about Garth, but that was something she needed to get over. He was dead, and Rodric had helped her realize she was still alive.

She rubbed her palms along the muscles of his forearms, and desire stirred inside her. She turned to face him. He'd discarded his glasses, and the warmth in his brown eyes comforted her.

"Yes, I wanted to run away. Now I'm glad I didn't."

His hands cupped her face. "Dear Eva Grace. I wish I could take your pain, the way you take it from others. The coven wouldn't have made it through today without you. Especially the elder aunts."

"It became real to them today."

He kissed her gently. "You were their rock. And Brenna's right hand. She couldn't step into her role without you."

"She was born for this role—a leader."

"And you're her chief lieutenant." His lips strayed to the curve of her jaw. "I have a confession. I was really turned on during that fight with Willow."

The deep timbre of his voice caused her pulse to quicken. "Really? Tell me about it."

He stroked her arms. "You were fierce, like caged heat. I loved it when the fireballs were flying. You stood your ground. It was very arousing."

"And yet you were able to fight," Eva Grace said.

"We men are such multitaskers."

She laughed for what felt like the first time in weeks, and Rodric captured her mouth with his.

Damn but he could kiss. She lost herself in the movement of his lips against hers.

Lorcan demanded their attention with a short, sharp bark.

"Back off," Rodric told him with a laugh. "She's mine right now."

The dog padded to the hall, no doubt to take up his usual post at her door.

"Now, where were we?" Rodric's lips took hers again.

"I love that you're a real warrior," she murmured as he drew away. "It's kind of primitive of me, not at all enlightened or suitable for a true feminist. But I like the idea of you being powerful and in control."

He chuckled. "I can't imagine you being told what to do for very long."

"Maybe just for a night?"

The question silenced him, but there was a glint in his eyes that made her throb.

Feeling bold, she slipped her hand down to cup his already rigid penis. She squeezed gently, and he groaned.

"What would you tell me to do about this?" she whispered as she unbuckled his belt.

He seemed at a loss for words, so she unzipped his pants and tugged them and his boxers down. His erection sprang free. Her fingers closed around him, and he took a deep, shuddering breath.

"Would you tell me to do this?" she murmured as she knelt in front of him.

"Eva Grace." Her name was a hoarse croak.

"Do you have a command?" She blew softly on the tip of his penis.

"Yeah," he managed to say as his right hand curved around her head and drew her forward.

She laughed just before she took him into her mouth. Then, with her eyes locked on his, she lavished every inch of him with worship until his breath was hitching, and she felt his legs tremble.

"I need you...to stop," he whispered.

She drew back. "Is that an order?"

"I don't give you ord..." His words trailed away at her smile. A grin touched his lips. "All right, get up here." She started to stand, and he tugged her to her feet.

"There's only one way for this to end," he said as he took off his shirt. The muscles of his chest and torso begged for her touch, but he backed away.

She knew what she wanted. She was aching to have him inside her.

He sat on the bed, back propped against the pillows and legs sprawled out on the comforter.

"Strip," he said with a wicked grin.

Eva Grace needed this moment, this playful interlude in the midst of the darkness she could feel at the edges of their lives. Somehow, she thought Sarah would understand and approve.

She said, "Slow or fast?"

"Slow." The muscles in his throat worked as he watched her unbutton her white silk blouse and pull it free of her skirt.

She turned away as she slipped it off, giving him a flirtatious look over her shoulder. "Is this the way you like it?"

He nodded. "Now the skirt."

With infinite care, she pulled down the zipper of her black pencil skirt and let it slide to the floor. She stepped out of it, clad now only in white silk panties and bra.

"The bra first," Rodric whispered.

She turned away again as she unhooked it, then she faced him, hands covering her breasts.

"None of that. Show me."

She did, and he licked his lips. "Come here." There was a ragged note in the command.

He swung his legs to the floor and sat up as she approached the bed. "You did very well."

"Do I get a reward?"

He laughed as his hands bracketed her hips and pulled her between his legs. Then his palms covered her breasts, thumbs stroking her nipples into peaks that begged for his lips. As if he knew just what she wanted, he drew her downward and kissed first one breast, then the other.

Heat flooded her body as his mouth moved south. His fingers hooked both sides of her panties, peeled them down her legs and threw them aside. His touch gentle but confident, he slipped a hand between her legs.

Eva Grace opened her thighs and moved against his hand, and he quickened the pace. Her knees nearly buckled when he slipped one and then another finger inside her while his thumb kept pressure on the spot where she pulsed. Her breath came in gasps as he increased the pressure, and the room began to glow—

yellow, orange and red—the colors of fire. It built like the blaze she had inside.

With an appreciative groan, Rodric looked into her eyes. "I have a final request."

She would have agreed to almost anything as long as he didn't stop what he was doing.

"Come for me," he whispered. "Please."

She fell apart under his touch, trembling, calling his name and hanging onto him as if her life depended on it.

Then she was on the bed, and he was inside her, and it took every bit of concentration she possessed to keep the curtains from catching fire as he found his own release.

****

Deep in the night, she woke as Rodric pulled a quilt over them both.

"That heat we made finally died down," he said as he drew her back into his arms. "Lorcan woke me up before we could freeze to death."

"Why isn't he on the bed?"

"I think we may have traumatized him tonight."

She giggled against his neck. "Do you think it's a combination of our magic that made it so hot?"

"I think it was just an incredible, mind-blowing shag," he retorted. "Combustible."

"But most people don't almost burn down their houses."

"Too bad for them."

"Yeah." The memory sent a shiver over her. She had never been so free and uninhibited. She drew back and touched his face. "Thank you."

"The pleasure was mine, I assure you." Laughter rumbled deep in his chest.

"It's more than that," she said. "Thank you for taking me away from everything for a while. I needed that."

He sobered. The only sound was the sigh of wind against the house.

"Tomorrow we have to figure out why Sarah was bringing me that agreement with Fred Williams' father. I think that could be the next key to defeating the Woman."

He nodded and drew her closer.

"Because I want to live," she added as emotion clogged her throat. "With you. I love you."

"And I love you." He gently stroked a hand through her hair. "I was brought here. You realize that, I hope. For some reason, I've been involved in this since before I arrived in New Mourne."

"Maybe it's why you met Garth." She took a deep breath. "And why he died."

Rodric stilled. "I never would have wanted that. I thank the gods and my ancestors every day that I'm here with you, but I never wished Garth any harm."

"Of course not." She put her arms around him. "But I'm not going to argue with fate or destiny. I just want to find a way out of our family's nightmare—once and for all."

"Then let's do it." His lips dipped to hers again. "Tomorrow. But tonight …" His penis stirred against her hip—hot and hard.

"Really?" she said, laughing. "Again?"

"Just to piss Lorcan off."

The dog barked from the hallway, and they built another fire.

Chapter 20

The day after the funeral, Brenna asked that all the younger witches meet at Eva Grace's house. Though Eva Grace wondered about the exclusion of the rest of the coven, she knew her cousin had good reasons. She was now their leader.

Rodric had gone to talk with Jake, and she spent the morning setting her house to rights. A little work and some magic cleared away the remaining broken china and other keepsakes from the night Sarah was murdered. Some Eva Grace knit together with a restorative spell, some she discarded, some made her hesitate to put them in their previous spots.

In the cabinet at the bottom of her study's built-in shelves, she tucked several items that reminded her of Garth—a shell from a beach vacation, flowers pressed between two pieces of glass. She left a small photograph of the two of them on a shelf.

She touched Garth's image. "You will always own part of my heart." A warm glow, like a hug, enveloped her.

"Mother," she whispered. "How I wish you were here." She listened, hoping for a response, but the only sound was the chime of the clock and the rattle of tree branches outside in the steady, cold wind.

Shivering, she hurried to the kitchen, eager to lose herself in cooking.

Several hours later, the air was redolent with the scents of spiced tea, coffee, pumpkin bread and cinnamon scones. The cousins were gathered around the round oak table in the kitchen. Maggie had brought fresh butter, Lauren contributed some of her mother's blackberry jelly.

Eva Grace smiled, enjoying the chatter about happier times—tea parties in the home place dining room, climbing trees in the woods behind the house, chasing fireflies in summer, trying to be serious while learning their craft, and then trying spells on the field mice in the barn.

"We have some things to discuss," Brenna said at last.

With the ease of long practice, they cleared the table and put the food away. Eva Grace saw Brenna slip away to the foyer and return with two wooden boxes.

Once they were gathered again at the table, Brenna opened a box and brought out the family wand.

"It always fit your hand perfectly," Maggie said.

Lauren nodded. "When you fought the demon back this summer."

"And kicking Willow's butt," Fiona agreed, her eyes gleaming.

"It's yours now," Eva Grace said.

"It's for the family." Brenna returned the wand to its box and reached for the other wooden case which was shallow but wide. She opened it, and Eva Grace gasped along with the others.

The box held four additional wands, each delicately carved and covered with etching or crystals.

"Marcus made these," Fiona said. "I'd recognize that handiwork anywhere."

"But when?" Lauren asked. "These would have taken him awhile."

"He said Sarah had him start on them years ago," Brenna explained. "He said she always believed having only one wand didn't give the coven enough power, so she decided you all should have your own." Her voice broke and Eva Grace comforted her.

Brenna's shoulders squared. "Marcus brought these to me before he left yesterday."

Eva Grace watched her cousins absorb the information. There had always been only one wand in the coven. It had been passed down from one coven leader to the next. Not only was it imbued with the power of the lightning, it had absorbed the powers of the coven leaders.

A new generation of witches with their own wands would be a different direction for the coven, but in her heart, Eva Grace felt it was right. This was the twenty-first century, and the witches around her table were strong and capable. They'd proven that in the meadow by standing united with Brenna when she faced Willow. It was time for change.

"Unless passed down in the coven, a wand chooses its user," Brenna said. "We all learned that as children."

She pushed the box to the middle of the table and picked up her own wand. "Take your time and let your emotions guide you."

Once again, the room was silent. Eva Grace looked at the beautiful woods, the carvings so lovingly made by Marcus, and suddenly knew hers would be the cedar. It would cleanse negativity in the atmosphere and would also be perfect for creating a sacred place, which she had been planning since moving to her new home.

She held out her hand, and the cedar wand rose toward her. Her fingers closed around it, and warmth moved up her arm to her heart. With this wand her magic would increase, and its power would be positive and personal. She smiled at Brenna, feeling the magical thread that bound them strengthen.

Fiona studied the remaining magical implements for a moment, then took the gleaming cherry wand. An intricate, carved line ran down one side, all the way to the tapered base.

"Oh my," Fiona whispered, a look of wonder on her face. Cherry would help keep Fiona grounded, especially when she interacted with several spirits at once. It stabilized and focused magic and helped its owner go beyond the obstacles in her path.

Without hesitation, Lauren picked up the ash wood wand and raised it to create a ring of sparkles over their heads. "Oh, yeah, this one is mine," she said and laughed with delight. The light-colored wood with polished moonstones pulsed with intelligence, curiosity and the elements. Eva Grace thought it suited her glamorous, passionate cousin.

"And this is mine." Maggie said, although she didn't touch the remaining wand.

"It's chestnut," Brenna said.

Still Maggie didn't move.

Eva Grace grew worried as the silence stretched. Maggie had shown her mettle at the battle with Willow, but Eva Grace suspected she still saw herself as the weak link.

"Chestnut is for those who seek justice," Brenna said.

Maggie lifted her chin. "Justice is needed in this

world." She grasped the wand and a bolt of light shot up to the ceiling.

"Holy goddess," she murmured as a smile spread across her face. "I didn't know it would feel like this, as if you're safely at home." She caressed the beautiful etchings that covered the deep reds and golds in the wood.

Around the table, her witch cousins tested their wands for heft and studied the carvings and crystals. There were four crystals on Eva Grace's wand that were essential for an empath. Rose quartz would force away negative feelings, the black tourmaline was for protection, the amethyst would strengthen her intuition, and malachite would remove emotional blockages.

Once again, Brenna picked up the family wand. "As you all know, a wand won't work unless you can focus all of your intention on what you want it to do. That's something you'll have to practice. I'm learning on the job myself." Her mischievous grin flashed.

"But it feels natural," Fiona said as her wand glowed.

"We mustn't forget these are weapons," Brenna said, teasing tone gone. "Sarah planned them for us to use together to end the curse for good. Marcus said she planned to give them to us this Samhain."

Eva Grace glanced around the table and realized all their faces held the same determination. She felt such pride and love that the tip of her wand glowed for a moment.

Brenna rose. "Come on, we need to imbue your wands with the Connelly power."

They each picked up the capes Brenna had asked them to bring and in moments were in a tight circle in the center of Eva Grace's back yard. Feeling they were being watched, Eva Grace glanced over to see the pixies sitting on the roof of their tiny home.

Brenna invited all of them to touch the tips of their wands together.

"Can I just say I love all of you?" she said as she raised her eyes to the points of the magic wands. Her voice was pure and strong as she spoke. "The Connelly wand with power imbued is centuries old, but always true. Another generation of power and pride, Connelly witches standing side by side. Sisters and cousins, all safe and free. As we will so mote it be."

Eva Grace felt her power move from her toes, through her upper body, and into her arm, coming out in a burst of sparkling green light. Colorful sparks that matched their capes shot from each cousin's wand. By the time they lowered them, they were all laughing and flowers and butterflies were dancing on the cold ground.

"Damn," Lauren said. "I feel like we should have Brian Adams, Rod Stewart, and Sting singing 'All for Love' for us."

"Sarah would love that." Fiona laughed. "Rod was surpassed only by Jagger in her esteem."

"You're right," Maggie said and giggled as a butterfly landed on her finger.

"Ladies, a little decorum, please," Brenna said. "Quit putting butterflies in danger. You know they can't take the cold."

But they were all still laughing and dancing when Rodric walked around the side of the house.

"We have wands," Eva Grace called out to him.

His grin was pure male appreciation. "*It is na, Jean, thy bonie face, nor shape that I admire; altho' thy beauty and thy grace might weel awauk desire.*'"

"Robert Burns," Lauren said.

"You know Robert Burns?" Maggie's face revealed her shock.

"He believed in women's rights and the beauty of love," Lauren said with a wicked grin. "All of us should quote Robert Burns."

"She's right," Rodric said, thickening his Scottish accent. "And I don't know what ye lovely ladies have been doing, but all of ye have a real glow."

"Just playing with magic," Brenna told him.

Eva Grace laughed and danced as the man she loved looked on in appreciation. Surely there was hope for them all.

Chapter 21

The morning after the wand ceremony, Eva Grace awoke with one thing on her mind — finding out what Fred Williams knew about the document signed by his father and her grandmother.

"I have a bad feeling about this," Rodric said as he reluctantly drove with her to the church. "Are you sure you're up to it? The funeral was just two days ago."

His concern annoyed rather than comforted her. Why was it that even enlightened males felt the need to protect females? "Samhain is only days away. You know things are going to get worse before then. We have to do something."

In the church parking lot, she was shocked to see Mick with Fred and Ginny on the church's front steps.

"That doesn't look good." Rodric's mouth tightened. "Do you think it's wise to interrupt?"

They could hear loud, angry voices. "What is Mick doing here?" she asked.

"Probably nothing good. Brenna thinks he may have something to do with the demon."

"Brenna is extremely smart. But she doesn't do well with forgiveness. She'll probably never forgive her parents for leaving her and Fiona here while they traveled. She's certainly not going to forgive our grandfather for his sins against Sarah, and she'll believe the worst of him."

"But those sins are what's on everyone's mind since Sarah was murdered. You and I sensed the black magic around him the night he asked you to come to Randi's aid. Your family has good reason to think he's demon possessed."

But she didn't want to believe that once again a member of her family was being used for evil as Maggie had been last summer. "Someone possessed by a demon wouldn't go near a church. He's my grandfather, and I'm not going to assume the worst about him."

She got out and hurried up the steps. Mick was standing between Fred and Ginny as they yelled at each other.

"You're not coming into my church," Fred said pointing an angry finger at Mick.

"It's called a sanctuary for a reason, Fred." Ginny put a hand on Mick's arm. "The women in the church have been taking coats and food out to Mr. Phillips' group. We can't turn him away. We're here for people in need."

Fred's lips thinned, but he pasted on a smile when he saw Eva Grace and Rodric.

"Hello." She nodded at Mick, who smiled. "What's going on?"

"Nothing you need to worry about, little witch," Ginny said, her tone venomous. "You're on sacred ground. It's a wonder you're not on fire."

"Ginny," Fred admonished.

"Oh, I see," Ginny said as her face reddened with anger. "She's welcome, but Mr. Phillips, a poor stranger in our town, isn't."

Eva Grace didn't flinch at Ginny's tone. The pastor's wife hated her family. "Actually, he's my grandfather. Can I help here?"

Before Ginny could retort, Fred said, "I was sorry to hear about Sarah. I know how awful it is to lose a grandmother you love. Is she why you're here?"

Ginny's eyes widened. "Surely you don't think you can have her funeral—"

"Dear," Fred interrupted. "You have no reason to think that."

"We had the funeral," Eva Grace said. "It was lovely and serene, much like my grandmother."

"Not an opinion shared by all," Ginny said. "There are those who feel our town is well rid of any witch."

Fred gasped, his face flushing. "Now see here, Ginny. That's enough."

But it was Mick who took control, taking Ginny's arm and leading her several steps away. "Now, now, my dear Mrs. Williams. I've upset you and the good reverend by coming here. I meant only to thank you for your kindness and inquire if you knew of anyone needing my group's skills."

"And what are those?" Fred asked.

Eva Grace was a bit puzzled by his animosity toward Mick.

"A good question," Rodric said.

"Rodric," Eva Grace warned. "Please don't start anything."

"It's fine, dear girl," Mick said easily. "Reverend, I know we Travelers don't always carry the best reputation, but my crew has been working hard since we arrived here. We've done a few roofs and some minor carpentry work. Bad weather's coming, and I wanted a few more jobs before it hits."

"Come to the office," Ginny told him. "I'll make a

few calls."

Fred glowered, and Mick shook his head. "I'll just wait here, I think."

No," Ginny said. "There's no reason you can't come into the church. All people are welcome."

"Really?" Eva Grace said with raised eyebrows.

Without looking away from Mick, Ginny said, "I said people, Eva Grace. That means humans, not creatures like you and your family."

Rodric's expression turned fierce. "Mrs. Williams, I'm not standing here letting you insult the Connellys."

Ginny took a challenging stance, her ice blue eyes narrowed as she swept her gaze over Rodric. "What sort of creature are you to have taken up with the Connellys?"

"Ginny," Fred implored. "Stop this."

"Yes, please," Mick said.

Ginny responded with an odd, defiant laugh.

Eva Grace thought the pastor's wife was acting very strange. While she never hid her contempt for the Connellys, she was being more unpleasant than normal, not bothering to sugarcoat her hatred. Before Eva Grace could say anything, a car pulled to a stop in the parking lot. They all turned to see a sheriff's cruiser.

"Did you call them?" Ginny demanded of her husband.

"Of course not," Fred said.

They watched in silence as Jake and Brian came up the steps. "Got a problem, Fred?" Jake asked.

"Nothing we can't handle," Fred said smoothly.

"We were told at the campground that Mick was coming over here," Jake said. "We'd like him to go to the office for a little talk."

"About what?" Eva Grace demanded.

Jake looked irritated. "We just need to talk to him."

Brian walked toward Mick. Every protective instinct Eva Grace had sprung into action.

She stepped in front of Brian and ignored Rodric's protest. "Do you have to haul him in like this?" Magic flared inside her.

Jake reached for her arm but yanked his hand back and cried out in pain. "Dammit, this is official business. You can't do that."

"I think I just did," Eva Grace said.

"Please get out of the way," Brian told her. He looked at Mick. "We need you to go with us."

"Of course," Mick said, his expression calm. "I'll be happy to." He started after Brian and reached out to pat Eva Grace's arm as he passed. She felt something familiar in his touch, like she knew him on a primeval level.

She turned to Jake. "He didn't kill Sarah."

"No, he didn't," Ginny added quickly.

The two women looked at each other in astonishment. Eva Grace turned back to Jake before anyone else could say more. "Why would Mick want to hurt Sarah?"

With forced patience, Jake said, "We're conducting an investigation, and I'm questioning everyone who may have had a reason to hurt Sarah."

"But why would he hurt her?" she insisted.

Rodric said, "You're being a bit unreasonable."

Her anger flared. "Leave me alone. This is outrageous."

"We're just going to talk to him," Jake said. "Nobody has said anything about arresting him."

"It's routine, Eva Grace. Sarah was murdered—"

Brian stopped as his voice broke. "Don't you want to know who killed her?"

Eva Grace felt like he had slapped her. Of course, she wanted Sarah's killer punished, but she couldn't believe it was this man whose blood ran in her veins. She turned from Brian to Mick. "Do you want me to go with you?"

"That's enough," Jake said angrily as he turned to Mick. "Can we go now?"

Mick nodded and followed him down the steps with Brian bringing up the rear.

When Eva Grace started to follow, Rodric took her arm. "You can't stop them."

Without another word to Ginny and Fred, she jerked her arm from Rodric's and watched the sheriff's cruiser pull away. She went to the car.

Once Rodric joined her and started the car, she asked, "Why are y'all so convinced Mick is a bad guy?"

"Why are you so convinced he's not? He left Sarah, knowing she was pregnant. Doesn't that give an inkling into his character? What kind of man does that?"

"He was a stupid young man. Maybe he's changed. He cares for Randi."

"And where are her parents? Is she with Mick because she wants to be or because he forces her?"

"That's unfair."

"She was under a spell the night he came for you."

"But he came for help. Doesn't that mean anything?"

"At this point, how can we know?"

Her head was pounding. She felt off. It was probably Ginny's poisonous attack. And maybe as Rodric had said, she was being a bit irrational.

"Take me home, please," she told him.

"Eva—"

"Just take me home. I'm full of confusion, sorrow, and just plain despair. I want to do a ritual."

"Is there any way I can help?"

"No, I just need some time alone," she said. "I may go to the clearing...I don't know. Just please take me home."

"All right, but promise you'll call me if you need me."

"I will."

They said nothing more on the drive to her house. She got out with a murmured goodbye. When he didn't pull out of the driveway, Eva Grace turned and gave a slight wave. Inside, she was grateful for Lorcan's welcome.

Dropping to her knees, she put her arms around him and murmured into the dog's soft fur.

Lorcan moved closer to her and stood unmoving as his fur soaked up her tears. After a few moments, she stood and the two of them walked into the kitchen.

"I'm going to have some of my grief tea." She stopped and looked down at the dog. "It's so strange to be the one who feels a need for help. I've always been the healer, the supporter, the person who shows up when there's a need."

As if on cue, her phone rang—Brenna. No doubt she had already heard from Jake about the confrontation at the church. Eva Grace knew what her cousin was going to say about her defense of Mick.

"I'm not going to argue with her," she told Lorcan as she turned off her phone. But she also felt the pull of the magical bonds between her and Brenna. She could feel the coven leader's anger.

"But I don't care." She felt compelled to check on Mick. "Let's go," she said to Lorcan and grabbed her keys and coat.

When she arrived at the sheriff's office, Mick and Randi were walking down the steps. She left Lorcan in the car and hurried over to them. "Is everything all right?"

Mick put a hand on Randi's arm before she could answer. The young woman looked pale and drawn.

"It's not a problem," he said with a smile. "I have an alibi. They checked it out. No harm done."

"I'm so glad," Eva Grace said.

"We're headed back to the park to fix a communal meal," he said. "We'll all be together all night, assuring no one is harmed by Sarah's spirit."

"Why would you think Sarah's spirit would harm you?"

"Romany tradition calls for this," he explained. "If we were handling the funeral, we would burn her belongings and cleanse everything. It's done after every death. Since we can't do that, we'll have a vigil to keep her spirit away."

"But she's not one of you."

"Her blood is mingled with mine," he said calmly. "So we'll stay together tonight. You should join us."

From the car, Lorcan let out an insistent bark. Eva Grace felt a prickle of unease. "No, thanks. We have our own traditions."

As they said goodbye, she looked closely at Randi who looked dazed. "Are you sure you're okay?"

Mick said, "She's very tired, and this was upsetting. She's just fine."

Eva Grace quickly said goodbye. In the car, Lorcan sniffed her and whined. Eva Grace felt even more troubled. She drove home in a hurry.

To calm her nerves, she took a bath with lavender essential oil in her diffuser. The delicate, relaxing aroma finally eased the tension that gripped her. She lay down in her bed, Lorcan on the floor beside her, and closed her eyes.

She found herself walking toward Sarah and Marcus's workshop. It wasn't the new structure built after this summer's fire. This was where Sarah had worked on her art and jewelry when Eva Grace was young. It was one of her favorite places.

A woman was seated at a table with a lamp overhead, working on an intricate silver design.

Celia turned and smiled. "Hello, sweet daughter."

"Mama?" Eva Grace said, shocked.

"I loved working here with Sarah when I was a girl." Celia picked up a pair of pliers. "We spent hours here. Delia never had any interest in it. She spent a lot of time on the low limb of the big oak at the side of the house reading."

"Can I touch you?" Eva Grace asked.

Instead of answering, Celia said, "You know the thing about making anything beautiful? You have to get a little rough with it before you're finished." She snipped a silver wire with a flourish and smiled. "Remember that when you're dealing with the coven and the family."

Feeling braver, Eva Grace moved in to hug her mother. She yearned to know her touch.

But she woke in her bed to the soft scent of lavender and crushing regret. Her mother was just a memory to those who loved her. Would Eva Grace be the same?

"No," she whispered to the deepening shadows as she sat up. She needed more strength to fight a final battle, and she knew where to find it—on Connelly land.

Chapter 22

In the woods near the RV park, Rodric listened to the laughter of the children playing soccer in front of the Traveler's campers. He had followed Mick and Randi to the campground and hidden behind a group of anise. He wasn't sure what he was looking for, but he was certain there was a connection between this man and Sarah's death.

On the way here, Jake had called to say that Mick had an alibi.

So here Rodric was, watching for signs of evil and traces of magic or odd behavior in the camp.

So far, he'd seen nothing untoward, but his attention sharpened as Mick emerged from his trailer. The man kicked the ball for a minute with the children and then sat on a stool not far from Rodric's hideout.

Unease swept over Rodric, and he glanced into the dense forest. He smelled the demon. Damn, this was frustrating. How could he so easily sense the evil surrounding Mick while Eva Grace could not? Was Mick using an obfuscation spell to keep her in the dark?

A rustle in the underbrush brought Rodric to his feet, and his axe appeared in his hand. A small group of does and a fawn stepped around the trees, and the axe vanished. The four deer were silent, watching him with knowing, dark eyes.

They quickly began to blur, and when he blinked,

four fae, two male and two females, stood where the deer had been. They smiled at him, stunning in their beauty, and dressed in sparkling robes that reflected the colors of the rainbow. They weren't tall like Willow but were close to humans in size. He could have sworn he'd seen them before.

Before he could speak, they surrounded him, turned their backs and spread their wings, sealing him inside a tight, protective circle. Rodric briefly worried that Mick would see them, but magic kindled in the air and grew in a powerful wave. He was cut off from the camp. Rodric rested his hand on the hilt of his sword, ready to fight if necessary.

Just beyond the fae he saw a fog form. It grew quickly and rose in a black billow. The fae's strong magic almost knocked Rodric to his knees as the evil roiled toward them.

A deep voice rose out of the fog. "Hiding behind faeries, Scotsman? Shameful."

Though Rodric tried to move forward to challenge the demon, he couldn't penetrate the wall of fairies. "Let me through. I want to face this evil once and for all."

One faerie looked over her shoulder at Rodric. "Now is not the time."

"When is the time?" How can I keep Eva Grace safe if I can't keep the evil from getting to her? I can't let that damn spirit or this demon take her."

"In time," the faerie said and turned away.

Rodric took a moment to catch his breath and then pulled his own magic forward. In seconds, he wore the warrior armor of Aife, but when he tried to move his foot to take a step forward, he couldn't move. "*Leig dhomh dol a—*" he yelled, begging the faeries in vain to let him go.

The demon laughed, taking the form of a man as it stepped out of the fog, wearing old-fashioned clothes and eyes glowing red.

The smell of sulfur nauseated Rodric.

The demon growled, an awful deep sound that made the trees tremble. "The faeries are right. It's not your time," the demon said. "You and I will have our battle, but I've got plans to make and things to do."

The wind rose as the demon dissolved into the black fog that darted around tree trunks. When it disappeared, there was a pop like a champagne cork, and the woods returned to normal.

But the faeries were still shielding Rodric from the camp. They rose around him, their wings soundless among the dry, brown leaves on the trees.

The faerie who had spoken to him smiled. "Today you survived. Thank your ancestors."

"Who are you?" Rodric demanded. "Who sent you? If you want to protect someone, try Eva Grace."

The fae looked at each other, then burst into laughter that trilled through the cold air like Christmas bells.

Fuming, Rodric watched until they cleared the tops of the trees and swooped away. He gave the camp another angry look. All was the same. They hadn't heard the demon or the faeries. If Mick was connected to the demon, shouldn't he have had some sense that the demon was nearby? There was no way to know.

Rodric turned and stalked through the woods, not bothering with stealth. He was almost back to his car when a shrill cry stopped him short. An eagle glided down and perched on top of a rotten stump. Intelligence gleamed in the bird's eyes, and Rodric stood back until he spied a small leather pouch around the eagle's neck. He moved closer, and the bird disappeared.

"What the hell?"

There was a noise behind him, and he turned to find an old man putting a loin cloth around his waist. Rodric stepped back in shock, his hand automatically reaching for his weapon.

The man raised his hands. "No worries, Dr. McGuire, I'm here to tell you a story." That's when Rodric noticed the man wore the same leather pouch as the bird.

There was no threat in the air, so Rodric remained as he was. "Magic is heavy in the woods today."

"Magic is always here if you know where to look." The man's skin was dark, his hair jet black and straight, flowing like silk down his back.

He sat on the ground with the agility of one much younger. Rodric sat on the stump and waited, sensing nothing was to be gained by impatience.

The older man took his time, gathering twigs and small sticks. When there was a suitable pile, he pulled a pack of matches out of the leather pouch.

Unable to resist, Rodric said, "You're not going to rub sticks together?"

The man laughed and lit the small fire. "Matches work much better and are much less trouble." Finally, he looked up at Rodric. "My name is Uwohali, which means eagle. I am a skinwalker, and I keep a feather with me always."

Rodric understood that a skinwalker needed the DNA of the form they could assume. For Uwohali, that was an eagle.

"You were in the meadow the night the witches

banished Willow," Rodric said. "I saw you close to where the little pixies went."

The old man smiled. "You're very observant, Dr. McGuire."

"Please call me Rodric." They shook hands.

"I'm the grandfather of Dr. Hargrave who saved Doris Connelly's life this past summer."

"Of course," Rodric said. "I thought you looked familiar. You must be proud of your grandson. He's a wonderful doctor."

Uwohali nodded as he tended to his small fire, adding more dried leaves and twigs. "I was a little disappointed when he decided to specialize in plastic surgery. But he works in the ER as well, to help those injured like Doris was. And he works a month each year on a reservation in Oklahoma, so I can't complain."

"You said you had a story to tell me," Rodric prompted. "Being Scottish, I love to hear someone spin a good tale."

"This is a story as old as the spirit that has cursed the Connelly witches," Uwohali said. "When my grandson told me that the Connellys were looking to find the story of the Woman in White, I began to talk with the old ones. And this is what they told me."

He stared into the fire that cracked and popped. In moments Rodric was also mesmerized by the flames. They seemed to grow until there was a full campfire in front of them. With a jerk, Rodric realized he was no longer in the woods around the RV park.

It was a different time. The forest was thick and green. A small house nearby was made of saplings with mud holding them together.

A young woman was pulling weeds in a small

garden. Her hair was blonde, her skin fair. Beside her a baby cooed and waved tiny arms in a small, woven basket. The woman sang softly as she worked down a row of squash and beans.

"Catriona," Rodric murmured in recognition. This was the Woman in White before she became the spirit who stalked the Connellys.

Uwohali spoke again. "Long ago, this land belonged to the people, and they loved it. They had no problem sharing it with others who moved nearby. All they wanted was to live in peace, raise their families and enjoy how they had been blessed by the good earth."

Catriona stopped and wiped her hands on the skirt of her colorful cotton dress. Standing, she stretched her back for a few moments, and then picked up the baby. The child snuggled and squirmed until she lowered her dress and let the baby nurse.

"Ahyoka?" a voice called.

"Back here, Devdas," she replied.

Rodric leaned forward, feeling the heat from the fire rise up to his face. "Is this her husband?"

Uwohali smiled. "I think you'll find my research blends with yours. He called her Ahyoka and loved her from the moment he saw her. She came with her father to save the 'soulless savages.' She was surprised when they welcomed them with feasts and celebrations. She was even more surprised to find love waiting for her."

"The Cherokee have never been separatists," Rodric said.

"All are equal and the earth is sacred," Uwohali said.

He moved his hands over the fire and the scene before them changed. The hut was burning. Catriona was screaming and struggling as two white men held her back and another held her wailing baby. Two others held her husband Devdas while an older white man whipped him until his screams rose above those of his wife and child.

"Stop it, Papa, stop it," Catriona pleaded. "I'll go with you. Just let me take the baby. Please stop! Don't kill Devdas."

Breathing heavily, the man she called Papa turned with an evil smile on his face. Rodric started, shocked. This was the same man who had appeared to him from the demon's smoke. Their suspicions were correct. Catriona's father was a demon worshiper, possessed by his master.

The soulless bastard laughed with vile glee. "Of course, you're going back with me, Catriona. You can bring that half-breed thing, too. This one," he said pointing to her husband. "He's going as far away from you as I can get him. Say your goodbyes."

She raced to the young brave and threw herself down beside him. She wiped the blood from his cheeks. "I'm so sorry. I'm so sorry."

Through swollen lips, he whispered something to her. Rodric couldn't hear over the baby's cries and the roar of the fire engulfing the little house.

Catriona laid her head against her husband's chest and sobbed. Her father jerked his head in her direction, and the men pulled her away while she fought and kicked and begged for her husband's life.

Rodric felt the heat of the fire on his face, thought it was the blazing house, but then realized he was back in the woods behind the RV park. Although the little campfire still burned, Uwohali was gone. Looking up, he saw an eagle soar above the trees in the late afternoon sky.

More pieces of the puzzle were clicking into place. Much of what Uwohali had shown him was what they'd expected. How could it help save a Connelly witch's life? Rodric wasn't certain, but he wanted to discuss it with Eva Grace.

Chapter 23

Eva Grace wanted the peace and clarity found only in the coven's sacred clearing. She left Lorcan at home, a move he protested so vehemently that she settled him with a sleeping spell. She felt a little guilty, but she wanted to be alone.

Ignoring a couple of calls and texts from Rodric and coven members, she took the back way to the clearing so she didn't have to park at the home place. She didn't want to see anyone.

The woods were cold and silent as she hiked to the familiar spot. With nightfall approaching, the temperature would be dropping fast. Not the best night to perform a ritual while skyclad, but she needed this.

In the center of the clearing, she sank to the ground, her green cloak pooling around her. She felt the power of the land—the energy from past rituals. Almost every significant event the Connelly coven faced ended here.

For a few moments, she sat in the lotus position, her eyes closed and her breathing slow and deliberate. When she felt sufficiently relaxed, she opened the velvet bag she'd brought with her.

First, she laid her wand to the side. Then she put out the crystals with care. The bloodstone would help her center herself and relieve the chaos she was struggling with. She added a green moss agate to boost her confidence and self-esteem, and last, she laid out the red snakeskin jasper, which always gave her insight in difficult situations.

Next came the candles—black to repel negativity, blue to create calm, and red to repair her waning strength. She waved a hand to light them and placed a small cauldron in the center of the circle of light.

Finally, she lit a bundle of herbs and dropped it in the cauldron. The aroma of sage and cedar wafted upward. She drew the smoke toward her, embracing the herbs' power to cleanse and reinvigorate. She relaxed and closed her eyes.

Hearing a rustle in the bushes, her eyes popped open. She bit back a gasp.

The Woman in White walked toward her.

The spirit's full lips twisted in a smirk. "Little witch, what are you up to?" The hem of her old-fashioned dress brushed the grass as she glided forward.

Was it really the Woman or the demon playing tricks as in the past? Not certain, Eva Grace rose from the ground, her wand in her hand. She should have set a circle of salt. Past experience should have taught her not to feel so safe here. But she maintained her calm and faced the Woman. "I'm sure you've watched us perform these cleansing rituals many times."

The ghost smiled at once beautiful and terrifying.

Calling on her power to remain calm, Eva Grace asked, "What are you doing? Ready for your next tribute?" As bravado, it sounded a little weak, but she needed to get the upper hand.

The Woman began to circle Eva Grace, "So you think you're the one I want? This generation has provided several candidates. That's why I'm taking my time. So many choices."

Eva Grace thought of her cousins and shivered. "Cold?"

"Winter has come early." Eva Grace was forced to turn to keep an eye on the Woman.

The spirit glowed, looking pleased. "I hope you're all enjoying the weather."

"Why do you do it?" Eva Grace said calmly. "Why torture the town?"

"Oh, that's not me." She came to a stop. "You know who's to blame for the misfortune that visits your little town."

"I don't understand the games you play with your demon."

"Oh, I think you do." The Woman lifted slightly off the ground, gaining a height advantage to look down on Eva Grace. "I think you've been very, very angry before. You hide it behind your sweet smile and your healing ways. But your anger is making you stronger than you've ever been."

The truth made Eva Grace uncomfortable, but she owned up to it. "Yes, I have many reasons to be angry. But after all of this time, why are you still so angry, Catriona?"

The mention of her name made the ghost's eyes go black. A sharp wind cut across the clearing, super-chilled air that made Eva Grace's lungs ache. The candles blew out and lit again. Menace spread in waves from the apparition. But Eva Grace stood still and faced her head on. "Your name is Catriona, right?"

"You heard that the last time your family and I were together. But it's been a long time since I was Catriona."

Was it Eva Grace's imagination or did the Woman soften a bit?

"My name is Gaelic for pure," the Woman said. "Do you think I'm pure, Eva Grace?"

"Pure evil maybe."

The Woman laughed, and the candles sputtered again. Eva Grace pulled on her empathy. She needed to find out what she could. Like Rodric said, power came from knowing your enemy.

"What brought you to this?" she asked the spirit.

"Love," the Woman said without hesitation.

"Love?" The answer shocked Eva Grace. "Love doesn't motivate killing. You've killed innocents for hundreds of years for something other than love."

"I've been merciful. I saved each of those witches from suffering."

"And gave their families and friends such pain."

"That was my price, the deal I struck. That was for me. When I take one of you, it's for me." The final word was an inhuman wail that echoed through the stark, barren trees.

Eva Grace imagined that cry was heard for miles. At the home place, certainly. Would the coven soon arrive? She didn't want them here. This was for her to do, for her to hear.

"I understand your pain," she told the Woman. "What happened to you? We keep thinking we know the story, but it's yours to tell. Can you tell me about your Devdas and what your father did to you and your child?"

The Woman grew more opaque. "Are you trying to comfort me, witch?"

"You said we're alike, that we both suffered. Maybe I could--"

The ghost cut her off with a snarl. "You fool! I don't want your comfort or your pity. My father set this in motion when he took all that I loved."

"That's why you killed him, isn't it? Why wasn't that enough?"

Instead of answering, the Woman said, "That's why we're alike, you know. Because of our fathers."

"Can you tell me about your father?" Eva Grace pressed.

"Who is *your* father?" The Woman's tone was mocking, her laughter cruel.

"Do you know?"

"I might." The Woman drifted across the ground, her form a misty outline.

Eva Grace followed her. "You know my father?"

"He left your mother to bear you alone. He tried to hide his sins just like my father. That's why I took your mother." The Woman giggled. "Poor, pitiful girl. I did her a favor."

"Noooooo." The word ripped from the well of hurt inside Eva Grace. She leapt toward the Woman. "My mother fought you. Just as I'll fight you." She flung her wand out and sent a ball of fire at the spirit.

It went straight through the Woman, who laughed again. Then she kicked out and sent Eva Grace to the ground.

She gasped for breath, and for several moments the black sky spun in dizzying circles overhead.

"You can't win," the Woman gloated. "I'm always stronger, you know. Stronger than my father, stronger than death, stronger than your poor, suffering family with their little spells and their plotting and planning to beat me."

Eva Grace was lifted, flipped over and slammed to the ground. She tasted blood. But it just fueled her determination. She pulled herself to her knees.

The Woman laughed while Eva Grace gathered her power.

"Feeling afraid, little witch?"

"Just wondering what you're going to do next. Bring it on."

"You're a tough one," the Woman said. "I'll give you that. You kept going when my demon took your man."

"I'm a realist. I know I can't change what's happened." Eva Grace pulled herself to her feet, feeling stronger by the second.

"That's the difference between you and me. I didn't just let it happen to me. I changed everything," the Woman said. "But I'm in a better place in the cold realm of in-between than you are in your little circle."

"You don't seem very happy with where you are."

The spirit began to levitate again. "We're so alike, stuck in a place with nowhere to go. But I make other people miserable, too. That makes it worthwhile."

Eva Grace took a deep breath, drew into herself, clutched her wand, and raised her hands over her head. She chanted, "Rush of wind and rise of dirt, water for power, air to work. Heed my call, hear my plea. As I will, so mote it be."

The Woman screamed as a wall of wind and water slammed into her. She flew forward, but the protective magic held fast. The ghost pushed against it, but she couldn't harm Eva Grace again.

"The Connellys will pay," the Woman screamed, pounding on the invisible wall. "The Connellys will pay."

Eva Grace held her ground as the spirit disappeared,

for now.

Behind her, she heard shouts. Her fellow witches with Jake and Rodric rushed to her side.

Rodric took her in his arms. "Thank the goddess. I was so afraid."

"Are you okay?" Brenna demanded. "You were in trouble."

"I'm just fine." Eva Grace stepped back from Rodric, lifting her chin as she looked around at them all.

She was no longer just the coven's healer. She was a warrior, and she had the strength to fight the evil that threatened her family.

Chapter 24

Eva Grace went back to the home place with her family and Rodric. While they were upset that she'd put herself in danger, at least Brenna and Fiona understood why she'd done it. The two of them had done the same thing for the family. Everyone was overjoyed that Eva Grace had turned their nemesis away.

The Woman was vulnerable. It was a ray of hope.

Rodric told them about his encounter with faeries, the demon and Uwohali. Once again, the coven laid out what they knew about the Woman and the demon. Her devil-worshipping father who masqueraded as a man of God. His murderous rage when she fell in love with a Cherokee. How he condemned her Devdas to slavery and perhaps murdered their child.

Catriona had killed her father. No doubt he deserved to die, but was that one of the reasons she couldn't be at peace? Tonight, Eva Grace had felt her deep pain.

How could this information help them end the curse? As the debate went on, weariness overtook Eva Grace, and Rodric took her home. Grateful for his protectiveness this time, she fell asleep in his arms.

But the next morning he was serious as they finished breakfast. "You can't go off on your own again."

She stiffened. "I have to do what I think is right. And she didn't take me." Eva Grace smiled, still savoring the satisfaction she'd felt last night.

"It was dangerous, but you did kick some ghostly ass."

"Yes, I did." While she felt victorious, Eva Grace also thought of the Woman's words from last night, *You've been where I've been.*

Rodric looked concerned. "What is it?"

"I'm connected to her, and I can't understand why."

"Perhaps it's the losses you've known—your mother, Garth and now Sarah."

"But few Connelly tributes were untouched by death or suffering."

"Could it be because you're an empath? You have such a caring nature. It's natural for you to pick up on things that others don't."

"I wonder if my mother felt this, too? She was a healer. The Woman mentioned her last night. Her words were cruel…" She focused on the memory. "But I think she was just trying to provoke me."

Rodric's brow knit. "Maybe the vengeance she takes and the pain she causes aren't satisfying her any longer."

"Let's hope she's not somewhere now, recharging." Eva Grace wished she knew where to go from here.

"We're supposed to help Brenna and Jake move to the home place today," Rodric said.

The coven's rules, outlined in the *Book of Magic*, said a new leader should be in full residence at the home place within five days of taking the wand. While Brenna and Jake had been staying there, today they'd make it official. There was a small ceremony the coven needed to do. Eva Grace sighed. The traditions had to be observed, but they were running out of time.

Her phone's ringtone cut off her thoughts. She was shocked to see who was on the phone.

"Hello, Reverend Williams," she said, her gaze meeting Rodric's. "What can I do for you?"

****

A half hour later, Rodric and Eva Grace walked into the pastor's office at the church. Fred had apologized for his wife's conduct yesterday and asked if Eva Grace had wanted to see him. She could come by at 10, while Ginny was away from the church.

The administrative part of the church was through a side entrance, and it was quiet on this cold morning. The outer office was empty, and Fred appeared in a doorway, one hand over the phone he held to his ear. "I'll be just a moment," he said and turned away to talk. From what Eva Grace could hear, tithes were down. The town's economic woes must be hitting the church, as well.

Shaking her head, she studied the tasteful decor. The room had beautiful oak paneling and leather upholstery. She wasn't sure why she was surprised. They could afford the best.

She examined four paintings grouped on a wall. All originals, they captured the church in all four seasons. The one with the mountains bursting in glorious fall colors made her sad. They were being robbed of that this year.

"I'll see you now." Fred said.

In his office, they took a seat around a mahogany table graced by a bowl of autumn flowers. "Now how can I help you?" His fingers tapped on the polished table.

He was nervous, Eva Grace thought as she took out the note that had been found with Sarah. "We're hoping you might know where this came from. It was signed by Sarah and your father."

Fred's face went white.

"Let me just read it to you."

She unfolded the paper and read, "'We agree to this pact this day, with words from both parties recorded here.'"

"There's a quote beneath that. 'But for the cowardly and unbelieving and abominable and murderers and immoral persons and sorcerers and idolaters and all liars, their part will be in the lake that burns with fire and brimstone, which is the second death.'"

"A verse from the book of Revelations." Fred nodded. "One of Father's favorites."

Grace looked at him expectantly. "His signature is below it."

Fred studied the table without moving.

Finally, Rodric said, "Are you all right?"

"I'm fine." He stood and selected a book from a nearby shelf. "I found the same note in my father's desk after his fatal heart attack."

Eva Grace exchanged a startled look with Rodric.

Fred took a note from the book and read the remaining contents. "'Kahlil Gibran says, 'If you reveal your secrets to the wind, you should not blame the wind for revealing them to the trees.' That part is signed and dated by your grandmother."

He looked at Eva Grace. "As you know, my father didn't approve of your family. I can't believe he'd sign something with Sarah. I don't know if it's real."

"Then why would both of them have it?" Eva Grace asked, irritated by his insinuation that this was a lie.

"It was found under Sarah's body," Rodric said.

"And it came from my family's..." she broke off, realizing a book of magic wouldn't mean much to Fred.

"It was kept with other important papers. So why wouldn't it be real?"

At Fred's silence, Rodric said, "What does the scripture mean to you?"

"It condemns sins of the day and of the flesh and unbelievers." Fred's gaze met Eva Grace's, but he quickly looked away.

"Why would that be in an agreement?" she said. "Was this a temporary truce, sort like 'let's agree to disagree'? If so, it didn't last. While we've been civil for the most part, you've often spoken out against evil forces in New Mourne and our family in particular."

"I stand by my beliefs."

"But you did try to help this summer," Rodric said.

Eva Grace chose her words carefully. "Of course, the scripture you shared with us led Brenna to believe she was our generation's sacrifice."

"It was not my intent to push Brenna toward harm," Fred said.

"Why did you want to help?"

"Because I'm a Christian." He sat down heavily in the chair behind his desk, looking strained. "Your family was suffering. The whole town was suffering. Though I abhor your beliefs, I felt it was my duty to help. I remember that my father went to Sarah after Celia died. Perhaps he was there in the same Christian spirit."

Eva Grace was doubtful, given the tone of the note. "I can't imagine he had any sympathy for my family. I've never heard any of the elder aunts say a kind word about him."

Fred gave a rueful smile. "He was a hard man, and once he had an opinion, he never swayed from it. I'm as baffled as you are about this note."

Eva Grace didn't quite believe him, so she went at the subject a little differently. "You and my mother were close for a while. I imagine your father hated that."

Fred hesitated, then answered smoothly, "Your mother was friendly to everyone, very kind and different from a lot of people our age at school. We'd meet each other and talk for hours. Then my father discovered I was spending time with her, and he ordered me to stop seeing the wretched witch."

He stopped, contrite. "I'm sorry. That's what my father called her. I didn't think of your mother that way."

"Well, that's good to know, since she was so kind to you."

Fred leaned forward. "She left town that summer for college. The last time we spoke, she said she wanted some independence, and your grandmother wasn't too happy about it. When she came back that winter, she was pregnant with another man's child." His lips thinned, and Eva Grace sensed his struggle to maintain his composure.

"Did you love her?" Rodric asked, surprising Eva Grace. When did that become a possibility?

Fred flinched. "It was infatuation," he admitted. "And perhaps some teenage rebellion. Our paths were set by then, in opposite directions."

They were quiet until Eva Grace said, "Did she love you?"

"She moved on to someone else pretty fast, so I guess not." Fred stood abruptly. "I have a meeting with the chairman of the budget committee in ten minutes and I need to prepare for it."

He came around the desk. Rodric stood but Eva Grace stayed where she was, reluctant to end the conversation. Fred waited impatiently at the door. She stood only when Rodric touched her shoulder.

"Thanks," she told Fred, feeling awkward.

He checked his watch, not meeting her gaze. "Sorry I couldn't shed any more light on this. I just don't know how that note links to Sarah's death."

When they were in the car, Rodric said, "What do you make of that?"

"I'm not sure he knows why Sarah had that note, but he's holding back."

"I agree." Rodric drove out of the parking lot.

Eva Grace looked at the sprawling church and school compound. Fred had taken his father's legacy and made it into his own kingdom. "Do you think they were in love?" she asked.

Rodric took a moment to answer. "I do."

The next and most natural question trembled on her lips, but she couldn't say it, and Rodric, may the goddess bless him, didn't ask either.

Was there any way that Fred Williams was her father? Chronologically, it was possible. Her mother left New Mourne that summer. Eva Grace was born in February. But Fred Williams? She just couldn't consider it.

"Let's go help Brenna and Jake. It's something positive to do before we decide on the next move."

Chapter 25

After helping Brenna unpack, Eva Grace and Rodric stopped at Siren's Call. Lauren had manned the shop all day with no customers, but they decided to open again tomorrow. The day after next was Samhain, and perhaps someone would need their wares.

On Main Street, most of the businesses had "Closed" signs in their windows. No tempting smells emanated from the kitchen witch's bakery. On a normal October evening there'd be pumpkin carving in the park, a haunted house open, and happy tourists crowding the street. Tonight, it was bitter cold, empty and dark.

"We can't take much more of this," Eva Grace said.

"It's like the Connelly's first Samhain here."

"At least we're not starving." Eva Grace thought of the food the family had put on the table today. "But how long before people lose their businesses and move? Even the supers have to make a living. If they have to leave New Mourne, where they're protected, what happens to them? Or worse, the Woman lets the demon take all of our magic."

"It's not going to happen," Rodric said in a flat, determined tone. "We're stronger than the demon or the Woman. Don't forget what you did last night. I know you're close to reaching her."

"It needs to happen soon." The blinking Vacancy sign on one of the town's small motels seemed to mock her.

At home they hurried inside and tried to warm up. Even Lorcan didn't tarry long in the yard. All three of them retreated to the bedroom where Eva Grace lit a fire. Still the air was frosty, and she was grateful for Rodric's warmth under quilts made by the elder aunts.

Much later, she awoke to light from the arrowhead around her neck. She roused Rodric.

"What do you think this means?"

He sat up just as another glow came from the windows. Balls of light danced outside. "Something tells me the pixies want to talk."

They pulled on some clothes and went to the back yard with Lorcan at their heels. Pixies filled the garden with shiny wings and magical light. Eva Grace laughed and followed their sparkling trail to the oak tree.

She and Rodric sat on the grass, which was as warm as on a summer's day. Lorcan settled beside Eva Grace, remaining quiet as the pixies gathered round. Several alighted on his back. Others perched on Eva Grace and Rodric's shoulders, light as butterflies. Once they were still, the door to the fairy house opened. A pixie with golden wings and a glow brighter than the rest flew toward them. Behind her were four others.

"I am Aine," the golden fairy said. "I bring you the treasures we have held for you these many years."

"Aine means radiance in Celtic lore," Rodric said, nodding in deference to the faerie. "You embody that word."

Aine smiled. "You are kin to us and full of charm like most of your kind."

"My nanny taught me well."

Aine turned to Eva Grace. "For you, young witch."

At her gesture, two of the pixies came forward and dropped a silver locket on the ground.

Eva Grace picked it up, the silver warmed her skin.

"This locket is precious," Aine said. "Open it and see why."

Enchanted, Eva Grace studied the delicate locket. Though it shone like new, the etching on the top side was worn. "Who does this belong to?"

"You now, like the other treasure around your neck." Aine's smile was radiant. "We gave the arrowhead to a Connelly years ago, for safekeeping. He was kind to us as a child."

"Inez's husband," Eva Grace murmured.

"He was a good man. We knew someone in his family would give it to the coven when it was time."

"Is it time now?" Rodric said. "Is that why you've brought this to us?"

"Open it," Aine suggested. "See what you see, young witch."

The tiny clasp was stubborn, but Eva Grace was able to pry it open. Inside was a braid of golden blond and silky black hair. Tears sprang to her eyes.

"It's hers," she said, looking into Aine's blue eyes. "This belongs to Catriona and her husband."

Aine nodded while the other pixies tittered and moved.

"Why not give them to their owners?" Rodric asked.

"She wasn't ready," Aine replied mysteriously.

"And now?"

Aine said, "We found the arrowhead and the locket long ago at the base of Mulligan Falls. We knew they would be powerful if in the right hands. We hid them from Willow."

As suddenly as the pixies had sprung to life, they stilled. Eva Grace could feel their fear.

"She will never know this," Eva Grace told them. "I promise."

"I swear by my ancestors," Rodric agreed. "And you know these witches sent Willow away."

Aine blinked. "She will be back." The others trilled their agreement.

"And she's already very angry at you," Eva Grace said to Aine. "Because you sided with the coven."

"Yes. No reason to give her more cause for retribution," Aine said. She turned to Rodric, her brilliant wings sparkling. "We have something for you, as well, Warrior."

The last two pixies presented him with a snowflake obsidian crystal. "You will face great evil," Aine warned. "Keep this with you always for protection."

A chill crept into the air. Aine moved backward. "Evil is close. Use these gifts well."

The pixies danced and made music as their leader flew back through the doorway of their little house. The tiny folk frolicked for several minutes before disappearing into the night sky.

Although the bubble of warmth around them was replaced with cold, Eva Grace was filled with hope. Rodric stood and gave her a hand up.

She took a couple of steps then turned back to look at the tiny fairy house. "Remember Randi's prophecy? She also said great evil was coming, and we witches couldn't fight it."

"I remember it, of course, although I never believed you couldn't fight."

Eva Grace rubbed her fingers across the smooth

locket. "Maybe she meant we can't fight it alone. Whatever I face, I know you'll be by my side. You're here for the coven. With you, I have a chance."

He took her hand. "You have my heart, my soul and whatever gifts and power I can give you."

"The pixies want to help. They want you protected." In her hand the locket warmed again. "We should go now."

"Go where?"

"To search for more treasures where they found these at Mulligan Falls." She pointed to the glow on the horizon. "It'll be light soon. We may find something else to help us."

"We should contact the others and tell them what's happened."

"We have to end this before Samhain," Eva Grace insisted. "If we don't find anything, we'll contact the coven to talk. Please, let's go."

With reluctance, he agreed, and they went inside for her to gather her magical aids once more. She threaded the Woman's locket onto the silver chain with the arrowhead.

Less than an hour later, they stood in the cold dawn near the base of the falls. The water dropped from the cliff above, churned over sharp rocks, and into the rapids of the Chattooga River.

On a flat rock near the river's edge, Eva Grace placed candles and crystals in a circle. She closed her eyes and lifted her hands to the sky, chanting over the roar of the water. "Something lost long ago, please show yourself now. A trinket or treasure, allow us to take measure. In the water, the ground or a tree, as I will so mote it be."

She opened her eyes and waited expectantly.

Rodric murmured, "What is it that I see there?" He pointed toward the falls. "Do you see it?"

Something flashed under the cascade of water. Eva Grace knew there was a pathway carved deep in the rocks behind the falls. She and her cousins had been warned against exploring it their whole lives, so of course they had. Ignoring Rodric's protests, she moved nimbly from rock to rock.

She was grabbed from behind, thought it was Rodric and turned. He was some distance away, struggling toward her on the slippery rocks. She couldn't hear him over the water's noise.

An invisible force pushed her forward. Caught by surprise, she couldn't fight the evil that shoved her to the edge of the rocks.

Chapter 26

Unable to move, Rodric watched as Eva Grace fell into the raging river. A wicked and powerful energy kept him in place.

He stopped struggling, drew on his power, and was immediately dressed in his *féeleadh mór, a* winter kilt. The tartan wrapped through his legs and over his left shoulder, giving him the warmth he needed.

With renewed strength, he made it to where she had disappeared. Below, she was caught in the swirling waters of a huge vortex.

He watched helplessly as she was tossed upward and sucked back down. She reached out to him again and again, but the water held her in its grip. He considered climbing down to her, but the rocks were like glass. He would end up in the water too, with no way to get either of them out.

She just kept slipping, sinking under the cold water, and coming up gasping for air.

The wind picked up and clouds darkened. A deep rumble moved through the air. Laughter, Rodric realized. The demon was laughing.

"Damn you!" he yelled. "You're a coward controlled by your mistress."

As thunder boomed, the water shot up and Eva Grace was level with Rodric. The arrowhead and locket gleamed at her throat, and the demon made the earth shake.

"Give those to me," the creature roared.

It wanted the treasures the faeries had given Eva Grace. The demon couldn't just take them, she'd have to give them to him. Which meant Rodric could save her. But how?

The water sucked her back down. Her movements slowed. Fatigue was taking over.

"Help me," he called to his ancestors. "Help us!"

A thick rope appeared in his hands. He made a loop as Eva Grace fought the water's rage.

He threw the loop with all his strength toward her. The wind was strong, and he couldn't get it close enough for her to grab it.

Rodric focused his magic into his arms and once again tossed the rope. This time she caught it.

"Try to get it around your waist," he yelled.

She seemed to understand and fought to get the loop over her head. She succeeded, but the effort cost her. She sank into the water, her weight pulling against the rope.

"Spawn of Aife," the demon roared at Rodric. "Tell her to save herself. Give me what I need."

"She's not giving you anything," Rodric shouted.

"Maybe to save you." A lightning bolt struck just feet from Rodric.

"Shield wall," he shouted. Interlocking metal shields sprang up between him and the monster who held Eva Grace.

The demon cursed and the wind blew harder, but the wall held.

"Just something I learned from our Viking invaders," Rodric jeered. "How do you like it?" Summoning all the magic in his blood, he looped the other end of the rope around his waist and slowly began to pull Eva Grace up from the river.

The rope cinched his middle, and he struggled to breathe. His legs ached with the strain. Eva Grace was dead weight, and the demon was pulling her away. Rodric planted his feet. His legs shook and muscles cramped as he slowly backed up.

The rock beneath him gave way to dirt, and he fought for purchase. Every muscle in his body burned as he gritted his teeth and kept pulling until he could go no farther.

He fell with a hard thump and lost some ground. He wrapped the rope around his wrists and held steady. He had to rest a minute, or he was going to join Eva Grace. Gripping the rope, his hands began to turn blue.

His love was dying even as he sat on his ass gasping for breath with numbness spreading up his arms. His shields slowly disappeared, leaving him vulnerable again.

As he fought to stand, the air around him sparkled. Then Maggie and Lauren were on either side of him, taking the weight off his hands and adding their magic to his grip.

As they began to pull Eva Grace with him, Brenna and Fiona flew over the river's edge and swooped down, taking Eva Grace's arms. The demon was howling, but the wind and rain were letting up.

The tremendous pressure on Rodric's weakening body disappeared. After shaking the rope free with Lauren and Maggie's help, he rubbed at the thousand needles pricking his arms. He wanted to move, to help them lift Eva Grace, but his body wouldn't cooperate.

Lauren massaged his right arm. "I felt Eva Grace,

and I just flew. Without even a thought."

On his left, Maggie said, "We all did. And got here at the same time from different places."

As feeling came back to his body, Rodric pushed to his feet. The air turned so frigid it hurt to breathe. But hope sparked inside him as he saw Brenna and Fiona fly over the river's edge, Eva Grace between them. Water rose behind them but froze into a black mass.

Rodric ran forward as they landed on the grass with Eva Grace's lifeless body. The wind ceased, and the rising column of ice shattered. The demon's scream pierced the early morning air.

"Take that, you evil bastard," Brenna yelled.

One of the witches cleverly made a bubble around all of them before debris rained down like a plague of frogs. Each piece fell to the ground, burst into a small flame and sputtered out.

"Help me," Brenna said as she frantically rubbed Eva Grace's limbs.

Rodric dropped to his knees to help her. Fiona cast a spell for warmth. Enveloped by a warm cushion of air, all their clothes dried. But Eva Grace remained unresponsive and cold to the touch. Rodric pushed her cousins aside and took her in his arms.

"Come back to me." He lightly tapped her cheek, still getting no response.

The flaming debris stopped and Maggie said, *"Bheith imithe,"* making the bubble disappear.

Snow fell on Eva Grace, and her chilled skin kept the flakes from melting. Leaves whirled around them when the wind picked up again.

Brenna wrapped her arms around herself. "Snow before Samhain. Our ancestor's woes are repeating."

Rodric rubbed Eva Grace's arms and begged her to wake up. Though she was breathing, he couldn't rouse her. The magical trinkets at her throat weren't glowing, either. Surely that was a bad sign. The pixies said she'd need them to fight.

He jerked as Jake came crashing through the woods in tiger form, no doubt drawn to Brenna by their mating bond.

The white tiger lowered his massive head and approached, blue eyes glimmering and a low rumble in his throat.

"She's alive," Rodric assured him as a siren wailed in the distance.

"There's Brian," Fiona murmured, holding up her cell phone. "He and Bailey are headed this way."

"We could try to fly again," Brenna said with a worried frown. "But we've expended so much magic, I feel weak."

"It's better to drive her," Rodric said, trying to reassure himself.

Then Eva Grace began to convulse.

Chapter 27

Eva Grace woke to complete blackness, so dark she couldn't even see her hand. She could move but didn't know if she should.

"Hello?" she said but received no response. "How did I get here?" She carefully raised herself on her elbows. "And...where am I?"

Feeling around, she found nothing but a hard surface. It didn't feel like concrete or wood, but what else could it be? The only thing she could imagine was granite. But where was she and how did she get here?

A bright light burst through the darkness. She screamed and fell back hard. Pain pierced her head. The glaring light made her eyes burn.

"Now, you're in my realm," a dark voice whispered. "At last, I've got a witch in my lair."

Demon. Her body tensed and her magic grew in response. Once again, she tried to determine her environment. He'd said she was in his realm. That had to mean she was "in-between," the place where spirits and demons reigned.

She knew little about the "in-between." It was mentioned briefly in craft school. She knew a witch could disappear there, never to be seen again. The light went out.

She heard a hiss and wondered if the demon was slithering in snake form again. She hated snakes, and it probably knew that. But if she could see, she could prepare. Damn the darkness. With a small swish of her wrist, she brought light, though it barely penetrated the space around her.

A snakehead rose in front of her, its mouth wide, fangs glistening. It swooped down and pulled the light into its enormous jaws.

Eva Grace shrieked and crab-walked away. Again, the cackle of evil laughter rose above her. Pulling herself into a sitting position, she pushed a ball of magic straight at the giant snake.

With a hiss, the head grew bigger and the jaw went wider as he gobbled the ball of magic like a tasty treat. When she quickly threw a stronger ball of magic, the snake again snapped it up.

This time Eva Grace didn't move. She could hear the snake's body slithering around her. She tried to make herself smaller and frantically searched her spells for something that would work against the giant reptile.

She slowly began an incantation in her head. *Stars in the air above, and earth dense in the space below...*

"Yesssssssss," came the whisper from the darkness.

Her blood chilled, the incantation forgotten. When she heard the snake slithering closer, her breath stopped as fear overwhelmed her.

A loud hiss echoed, making Eva Grace feel as if the snake was everywhere. Nausea roiled up as she pictured the gleaming fangs. With fear making it difficult to breathe, she couldn't summon enough energy to begin the incantation again.

A flurry of movement put her in motion. She had no idea which way to go, just an overwhelming urge to move as far from the creature as possible. Her breathing was shallow and fast. In moments, she felt lightheaded and weak. "Leave me alone," she said, though it was little more than a squeak.

"Come, witch, give me what I need." The sibilant voice held longing and desire. "Give me your magic, and I promise you'll wake safe and warm in your own bed."

Eva Grace could hear the lie in the demon's voice.

She wrapped her arms around her knees, longing for her cousins and the coven to help her. The darkness was as cold and solid as a block of ice. There were no connections to the bonds of magic she sent out for her family. She was completely alone.

"Just give me what I want, witch, and you're free."

Eva Grace's head jerked as the voice came from another direction. Still, she couldn't pinpoint where it was. She fought against the blackness, so she could think straight and create strong magic to help herself out of this situation.

She froze. *Magic.* The demon had urged her to give him her magic. She recalled the way its jaws had opened to gulp down the magic she threw at it. It was the same thing he'd tried with her cousins. He'd possessed Maggie and bargained unsuccessfully with Brenna and Fiona. Their magic was what he *needed.*

Last summer he had joined forces with the ghost of one of their ancestors who had dabbled in the dark arts. The spirit's magic was too weak to help the demon. But if he could steal the magic of a Connelly, he'd be able to take over the coven and defeat the Woman in White.

At last, she felt calm and focused. She rested her chin on her knees and thought about what Brenna and Fiona had experienced. It was always the magic. He needed a witch's magic.

She closed her eyes, took three deep breaths and turned her focus inward. With care and concentration, she minimized her magic. She pictured her powers as a ball of light dimming with each of her breaths. When it was small enough, she began to construct a wall to protect her magic. She needed to protect her magic just as Rodric had taught her to protect her feelings. Once the wall was strong and tall, her magic was locked away.

The demon roared in fury as darkness pulled her under again.

Chapter 28

In the center of a circle of witches, Eva Grace lay white and still on the dining room table at the Connelly home place.

Brian had broken every traffic law getting her here. When they arrived, she was breathing. That's all that mattered.

Rodric stood to the side with the men while the coven discussed what steps to take to bring Eva Grace back from wherever she'd gone.

With a decision made, Brenna set *The Connelly Book of Magic* at Eva Grace's feet. She turned to Delia, "Now for the crystals."

Though she wasn't a healer, Delia had vast knowledge through her studies with her husband. She placed one crystal on Eva Grace's forehead. "This is picture jasper for emotional and psychological healing."

She laid another on Eva Grace's stomach. "Hematite will penetrate her bloodstream and resist her body's stress."

She put the third crystal above Eva Grace's head. "An aventurine purifies mental, emotional, and etheric healing while releasing anxiety. It will support her independent spirit."

Delia stepped back and joined the circle again. Brenna, Fiona, Lauren and Maggie raised their wands.

Silence. A small gust of wind moved around the

room, making glasses tinkle and curtains swirl. When it reached the book, pages flipped and stilled.

Tension twisted Rodric's gut. Eva Grace still didn't move.

"Faithful healer, beloved sister witch, hear my plea," the book said, the voice female with the lilt of Ireland.

The witches collective gasp sent Rodric toward the table, but Jake and Brian held him back.

The book continued, "Wake from your sleep, and come back to your sisters. Otherwise, you'll end up with warts and blisters."

A stream of magic burst from the wands and encircled Eva Grace as the book repeated the chant.

"Who knew the book had a sense of humor?" Jake whispered.

"Circle of love, power of magic, physical healing helped by enchantment," the book intoned. "Evil is banished; the spirit is free."

The witches joined the final phrase, "As we will, so mote it be."

But Eva Grace was still as death, and the locket and arrowhead still didn't glow. Rodric's heart pounded.

Brenna turned to him. "Come on, warrior. Kiss her and wake her up."

Rodric was at Eva Grace's side in an instant. Her face was so pale, tiny blue veins prominent under her skin. He touched her cold lips with his, and then added gentle pressure.

Nothing happened.

Rodric looked at Brenna, whose cheeks were wet with tears.

Fiona said, "Try again."

Hands cupping Eva Grace's face, he put all his love into the kiss. He pulled her into his arms, resting her face against his neck as the crystals fell to the floor. He held her for a moment before he felt her breath against his beard. She gasped and started to cough.

"Blessed be," the witches murmured in unison, their relief palpable.

Rodric helped her sit up and scoot to the edge of the table. When she started to stand, he stopped her. "Just wait a minute until everything settles."

"What happened?" she asked weakly. "I remember something about warts and blisters."

"Not to worry," Fiona said. "That was just the book of magic being snarky."

Eva Grace looked confused. "The book?"

"She's weak as a kitten," Frances said matter-of-factly. "We'd better get her some food. I think we've got some leftover chicken casserole."

"I'll make some slaw," Doris added and patted Eva Grace's hand. "You're going to be fine, sweetie. We'll have a snack for you in a few minutes."

The elder aunts and their daughters bustled into the kitchen while the other men drifted into the hallway. The normalcy of the moment almost overwhelmed Rodric.

"You should sit down," Brenna said and moved a chair across the room with the crook of her finger.

"It's freezing in here." Lauren made the fire blaze with the flick of a hand.

Maggie produced a bottle of water and pressed it into Eva Grace's hands. "I think you need this."

"And this." Fiona snapped her fingers, and Rodric sat down with Eva Grace in his lap.

"My, my," said Delia as she carried a tray of cookies

into the room. "We're all feeling powerful tonight, aren't we?"

Indeed, the younger witches were glowing with power. Rodric felt their strength flowing into Eva Grace. Her body warmed in his arms, and her color returned as she took a long drink of water.

"Are you all right? Really all right?" he murmured to her. "I was so frightened. I couldna help you when I wanted to, not even with my magic. Can you tell us what happened?"

She nodded, then her hand flew to her chest. "The locket! Is it still there?"

The chain had twisted around, but the locket and the arrowhead were still on it.

"What's that?" Brenna asked.

Rodric and Eva Grace explained the gift from the pixies.

"And it's the Woman's?" Fiona said.

"Look inside," Eva Grace said.

Fiona undid the clasp to reveal the entwined blond and black hair.

"It's hers," Brenna agreed.

"The demon wanted it," Rodric said. "But Eva Grace would not give it up."

"The demon knows the end is near. He desperately wanted my magic. He took me to the 'in-between.'"

The witches gasped.

Delia was white. "You're sure? Few return from there."

Eva Grace rubbed her aching forehead. "It was utterly black darkness. The only thing I knew was that it was him." She shuddered. "He came to me as a giant snake."

"As we've seen him before," Brenna murmured.

Eva Grace explained how she had protected her magic and escaped.

Brenna was alarmed. "But do you have your magic now?"

Eva Grace stiffened, and Rodric was relieved when she lit the candles on the mantle with merely a glance.

"Thank God," he whispered to her.

Touching her necklace, she mused, "Maybe these are why I was able to get away from him."

From the kitchen doorway, Doris said, "Here's the food, my dears."

Eva Grace eased from Rodric's lap as platters of food began to fill the sideboard—ham, cheese and chicken casserole, homemade bread, a chocolate cake and apple pie. Rodric had no doubt the preparation had been helped by magic. As everyone gathered around and began filling plates, he realized Eva Grace was still not herself. "Would you like to lie down?"

"No, but I'd like to clean up. Brenna, can I borrow some clothes?"

"Sure. Let's go upstairs."

When they came back, Eva Grace looked stronger. She eagerly accepted a plate of food and seemed to improve with each bite.

Finally, she took a cup of chamomile tea and sat in a rocker near the fireplace. Rodric drew up a chair beside her.

Brenna came over, a protective hand on her stomach. "We need to talk about our next steps. What the pixies shared with you gives us a lot to think about. What can we do with the arrowhead and the locket? Perhaps the pixies could tell us more."

"They're frightened of Willow," Rodric answered. "I don't believe we should push them."

"What about going back to the falls to look again for more treasures," Fiona suggested.

"I think that was futile." Eva Grace sipped her tea. "I've been thinking. Mick's granddaughter gave us a strong warning the night I went to the campground. I can't help but believe there's something they could tell us."

"You can't go to him," Brenna said.

Eva Grace's eyes narrowed. "Why not explore every avenue?"

"He could have killed Sarah."

"He has an alibi."

"Bogus, no doubt," Brenna returned, her voice rising. "Jake's investigating his claims."

Eva Grace got to her feet, and Rodric stood. The room around them had silenced, all eyes and ears on the two witches.

Brenna said, "Did you know Mick claims Ginny Williams is his alibi?"

Rodric was as startled as Eva Grace looked.

Jake explained, "Ginny says she went out to the camp the night Sarah died with some medicine for the children. She claims she and Mick talked until after midnight."

"What does Fred have to say about that?" Eva Grace asked.

"He says Ginny was out late that night, and he didn't ask where."

Brenna raised one eyebrow. "It's bullshit."

"And it might be the truth," Eva Grace said. "It's obvious she's made the children in the camp one of her causes. Why couldn't she be there?"

"Are you out of your mind?" Brenna said. "Why would you believe either of these people?"

"What would be in it for Ginny to lie?" Eva Grace countered. "We should at least give Mick and her the benefit of a doubt. If not, we're acting just as she does about us."

"He doesn't deserve the benefit of a doubt," Brenna said sharply. "There's nothing between him and us."

"Except blood."

"Sarah dismissed him before our mothers were born. He contributed nothing to any of our lives."

"But why would he kill her?" Eva Grace asked. "What would be the motive?"

"Anger?" Jake suggested. "A demand for money that she refused?"

Fiona joined the argument. "He's not a good person, Eva Grace. Jake says he has a record for fraud, assault and forgery. He doesn't need to be in our lives."

Eva Grace took a deep breath, and Rodric saw she was barely holding her temper in check. She glared at Brenna and Fiona.

"I love you two more than anyone else, but I've lost too many people, and I'm not going to dismiss another blood relative without talking this out with him. I'm going to see him and Randi later today."

"Please don't," Brenna begged, her eyes filling with tears.

"Don't worry about me." Eva Grace patted her cousin's hand. "Right now, I need to go home." She looked at Rodric, and he had no choice but to follow her to the door.

They left with a few strained goodbyes.

On the porch, Rodric said, "Don't you think you should—"

She cut him off with a glare. "I'm not discussing this."

He realized there was nothing he could do. A storm named Eva Grace was brewing.

Chapter 29

Eva Grace stepped into the shower with a tired sigh. It had taken her thirty minutes to convince Rodric to give her some time alone. She just wanted a shower and to rest.

Hot water and fragrant shower gel did wash away the residual pain and exhaustion, but she was restless. Lorcan padded after her as she moved through the house. She tried to nap, but when she closed her eyes, she remembered the dark, dismal 'in-between.'

As the afternoon slipped away, the tick of her grandfather clock mocked her. Time was running out. Tomorrow was Samhain, and she believed it wouldn't pass without the Woman making her move.

Randi still loomed in the back of her thoughts. What role did she or Mick have in what was happening? Eva Grace admitted her family could be right. Mick could be evil. Or he and Randi could hold the key to ending the curse. Fate placed them here for some reason.

Going to the camp alone would anger everyone, especially Rodric, but Eva Grace didn't care. She wanted answers. Besides, she had some protection, she thought as she touched the Woman's locket.

Now was as good a time as any to go check on Randi. Maybe the surprise element would help her catch the gypsy clan unaware and see if someone was intentionally making Randi ill.

Lorcan whined and followed her to the door. He pressed his big body against her leg, and she dropped down to rub him thoroughly. Planting a kiss on top of his soft head, she gave him the command to stay, and he did. Her guilt returned when she heard him whining as she locked the door.

Halfway to the campground, she rounded a curve and slammed on the brakes. Lorcan stood defiantly in the middle of the road.

"Damn you, dog," she muttered. She got out and opened the passenger door for him. He immediately lay down and put his head in her lap. "You're staying in the car at the campground, and I mean it."

As they pulled into the entrance, Lorcan's head rose and a deep, low growl came from his belly. Eva Grace scanned the area but could see nothing to merit the dog's reaction. She pulled in near Mick's trailer just as the door opened. Expecting Randi to be the female form coming out, Eva Grace reached for her door handle.

Her hand went slack, and she gasped audibly as Ginny Williams stepped out of the RV and turned back to give Mick a lingering kiss. The tousled hair and the relaxed smile on the woman's face were a testament to her recent activity with the gypsy.

Feeling sick, Eva Grace slumped in her seat hoping Ginny wouldn't see her. She jumped at a light tap on the passenger window. She met Mick's laughing eyes.

"What brings you out here?" he said when Eva Grace lowered the window.

"Were you spying on me?" Ginny demanded. "Gonna run over and tell Freddy what I've been doing?"

"No, I came to see Randi. I wanted to see if she's still not feeling well."

Mick yelled sharply. "Randi."

She appeared in the doorway of another trailer.

"Come here," he said.

"I'm going home," Ginny said and gave him a loud kiss on the mouth before walking away.

Eva Grace said nothing as Mick smiled. "Don't worry, Ginny's just another willing woman I've obliged."

A chill crept through her as she thought of the hatred her aunts had always felt for the man who'd left Sarah. Her empathy rose as she realized he probably had the same flippant attitude with her grandmother.

A knock on the driver's window made her jump. She was more upset than she thought. She was thankful it was Randi, looking pale and tired.

"Hi, Eva Grace, did you need something?"

Walking around the car, Mick put a possessive arm around the girl's thin shoulders. "As you can see, she's doing fine. No need to worry."

Randi gave a weak smile but Eva Grace saw she'd stiffened under her grandfather's arm. "Sure, I'm right as rain."

"Did you need anything else?" Mick asked, his face becoming a leering mask. "Want to come inside and get more comfortable?"

Eva Grace shuddered, repulsed. "I'm fine here." She locked eyes with Randi. "Are you sure you're all right? You look a little pale and tired."

"It's nothing," Mick answered. "She's been with the kids all day. They'll make anyone tired." He removed his arm and headed for his trailer. "Tell her goodbye and come inside."

Feeling an urgent need to help Randi, Eva Grace

hissed, "Get in the car. Let me take you away from here."

The young woman looked around helplessly. Mick now stood in the doorway. Once again, his voice was sharp and cold. "It's time to come in."

Lorcan growled and bared his teeth at Mick.

"Come on, Randi, I feel like something's really wrong here," Eva Grace said. "Get in!" She reached over Lorcan and opened the door. He shoved it open for Randi and got in the back seat.

"I can't," Randi said, her eyes filling with tears. "He'll be so angry."

"Don't worry about him. Just come with me." Eva Grace was pleading as she started her car. "I'll help you. Come on."

Mick came down the steps.

She yelled again, "Get in!"

Randi seemed frozen but suddenly she jerked and rounded the convertible in two steps. Throwing herself in the passenger seat, she slammed the door.

Eva Grace pressed the gas pedal, and her rear tires spun in the gravel. Just as Mick reached the bottom step, she pulled forward and left him in the dust.

Chapter 30

As Eva Grace raced out of the park, Lorcan leaned his head between the seats to sniff at Randi. She offered a hand and he licked it.

"I thought about calling you earlier," Randi said.

"Why?" Eva Grace paused briefly at a stop sign before pulling onto the main road. "Were you upset about something?"

Randi cast a nervous glance over her shoulder. "There's been a lot of stuff going on lately, stuff that doesn't make sense to me."

"Like Mick getting visits from the local minister's wife?" Eva Grace said. She looked at Randi, who was biting her upper lip. "Tell me what's going on."

"I'm not like most of the people in the camp," Randi said, stroking Lorcan's soft head that now lay on the console. "Many of the elders can read and write enough to function in daily life, but that's about it. Though we have school for the children, it doesn't go beyond rudimentary teaching. I was in college before I came here."

"You haven't always lived with Mick?"

Randi shook her head.

"I lived most of my life with my mother in Minnesota. My father died when I was six or seven. He fell off a house his crew was roofing. We were with the Travelers then, but after the funeral, Mom took me away."

She stared out the window.

"What happened?" Eva Grace sensed this story was painful for Randi.

"Mom woke me up in the middle of the night, had our stuff packed, and said we were leaving. I was half asleep, but I remember telling her I didn't want to leave my cousins. She said she wasn't going to stick around for the Travelers to take over her life. Our car was parked outside the camp, and we took off."

"Where was Mick?" Eva Grace paused before pulling out onto Main Street.

"I don't…" Randi hesitated. "I don't know."

Eva Grace was surprised. "Mick is your grandfather. Why wouldn't he be there for your father's funeral?"

"All I remember is sadness and being taken away."

"Wait a minute," Eva Grace said. "Is Mick your mother's dad or your father's?"

Silence.

"Randi?"

"I don't know much," Randi replied, sounding tired. "My mother wouldn't talk about it. She met my dad when he was in the Army. He got out and came back to the Travelers. Mother hated it. I remember big arguments. Then we left after he died."

"You don't remember Mick?" A cold dread crept through Eva Grace. Who was this man?

"I'm sure I do. I was just so small. I'm sure…" Her voice trailed away.

"Did you have family in Minnesota?"

"No, it was just me and Mom. She warned me to never say a word about the Travelers. We kept to ourselves a lot. She got a job as a bookkeeper, went to school and became a CPA."

"Were you happy?"

"I was in junior college. To be honest, I didn't want to go too far away from Mom."

"Then why are you here now?"

"Would you believe me if I said I don't know?"

"What do you mean?" Eva Grace slowed the car and pulled to the side of the road so she could give Randi her full attention.

"I remember seeing Mick at our front door. He looked familiar," Randi said slowly. "Maybe like my dad?" She sounded uncertain.

Lorcan whined as Eva Grace prompted. "What happened?"

"The next thing I remember is waking up in his trailer frightened because I didn't know where I was. I tried to stand, I became ill—dizzy and really nauseous. I fell back on the bed. The next time I remember anything was the day after you had been to the trailer."

"Did Mick tell you I had been to see you?" Eva Grace reached for one of the girl's hands and found her palm was hot. "It feels like you've got a fever. Have you been feeling bad again?"

Randi sighed. "All the time now. I have no energy, and my stomach hurts."

Eva Grace rubbed her lower lip while trying to get her thoughts in order. It now seemed obvious that Mick had a magical hold on Randi. Finding out he had taken her against her will cemented that. But why?

"Have you talked to your mother? Does she know where you are?"

"Every time I try to talk to him about it, he has something important to do and walks away from me.

Yesterday he said my mother had no right to take me away from my family," Randi said softly. "I miss her, but I can't remember her phone number or our address. Every time I think about it, I get so sleepy." Her head nodded.

Lorcan's sharp bark jerked Randi awake. He licked her hand, whining deep in his throat.

"Try to stay awake," Eva Grace said. "I'm going to help you."

She pulled back out on the road, thinking of the Remember Not spells her grandmother and the elder aunts had used. Mick's magic wouldn't be like theirs, but the Romany people were known for curses. For Randi's sake, she hoped this wasn't permanent.

The young woman began to cry. "How could he do this to me? Why would he?"

Eva Grace gave her healing magic a little push.

"I don't know much about Romany magic, but I know when the Connelly women get together, there's very little that can defeat them. One thing we can do is find out where you're from. Jake can check missing person reports. I'm sure your mother has filed one."

They drove in silence until Randi bent double and moaned in pain. When she raised her head, she yelled, "Pull over. I'm going to be sick."

Eva Grace whipped the car to the side of the road. Randi jumped out and by the time Eva Grace and Lorcan got to her, she was dry heaving.

"Have you had anything to eat today?" Eva Grace asked.

"No, I couldn't." Randi pushed her hair behind her ears, still bent double.

Suddenly, the cold seemed to be closing in around

Eva Grace. Beside her, Lorcan growled. Black magic was here—very close. Was it from Randi? Surely not.

Going with her gut, she took hold of Randi's elbow. "We need to get to the coven right now." She helped her toward the car.

Once they were inside, she kept her foot heavy on the accelerator, anxiously watching for a car behind them. She pressed the button for her phone and was relieved when she heard Brenna's voice.

"Get everyone together. I need the coven's power."

Chapter 31

By the time Eva Grace reached the home place, it was sleeting. Randi shivered and hugged herself. Eva Grace was sure the thin cardigan sweater Randi wore was defenseless against the cold. Putting an arm around Randi, Eva Grace said, "We'll get you warm in a minute. I'm sure they have a fire going."

Eva Grace saw Brenna had summoned the family, and Rodric's car among the parked vehicles. Eva Grace headed for the front door. She stopped when she realized Randi was still in the car.

Eva Grace hurried back and opened the passenger door. "What's wrong?"

"I don't feel right going in there," Randi said, pulling her sweater around herself. "I don't think those people like me."

"Of course they do," Eva Grace said. "Once I tell them what Mick has done to you, they'll help you. I've never seen the Connellys turn their back on anyone in need. Come on, Randi, you're freezing, and we need to get you inside."

When they reached the front door, Eva Grace stepped over the threshold but Randi hesitated,

"I don't feel good about this," she said.

"Come on in. I want you here and that's all that matters."

Pulling Randi inside, Eva Grace closed the door.

"Come on, now, let's get you by the fire and I'll make some tea."

They were heading for the fireplace when Delia stepped out of the dining room.

"What's she doing here?" Delia demanded.

Brenna came up behind her mother. "How did she get past our wards? We have them set so only the family can enter tonight."

"She is family," Eva Grace said. "And she's been affected by black magic. We need to help her."

"How do you know bringing her here isn't going to make things worse," Brenna added. "After all, she's Mick's granddaughter. For all we know, he murdered Sarah."

"I just feel we need to help Randi."

"Is she why you asked for the coven to assemble?" Delia asked.

Eva Grace was shocked by the vehemence in her aunt's voice. "I think Mick may be holding her with magic. I thought we might do a cleansing ritual."

When Brenna and Delia didn't move, Eva Grace steered Randi to walk around them. "Let's at least let her get warm, and we'll talk in the dining room."

The rest of the family gathered in the room.

"Oh my goodness," Doris said as she entered the room. "How did she get past our wards?"

"I invited her in," Eva Grace said, her voice now sharp with anger. "I don't understand why you all are upset over a young woman who's obviously in distress being here."

Doris walked closer to Eva Grace. "Bad things happen when you invite evil into your home."

"By the goddess," Eva Grace yelled. "What do you

see that's evil in her?"

Rodric came out of the kitchen, his face lined with concern. "What do you think is wrong with Randi?"

"Mick has been controlling her," Eva Grace said. "She can't even remember her home address. She lived in Minnesota and vaguely remembers Mick showing up at her front door one day. You've all been saying Mick is evil, and I believe this proves it. Even I know I was wrong about him. Doesn't she strike you as someone who needs our help?"

Eva Grace's tone reflected her frustration and anger. "I don't think Randi is evil. Something is making her sick, and I can feel the black magic."

"Maybe the evil isn't in her," Mick stood in the dining room doorway.

There were audible gasps throughout the room. Jake came in from the kitchen.

He headed toward Mick and said, "You need to leave."

"You need to get out of my way," Mick said and swung his left arm out.

Jake flew across the room and hit the wall. The other men surged forward as a group, but Mick's outstretched hand knocked them back like pins hit by a bowling ball.

Eva Grace watched in horror as Mick's face melted into the face of Finn MacCuindlis, the father of the Woman in White who was the demon.

The demon said, "I finally found a man who willingly gave me his magic. Gypsy magic isn't as strong as witch magic, but it can be manipulated just as easily. Greed is good." His gleeful laughter grated on her nerves.

Jake reached for his gun. Raising his hand, the

demon sent the gun into the fireplace. "When are you going to realize you have no defense against me?"

He walked to Randi's side and took her hand. She whimpered but moved closer to him. "I almost had Sarah's magic, but the cranky hag kept pulling it within herself. When she became too weak to be of any use, I let Ginny stab her."

The elder aunts began to weep. Eva Grace realized her own face was wet as she fought back a sob. "You did the same thing to me when I was trapped in the 'in between,' you bastard."

"You bitches have no idea how good power can feel," Mick said, giving Eva Grace a gut punch with his magic.

When she folded under its impact, Rodric ran to her, putting himself in front of her. In a moment, he was wearing his warrior garb and holding a broadsword.

Going to her side, the other young witches helped Eva Grace regain her strength. They joined hands behind Rodric as he raised the broadsword. Before it made contact with Mick's flesh, Eva Grace watched the metal melt. Rodric threw it aside.

Outside, the sleet was coming down so hard and fast, the windows rattled, and the cold began seeping into the old house. Brenna pulled her wand out and raised it. The other witches placed their hands on one another as they had done in the meadow. However, the magic ball Brenna sent toward Mick and Randi fell helplessly to the floor and disappeared.

The demon raised its arms, still holding Randi's limp hand. A wave of black magic swept through the room, causing the witches to feel ill and the humans to collapse.

Eva Grace struggled against the waves of nausea and pain as Rodric pulled her into his arms. She wanted to resist him and face the demon but didn't have the strength.

Stepping forward, the demon put his arms around the couple with Randi's help. He uttered a guttural spell.

Eva Grace tightened her hold on Rodric as they were moved from the house into the bitter cold of the yard. Her arms were suddenly empty and as she called his name, it disappeared into the chaos of the winter storm.

When she looked back at the house, it was under a dome, much like a snow globe. The wind swirled the sleet and snow, and Rodric lay in a crumpled heap in the dirt of the driveway. She struggled to move, to go to him, but her body was completely trapped.

When she realized hope was lost, Eva Grace escaped into the past with thoughts of her childhood, her longing for her mother, the wonderful years of learning her craft with Sarah and the elder aunts. Her mind circled to her precious time with Garth, their years together and the horrible loss she felt when he was ripped from her side. The thrill of defeating the demon with Brenna and Fiona and now knowing she was helpless and in the hands of the evil monster. The comfort and warmth of finding Rodric and knowing love again.

Gone. It was all gone.

Chapter 32

Rodric moved and pain shot through his body. He was dazed. It had been a long time since he'd awakened wondering "Where am I?" He was lying on his belly in the grass and it was snowing. He pushed up to his elbows and recognized the Connelly home place.

Jake lay in a heap on the porch. Brian was on the walkway with a bloody forehead. Blinking his eyes and working to clear his confusion, Rodric fought his way to his feet. As he staggered forward to help his friends, he felt something warm in his right palm.

The snowflake obsidian the faeries had given him was glowing, and, as he watched, it beamed up his right arm into his bones. He began to feel clearer and stronger. Eva Grace had told him the crystal had healing properties. Clasping it harder, he closed his eyes and took a deep breath, using the power of the volcanic glass to center himself.

His confusion cleared as he remembered Eva Grace being taken by Mick.

"Goddess, I've got to get to her."

He ran forward and hit an invisible barrier that knocked him to the ground. Once again, he relied on the snowflake obsidian to help him clear his head.

What was holding him back?

Peering into the darkness, he could see the edges of the barrier. It wasn't snowing beyond the invisible wall.

A groan sounded behind him, and he turned to find Jake helping Brian to his feet. The sheriff pulled out a bandana and told the younger man to press it against the bleeding on his forehead.

"You all right, Rodric?" Jake asked.

"I think so. We seem to be trapped inside a bubble of some kind. It's very strong," Rodric said as he walked back toward them.

"I saw you stumble when you tried to run." Jake paused to take a deep breath. "Man, something knocked us cold." He jerked around. "I need to see if Brenna is all right." He ran into the house.

Brian sat down on the front step, and Rodric could see the purpling bruise growing on the young deputy's forehead.

"Mick took Eva Grace and Randi." Rodric wasn't sure why he thought the younger woman had been taken, but that's how it felt to him. "We've got to find a way to get out of this bubble."

"Maybe the coven will know a spell or an enchantment that will work," Brian said, grimacing as he touched his forehead. "Or I'm afraid we're stuck."

"We can't be," Rodric said, pressing the crystal harder in his palm. Its pulse sent calming warmth through his bones.

He went to the edge of the bubble again feeling for openings for weakened spots but found nothing. Looking back at Brian, he said, "I'm going to use some magic."

Brian got to his feet. "Thank the goddess you have magic."

Rodric concentrated, and his sword and armament came to him. He swung the sword at the bubble. The sword bounced to the ground. He tried again and again with the same result. In frustration, he sheathed the sword and began to pace.

How was he going to get to Eva Grace? There had to be a way out.

He turned at the sound of Brenna's voice.

"Can I help you?" she called as she came through the snow with Jake behind her.

"I'm so relieved you're okay," he said.

"All that happened was I fell asleep in my chair. What can I do here?" She didn't even blink at his armor.

"My weapons aren't piercing this," he said and rapped on the barrier.

Jake shifted to tiger form and dove at it with his razor-sharp claws. Though there was a break in the magic field, it repaired itself.

Brenna touched the barrier and jerked back. "We've got some black magic going here. Get the others," she told Brian.

In a few moments, the coven was in a circle, chanting.

Rodric felt their magic grow stronger. He gave it a push from his own gifts. Fire rose from the center of the circle, swooped, and slammed into the barrier, leaving a thick black plume of smoke.

They all coughed, and Rodric felt his heart fill with desperation. Hopelessness was as strong in his senses as the overwhelming smell of sulfur that now surrounded them.

Stepping back, he grasped the handle of his sword, took a firm stance and began to shout, "Aife, warrior goddess, great protector and healer, I call on you to aid me in my quest."

The air around him grew heavier, and the hilt on his

sword changed. When he raised the weapon, it was not a sword, but a dirk, the ancient dagger of Aife.

According to the Ferguson family legend, the dirk would come to him when he needed to save his true love.

"Take me there. I'm ready."

His armor began to shimmer, and he grasped the dirk tighter. He sensed movement in time. Strengthening his stance, he prayed he would end up with Eva Grace and not in the middle of a medieval battle.

Chapter 33

Eva Grace came to herself standing in the Connelly clearing. She knew she was near the edge of the cliff by the roar of Mulligan Falls behind her. She tried to move, but her body was held in place.

"You're not going anywhere," a man's voice said.

She looked around and found Mick holding a weeping Randi close to his side. "We have business to take care of, and then you'll take a little tumble over the falls."

His laughter was maniacal. In the glow of torches that had been set at intervals around the clearing, his handsome features twisted. The demon had him.

Remembering her escape from the 'in-between,' Eva Grace pulled her magic to herself. "I don't have any plans to take a swim today," she said with strength in her voice.

"Your plans no longer matter," he said.

"Please, Grandfather, let me go. I don't want to be here," Randi said, with tears streaming down her face. "Please."

"Shut up," he growled.

Once again, Eva Grace tried to move, but her body was paralyzed. She fought against her urge to help Randi and to suppress her magic.

"All I need from you is that shiny jewelry that's around your neck," Mick said. "Once you give me that,

I'll have what I want."

"I'm not giving you anything," Eva Grace said. "And you can't take it."

Mick roared his frustration and let go of Randi. She dropped to her knees, weeping into her hands.

Eva Grace yelled, "Run, Randi."

Randi tried to rise, but Mick pushed her back down and stomped his foot on her leg, making her scream.

Fighting the need to send healing magic to her, Eva Grace closed her eyes.

"Come on, you know you want to help her," Mick purred like an evil cat. "She's in pain."

Eva Grace cringed as he put more pressure on Randi's leg. "You're a monster," she said through gritted teeth.

"You have no idea, little witch."

"I'm facing a demon who thinks it can steal my magic, but I've got its secret," Eva Grace said. "It can't get my magic."

"That's where you're wrong." Mick's menacing laughter echoed to the water. "All I need is your pretty jewelry."

He reached for the locket and arrowhead nestled against her chest.

Rodric suddenly stood in front of her. His power and warmth spread through her like a healing balm. She was finally able to move. However, it wasn't Rodric that stopped Mick from touching her necklace, it was a burst of bright, intense magic that knocked the gypsy to the ground.

As Mick fell, a vivid black shadow rose and out of his body. Eva Grace watched in horror as Mick disappeared with a pop, leaving only the black demon behind.

"Come to me," a woman's voice drifted across the clearing. "Come to me. I'm here for you."

The oily black shadow moved across the grass and entered Ginny Williams's body. The woman's skin moved in fascinating and frightening ways. As it settled, she cried out in pleasure and then smiled at them with the evil still roiling in her body. Rodric continued to protect Eva Grace.

Ginny said, "They say you should never make a deal with the devil. But what the hell. I'd already had to live with a preacher."

When another figure came out of the trees, Eva Grace braced herself. It was Fred following his wife.

"This time I'm going to win, you stupid witch." Ginny headed toward them, her feet barely touching the ground. "I'm in control. I've been in control for a long time. Who do you think found Mick and brought him back to his sweet Sarah to sow discord within your evil family?"

"Ginny, what are you doing?" Fred yelled. The minister was crying, and his clothes were rumpled and dirty. He looked like a defeated man, worn down by life's horrors.

"This isn't Ginny. She's in league with the devil," Rodric shouted as Eva Grace moved beside him and pulled out her wand.

Ginny laughed again and with a wave of her hand sent her husband to his knees. Flames erupted at her fingertips. "Look at that. I've got magic, too."

"Don't, Ginny," Eva Grace said, feeling steady at last. "The demon will destroy you."

"Do I look like I care? I know about the demon and

your curse. I know why your mother died. It's what she deserved."

"Don't say that," Eva Grace yelled.

"I asked the demon to come to me," Ginny said. "I put him into Mick's body." She looked over at Fred. "He screwed me better than you ever have."

"Ginny," Fred bowed his head and sobbed.

Rubbing her hands together, Ginny carelessly flung fire at Eva Grace, who moved aside as it fell into the water.

"That was fun. I wondered what else I can do," Ginny said and clapped her hands. "Oh, I know, I can kill witches."

"Never," Rodric said, brandishing the dirk.

"You'll never stop me," Ginny hissed. "I knew you'd be here, too. Your uncle was in league with my followers. He promised to kill you, but he couldn't get past that stubborn old woman who raised you. When he failed, they killed him along with those people he liked to torture."

Eva Grace felt the ripple of horror that moved through Rodric. What he feared about his uncle was true.

Ginny cackled. "I'm one step ahead of you all. Guess who had Mick kill Sarah when she came looking for this sappy little empath? Mick shared your blood, so he was able to get onto your land. I sent him there."

Eva Grace gasped. "You had him kill Sarah?"

"I wanted your pretty stone house to fall on her, but the little dagger stopped her instead." Ginny's hysterical laughter echoed throughout the woods. "It was me. I killed the wicked witch of New Mourne."

"Ginny, please come home with me," Fred said, getting to his feet. "We can fight this thing that has you in its power. Pray to God for help. You can beat it."

"You sniveling coward, get away from me," Ginny growled. "I've known all along that you were the father of that redhaired slut's child."

"So it's true." The words burst out of Eva Grace as she swung to face Fred. "You are my father."

"I didn't know until later," Fred said. "I suspected, but when I found the note…"

"That you denied," Rodric gritted out. "You are a coward."

Ginny advanced toward Fred, shooting fire at his feet that he had to dodge. "Your pretty witch didn't really want you, did she, Fred? She never told you she was carrying your child, did she?"

Fred smothered a flame on his pants leg.

"And then I guess your little swimmers dried up." Ginny's voice rose to a scream. "You never planted a baby inside me."

Fred jumped back.

Ginny's brilliant blue eyes were now black. "Oh, I know, Mr. Goody Two Shoes, not having children was my fault. Damn useless ovaries. But that's no problem, I just grew a pair of balls since you didn't have any. Now go away."

With a swing of her hand, she knocked Fred on the ground where he lay unmoving.

The older woman's body suddenly stiffened, and the voice that came out of her was raspy and deep. "Give me the necklace, Eva Grace Connelly…now! The Woman in White is weak or she would have already taken you. I'm stronger now. She's done nothing but walk around weeping while she watched you stupid witches find ways to destroy her."

The demon rose up and out of Ginny's body and she collapsed on the grass beside Fred. What stood in the clearing now was the black, oozing monster the Connellys had previously faced.

"Give me your magic, witch, or I will kill your man!"

Chapter 34

Eva Grace watched helplessly as Rodric was dragged away by the demon. It was obvious he couldn't move anything but his eyes. And they were filled with pleading. She knew instinctively that he wanted her to sacrifice him to save herself. But Eva Grace was sure she couldn't do that.

For months, she had wondered if she'd have surrendered her magic to the Woman in the White if the spirit had come to her before Garth died. She had loved him with all her heart. They were going to marry, have children and live a long life.

Of course, that didn't happen. The demon disguised as the Woman had killed Garth, taking her lover's last breath from his body while she looked on. Once again, she felt the piercing pain in her heart as she remembered that horrible moment.

She looked around, searching for anything she could use in a fight with this black devil. Randi lay unconscious on the ground. There was nothing but her wand. One thing she was sure about: she could not use her magic to help him.

"All you have to do is hand me the necklace," the demon said.

Once again, she was drawn to Rodric's eyes. They were fierce with emotion. She could almost hear him saying, "Let me go and save yourself, your town, and your family."

Careful to keep a tight rein on her magic, Eva Grace gripped the locket and arrowhead. Must everything she loved be taken away? Her mother was taken. Garth and Sarah were killed because of her. People were dead because they loved her.

Snow fell as Eva Grace made her decision. There was no question she would give away her magic to save Rodric. She could not lose anyone else. It was too much.

The wind grew cold and began to swirl the snow. The Woman in White was a slow-motion figure coming into view. She moved between the two women and the demon and Rodric.

While the demon was focused on the rising spirit, Eva Grace whispered, "Can you stand up, Randi?"

Visibly trembling, Randi looked at Eva Grace with eyes full of fear.

"Please get up." Eva Grace stood straight but offered her left hand. "I'll help you."

"You've come for your tribute, but tonight I'm the one who will win," the demon shouted.

The Woman watched the demon in silence.

Eva Grace held her breath as she grasped Randi's cold fingers and steadied herself. Randi stood slowly and didn't draw the attention of the demon and the ghost.

"You've never won before," the Woman said to the demon. "What makes you think you can win now?"

"I am stronger than you, and I have her man." The demon squeezed Rodric's neck, and his body slumped.

As she fought not to scream in panic, Eva Grace saw his eyes flutter and thanked the goddess.

The Woman addressed the demon again. "You've never been stronger than me, and you're not now."

Eva Grace was startled as the ghost turned to her. Beside her, Randi swayed but held on tight.

"Would you like to know what led us to this moment?" the Woman asked.

"Of course," Eva Grace said. "We think we know your story, but I'd like to hear it from you."

"Yes, you already know this monster was once my father," the Woman said, gesturing toward the demon. "He proclaimed himself a man of god and came to this country to save savages. My mother was a frail woman and she died shortly after we arrived. Being a man, he couldn't be alone, so he decided I should never marry."

The demon pulled its arm tight around Rodric's neck again and growled, "I don't have time for stories."

The Woman raised her arm and said, "*Bí fós.*"

The demon's body was stilled and its hold on Rodric loosened. Eva Grace breathed easier as he appeared to revive. She translated the Woman's Irish Gaelic words. The spirit had commanded the demon to be still. Breathing a small sigh of relief, Eva Grace turned back to the Woman.

"I became close to the Cherokee tribe that lived near us," the Woman continued. "Their lifestyle was not too different from ours. I even came to believe the Great Spirit they drew upon was simply their version of our god. Their love of the land and of peace was wonderful.

"Devdas was a kind man. He took care of his mother. When he went out with a hunting party, he always brought me some rabbits or a wild turkey. He helped me learn the Cherokee language, and I found many friends in the camp. I would visit whenever my father was gone for days with his friends."

The Woman in White looked around sadly and Eva

Grace realized the ice crystals she saw falling at the spirit's feet were tears.

"I fell in love with Devdas and, for the first time since my mother died, I knew someone loved me—truly and unconditionally. I knew my father would be furious."

There was a growl from the demon, but he did not move.

"Devdas and I worked on our plans for weeks. His best friend Isha had family in Tennessee, and he helped us escape. Devdas was sad to leave his mother, but she wanted us to live together in peace."

The Woman smiled for the first time. Eva Grace thought it made her appear almost human.

"We had almost a year of peace and happiness. Devdas called me Ahyoka because it means 'she brought happiness' in Cherokee. Isn't that beautiful?"

"Yes," Eva Grace said. "He must have loved you very much."

"He became my family, and I put away all the bad memories with my father. I no longer had anything to fear…or so I thought. Devdas and I were so happy when we knew I was with child. I was sure I would give him a son, though he said he would also be pleased with a daughter who had my beautiful blonde hair."

Eva Grace began to cry. Now she knew why she felt a connection with the woman. Great loss was a part of both their lives.

"We were so happy that I should have known it couldn't last. Devdas was fishing for our dinner when my father and three strange men came into our cabin and forced me to go with them. I was terrified they might hurt me and our baby, so I didn't fight them. My father burned our home and sold Devdas into slavery. I never saw him again."

Everything in the clearing went still. There was utter silence as the snowflakes drifted down.

"And then what happened?" Eva Graced asked softly. "We haven't learned the truth about this part of your story."

Instead of answering, the Woman grew until she towered over the demon, and Randi screamed. Eva Grace had to clutch Randi's hand to keep her from falling.

"You killed my baby." The Woman's voice echoed in the woods like a lion's roar.

"I knew you didn't kill the child of your heart," Eva Grace said.

"But I killed my father," the Woman said.

The demon shuddered, but he did not release Rodric.

The huge spirit moved about the clearing with fierce, jerky movements. Everywhere she stepped the ground became solid ice. "You took my baby from my breast and killed him," she thundered.

She swooped up and then behind the demon. It jerked around to face her, dragging Rodric.

Eva Grace clutched her necklace and silently summoned the coven.

The Woman looked at Eva Grace with fire in her eyes. "I waited until he slept in a drunken stupor, and I tied his arms to the bed with hemp rope. When he was snoring and deeply asleep, I sliced his ankles so he couldn't move."

The demon roared, reaching out for the ghost that moved away from him in a flash.

The Woman laughed, a sound that made Eva Grace

shudder. Randi fell to the ground and wrapped herself into a whimpering ball.

"I made cuts all over his body, little, tiny painful cuts that made him scream as I did when he beat me." She turned to Eva Grace with eyes filled with stark sadness.

The ghost swirled around the demon, who began to show fear for the first time although he still held Rodric motionless.

"When I grew tired, I made small, deep cuts in his neck so he would bleed to death slowly," the Woman said, her voice flat and emotionless. "I left him to die alone."

"I saw you in the scrying mirror," Eva Grace said. "You were covered in blood and running."

The Woman moved across the grass and hovered at the edge of the cliff. "I came here and threw myself into the cold depths to escape my own pain. When this demon came after me, I delighted in making him do my bidding. I've been doing that ever since."

"All you did was give me the power to keep fighting you," the demon said. "As soon as I get that necklace, I'll be the one ruling this land and giving these damned creatures a hell they can't imagine."

The Woman looked at Eva Grace. "When your ancestor came to cleanse this land and claim it for the coven, I was searching for the arrowhead Devdas had given me and the locket that belonged to my mother. I had lost them when I died."

Eva Grace touched her necklace. These were precious to the Woman. Why hadn't she taken them? Must they be given to her, too?

"I was so angry," the Woman continued. "I wanted

everyone to hurt as I had hurt, so I punished them as much as I could. Natives and settlers avoided this place. But the first Sarah Connelly was as strong a woman as me. She was willing to negotiate. I made a bargain, though I ensured it would be a painful one. I wanted your family to know that happiness only came with great pain."

Eva Grace spoke quietly, "But you were punishing innocents for the crimes of a monster."

The ghost gave a painful little cry. "I know. I couldn't stop myself."

"What about now? Are you going to take me?"

"I think I have taken enough from this family. No more bargains." The ghost turned to the demon.

In a flash, it took the form of an old man. Its arms were thin but strong with a smile of pure evil. "I took care of my problems, girl. I wasn't going to have a half-breed in my house. You let that savage ruin you."

Eva Grace gasped, and icy tears slid down her cheeks. No wonder this spirit had been angry and vengeful. She had experienced sorrow and brutal treatment that no woman should.

"But I," the Woman said, pounding her chest with her fist. "I took care of you, old man."

From the corner of her eye, Eva Grace saw movement. She gasped as Lorcan raced into the clearing and launched himself at the demon. That gave Rodric just enough room to twist away. Lorcan backed up as the demon swiped at him.

She screamed as the dog yelped.

As the demon focused on Lorcan, Rodric pulled his dirk upward. He sliced it across the demon's ankles, just as the Woman had so long ago. Magic crackled through the air.

The demon fell to its knees howling like a wounded animal while Lorcan moved away.

Eva Grace yanked the necklace from her neck. She tossed it to the Woman in White.

"Destroy him," Eva Grace pleaded.

"No," the demon bellowed.

Rodric stabbed the beast in its core. As he stepped back, the Woman threw the arrowhead at the demon with enough force to penetrate the wound. A huge roar filled the air, then the demon became a cloud of smoke.

The snow stopped, and the air grew warmer. The black particulates of the demon's magic drifted harmlessly to the ground. Eva Grace took a deep breath, hoping this was truly the end of the creature.

It grew quiet in the clearing as Rodric still stood with weapon drawn.

The Woman stared down at the locket Eva Grace had given her. "Thank you," she said as Eva Grace pushed healing magic toward her.

Rodric sheathed his dirk and Lorcan went to his side as Eva Grace pulled Randi to her feet. She saw Fred get up and crawl to Ginny who lay very still on the ground. They'd have to deal with her later, Eva Grace thought. But right now, she didn't care. Was it true this was over, truly over?

Chanting filled the clearing as members of the coven began coming out of the woods. But it wasn't just the witches. The entire Connelly family and many friends and neighbors soon filled the clearing. A gentle breeze blew. Eva Grace looked up and saw leaves falling from the trees. Fall foliage had returned.

She tensed as Fiona and Uwohali, the old Cherokee,

stepped close to the Woman in White. The man raised his hands and began to speak, "The Nunnehi bring you a gift from the spirits."

Faint music grew louder. Eva Grace recognized it as the drums and flutes of the Native Americans. Uwohali danced as a soft fog engulfed him. An eagle emerged and flew away. When the fog settled to the ground, a handsome Cherokee brave stood in the sacred place with a baby in his arms.

The Woman in White drew back, sobbing into her hands.

"We've brought your family, Catriona," Fiona said. "And we can help you take them with you to the other side."

The handsome brave walked to his wife and handed her the child, and then took them both in his arms. Behind them, a lighted opening spread slowly. Catriona raised her lips to her beloved, and then turned to Eva Grace.

"I leave you and your family in peace," she said. Then she and her husband stepped through the opening and faded from sight.

Chapter 35

Eva Grace sat in the grass with Lorcan and enjoyed her last bites of Coca Cola cake. She wasn't sure which elder aunt had prepared it, but it was moist and delicious. Rodric had gone back for another piece.

Samhain had been a day of festivity and celebration in New Mourne's city park. The giant pot-luck lunch featured barbeque with all the trimmings and fabulous desserts. Many shops were selling wares in the tents. As usual, most of the town turned out for the event. Best of all, many tourists had also arrived.

She watched Randi playing with Rose and other youngsters from town. Randi had called her mother last night. It turned out her mother had listed her as a missing person and would be at the Atlanta airport tomorrow for a joyful reunion.

Eva Grace was relieved that Randi had not been harmed by Mick's plan. They felt he'd just used Randi to make himself look like a caring person and prey on Eva Grace's sympathies.

It had worked, she was ashamed to admit. Perhaps he had used a Romany spell of some kind to influence her. Thank the goddess Mick was gone. The other Travelers had packed up in the middle of the night and disappeared.

For the first time in months, Eva Grace felt contentment and peace. There was no longer a curse hanging over her family, and the coven was united with a sense of purpose. Brenna was going to be a strong and fair leader—and a wonderful mother. They could return to planning weddings and living their lives. Their family's long torment was over.

She was startled when she looked up and saw Fred Williams walking toward her. Ginny was in a catatonic state awaiting transfer to the mental hospital in Milledgeville. Eva Grace couldn't imagine why he was here.

But she stood as he approached and dusted grass off her jeans. She tossed her paper plate in a nearby bin. Lorcan growled, and Eva Grace soothed him.

"Hello," Fred said, automatically offering his hand.

She gave him just the tips of her fingers and quickly pulled away.

"Do you think we could go somewhere and talk for a few minutes?"

Wary, Eva Grace said, "Why?"

"What Ginny did…" He swallowed hard. "I still can't believe it. I want you to know I had no idea she was planning any of that."

"I believe you," Eva Grace said. No matter what, she was sure he had no part in what transpired last night.

"I'd like for us to get acquainted," he said. "After all, I am your father."

The cold and anger that passed through Eva Grace's body were welcomed and strengthened her resolve. She took a step back. "I don't think so."

He appeared shocked at her reaction. "I don't understand. We have time now and—"

"I believe what you mean is Ginny is out of the picture and you have the freedom to visit me secretly so your congregation doesn't know."

"No…I mean…I just want to get to know you and show you I care."

"Sorry, you had a lifetime, and now it's too late."

She turned and walked away, meeting Rodric beside the dessert table.

"Are you all right? What did Fred want?"

She looked up at him and felt a surge of love replace the cold anger that had permeated her body. "Nothing important. I'm going to check on things at the Siren's Call booth."

Later that night, the coven gathered in the clearing. Only the witches and their families remained when it grew dark. They looked like a circle of jewels in their colorful cloaks, standing shoulder to shoulder around the bonfire. Eva Grace was filled with love and pride. The coven finished with their family's traditional chant in celebration of Samhain.

"The harvest is done, our bounty replete

All souls are remembered, their healing so sweet

With joy and relief, our circle is complete,

As we will, so mote it be."

When they dispersed, Eva Grace heard Lauren say, "Did you see that?"

All eyes rose to the bright full moon at its peak in the sky.

"It was probably just a cloud passing over the moon," Maggie said.

"I don't think so," Lauren retorted. "I could swear I saw a dragon fly over."

Eva Grace couldn't stop her chuckle. One never knew what could happen in a magical place like their home. When Rodric walked up, she moved into his arms and hugged him.

"What a blessed night," she said. "I'm so fortunate to be here with my family and you. Have I told you I love you?"

"Only about fifty times today, but that's certainly not enough."

What began as a warm kiss deepened and became a passionate joining that left both of them breathless.

Eva Grace laughed as she realized they were alone in the sacred clearing. Even Lorcan had deserted them. "I guess we ran everyone else off."

Rodric took her hand and led her toward the woods.

"You know, Samhain is the time you ponder what you've learned from the past and make plans for the future," Eva Grace said.

He stopped and reached into his pocket. Eva Grace was surprised when he took her hand and carefully slipped a ring on it. The emerald caught the moon's bright light and glowed.

"Marry me, Eva Grace, and let's plan our future together."

Moving closer, she put a hand on his face and felt she would burst with love and happiness as she said, "Yes."

A word about the author...

Neely Powell is the pseudonym for co-writers Leigh Neely and Jan Hamilton Powell. Long-time friends, they're the authors of "The Witches of New Mourne" a paranormal series about a family coven, a centuries-old curse, and an enchanted town. AWAKENING MAGIC and HAUNTING MAGIC, the first two books of the series, are available from The Wild Rose Press. Their first paranormal novel, TRUE NATURE, is also available from The Wild Rose Press. Writing as Celeste Hamilton, Jan published 24 bestselling romance novels for Silhouette and Avon Books while managing a career in corporate communications. Leigh has a long resume as a magazine editor and writer. Both are now writing fiction full-time. Neely Powell writes about shifters, witches, werewolves, faeries, and ghosts, mixing in shades of mystery, romance, and thrillers—the kinds of books they both enjoy reading.

http://www.neelypowellauthor.com
http://www.facebook.com/NeelyPowellAuthor
https://www.twitter.com/@NeelyPowell3
https://www.goodreads.com/author/Neely_Powell

CPSIA information can be obtained
at www.ICGtesting.com
Printed in the USA
LVHW031651300921
699149LV00012B/332